"I don't care. I will kill you, do you understand?" Willie was screaming. "I will cut your heart out and feed it to the dogs. I will . . ." The shouting ended in an apoplectic splutter, then the phone crashed against its cradle. A moment later bells jangled as the phone came cartwheeling through the open doorway, trailing its wire as if pursued by a serpent.

Almost immediately, Willie followed the wire and stood in the doorway, and it seemed as if the room grew suddenly dark. Hemenway didn't ask who had been on the other end. He didn't want to know.

"That was your Mr. Jones," he said. "He threatened me, and, my friend, he threatened you."

Hemenway felt his body begin to collapse. "What are we going to do?"

"I don't know about you, amigo, but I know what I will do. . . ."

Also by Philip Baxter

CRITICAL MASS
POWER TRIO*

*coming soon

Available from HarperPaperbacks

DOUBLE BLIND

PHILIP BAXTER

HarperPaperbacks
A Division of HarperCollinsPublishers

HarperPaperbacks   *A Division of* HarperCollins*Publishers*
10 East 53rd Street, New York, N.Y. 10022

Copyright © 1994 by HarperCollins*Publishers*
All rights reserved. No part of this book may be used or reproduced in any manner whatsoever without written permission of the publisher, except in the case of brief quotations embodied in critical articles and reviews. For information address HarperCollins*Publishers*,
10 East 53rd Street, New York, N.Y. 10022.

Cover photograph by Herman Estevez

First printing: February 1994

Printed in the United States of America

HarperPaperbacks and colophon are trademarks of HarperCollins*Publishers*

❖ 10 9 8 7 6 5 4 3 2 1

DOUBLE BLIND

- O N E - - -

THE TRAFFIC WAS MURDER. IN FACT, FOR PETE Flannery there wasn't much about New York in midsummer that wasn't murder. Add ninety-eight degrees to humidity in the high nineties, and you felt like your skin was dissolving, exposing every raw nerve to the toxic haze. That it was nearly ten o'clock at night meant nothing, not in the sixth day of a heat wave that had already brought tempers to the boiling point. More than one TV meteorologist had tried frying an egg on the pavement, with results that were no more or less edible than eggs produced by half the cheap diners on the West Side. The papers were already running a daily death toll, keeping track of murders as if they were scores in a pennant race.

Sitting in the cab of his truck, Pete Flannery reached for the volume button on his tape deck, cranked it up a couple of notches for some ZZ Top, and tugged an imaginary beard as he rolled through the freight gate at JFK. The buzz-saw rip of Billy Gibbons's guitar made the cab throb, and the vibration of the booming bass made Flannery's feet tingle, even through the thick soles of his work boots.

It was an easy run, and it was the last one of the day. As much as he hated working a double shift, the extra money would fatten his bank account for a couple of weeks, until the first payment for Kim's tuition came due in September. But it was what you did when you had kids and you wanted them to have an edge nobody ever gave you.

The Lufthansa freight terminal loomed up dead ahead, gray walls all but invisible overhead, where the haze drifted like fog in the yellow glare of the work lights. Instinctively, Flannery reached for his clipboard, glanced at the bill of lading as he rolled across the concrete apron, his tires thumping like a heartbeat over the heat-swollen tar strips.

At the front of the warehouse, he slowed, listened to the tired sigh of air from his brakes, and killed the engine. Grabbing the clipboard, he shoved the door open with his shoulder, dropped to the apron, and waved to Hans Schlutter, the crew chief of the night shift.

Hans waved back, turned to yell into the cavernous interior of the building, then walked across the apron. His fine blond hair was limp with humidity, sweat-darkened in places, and clung to his temples like strands of kelp. His blond mustache seemed to droop, but his smile was as ready as ever.

"Peter," he said, grinning broadly, "what the hell are you doing here this time of night?"

Schlutter's English was impeccable, his accent all but gone, and only an occasional imprecisely used idiom betraying his Teutonic origins.

Flannery shrugged, shook his head, then spread his hands widely. "You know how it is, Hans. Bills to pay, and all that."

"Double-dipping again, are you?"

Flannery grunted. "I guess you could call it that." He glanced at his clipboard, then handed it to Schlutter. "Three crates. Some sort of electronic parts, according to the paperwork."

Schlutter skimmed the bill, nodding almost imperceptibly. "Yeah, we have them. Came in from Frankfurt about three hours ago. Why don't you go on into my office? There's coffee, if you can stand it, and lemonade in the fridge."

Flannery grinned. "Strudel?"

Schlutter pursed his lips. "You like that kind of shit? Too German for me. Heavy stuff, makes you thick through the middle. But there's no accounting for taste. . . ."

Flannery walked past the crew chief and into the dimly lit interior of the warehouse. Schlutter's office sat in one corner, a cubicle, waist-high metal partitions topped by Plexiglas panels. It had no ceiling, and Flannery knew from his frequent visits that every noise in the huge building rattled around the girders under the roof then dropped into the cubicle with a deafening roar.

He walked to the small refrigerator, opened it, and found the pitcher of lemonade. Pouring himself a plastic cup full, he returned the pitcher and dropped into one of the rickety chairs. The sudden thunder of a forklift exploded against the sheet-metal roof and filled the cubicle with its clamor.

Flannery turned to watch the lumbering fork-lift, three large pallets strapped on edge, waddle like a ruptured duck, out toward his truck. The truck was sealed with a metal band, and he'd have to be there when it was broken. Hans would have to replace it with a new one, crimp it in place as soon as the freight had been loaded. One of those annoying rituals that everybody did by rote.

Sipping the lemonade, he swallowed loudly, then rolled the cold plastic against his forehead, enjoying the trickle of condensation as it dripped through his eyebrows and rolled down his cheeks. He tossed off the last of the lemonade, got to his feet, and walked back toward the apron.

The forklift sat beside his truck, belching shapeless gray clouds like a fat man trying to impress a nephew with smoke rings. More haze, Flannery thought, glancing at the sky. Between the low-hanging smog and the glare of the work lights, he couldn't see a thing above the roof level. He knew from the ride out that the stars weren't visible. There was supposed to be a full moon, but this night the city had to settle for a pale blob of light, gliding by like some prehistoric thing hauled up from the Mariana Trench.

Schlutter was waiting for him when he reached the truck. Flannery lowered the tailgate, the hydraulic snarl of the servos sounding almost petulant beside the threatening rumble of the forklift's diesel. When the tailgate was down, Flannery walked to the other side of the truck, nodded for Schlutter to join him, and waited while the German wrote down the number on the metal seal. Flannery twisted it three or four times to fatigue the soft metal, then snapped it, and rolled the corrugated door up toward the truck roof.

"Find the lemonade, Pete?" Schlutter asked.

Flannery nodded, pursed his lips. "Yeah, sour as hell."

"Pure." Schlutter grinned. "No sugar."

"Tell me about it." Flannery walked to the forklift, snatched his clipboard from the woven strap holding the pallets in place, and checked the numbers on his bill of lading. They corresponded, as they always did, and he nodded for the forklift operator to finish his job.

The forklift lurched forward a few feet, then shuddered as the fork rose above the floor level of Flannery's truck and stabbed forward. Flannery climbed up into the truck, undid the straps, and wrestled the three pallets clear of the lift, leaned them against the wall, and strapped them in place for the long ride to Manhattan.

The lift was already gone by the time he was satisfied that the pallets would stay in place, and when Flannery reached up for the pull rope on his door and dropped to the ground, pulling the door closed as he fell, Schlutter was waiting impatiently, a new seal in hand.

Closing the latch, Schlutter slipped the seal through, jammed the free end into the serrated jaws on the other end, and crimped them closed with a pair of pliers. Flannery noted the number stamped into the seal on his clipboard, then slapped the board against his thigh.

"Thanks for the lemonade, Hans," he said.

"You working nights next week, Pete?"

Flannery nodded. "Yup! No rest for the weary."

Schlutter laughed. "See you then."

Flannery waved as Schlutter walked back to the freight hangar, then climbed into the cab and started the engine. The gears argued for a moment, then slipped into first, and the truck started to roll. Flannery swung in a broad arc, until the hangar was a blur in his sideview mirror, and he headed for the gate.

He stopped long enough for the guard to note his plate number and check the seal on his truck, then ground another pound and headed out into the approach road for the Van Wyck, slowing just enough to check oncoming traffic. There wasn't much moving this late, and he headed for the city, cranking up ZZ Top again, letting the music numb him for the ride into Long Island City and the warehouse.

Even the lights in the skyscrapers were dimmed by the haze, the tip of the Empire State altogether invisible, somewhere up above the smoky pall. For half an hour he drove like a zombie, exhausted from the double shift, his eyes bleared by lack of sleep and helpless against the haze. He nearly missed the switch to the Grand Central Parkway and smacked himself in the face to wake up.

When the tape clicked into reverse, he stopped it, ejected it, and jammed in another, *The Allman Brothers Live at Fillmore East.* He'd been there the night it was recorded, and there were times when it seemed the highlight of an ordinary life, vying with the night he saw Graig Nettles give a clinic at third base in the series against the Dodgers in '78. It wasn't much to look back on, but he wasn't living for himself anymore. He was whatever he was gonna be. But the kids, that was something else. That was what was important. If he could manage to scrape together enough to get them both through college, then he could go to his rest knowing he'd given them a shot.

Leaving the Grand Central, he headed for Northern Boulevard, his favorite shortcut, which took him through the heart of Long Island City. It saved a little time and a lot of traffic. At night, the industrial section of Long Island City was a ghost town, and he could ignore traffic lights and relieve the tedium of the expressway, which reminded him all too forcefully of how much of a dead end his job was.

As he left Northern Boulevard lights appeared in his sideview all of a sudden, as if the car had sneaked up on him without them, then speared them on at the last second.

"What the fuck . . . ?"

He peered down as the car pulled alongside him, perilously close, and it took him a few seconds to realize the man in the passenger seat was pointing a gun at him, one of those ugly "Miami Vice" things that looked like it had been cobbled together from a black Erector set.

The man had his window down and was shouting, but Flannery couldn't hear him because his own window was closed and Duane Allman was in full flight. But there was no mistaking what he wanted.

Quickly, Flannery ran through the inventory in the back of the truck. He couldn't think of anything anybody would want. But that didn't seem to bother the men in the Buick alongside him. The passenger waved the gun again, and Flannery pulled over.

The car stopped in front of him, and he looked for headlights on the road behind him. But the road was deserted in either direction. Taking a deep breath, he rested his hands on the steering wheel. The passenger climbed out of the car and walked toward the front of the truck, leaving his door open. Flannery rolled down his window.

"What the hell is going on?" he demanded.

"You don't want to know, chico." The man had a slight Latin accent, and Flannery knit his brows trying to figure what the man wanted.

Nodding his head, the man gestured with the gun for Flannery to climb down out of the cab. Just to make sure, he snapped, "Get out, chico."

Flannery did as he was told. On the ground, he looked to the gunman for further instructions. The man pointed to the car, waiting with its front passenger door open, and Flannery started to move toward it, prodded by the muzzle of the ugly black gun. The rear door of the car opened, and Flannery bent over to look inside. The gunman shoved him in and slammed the door behind him. The car lurched into motion before Flannery had a chance to ask what was happening.

He turned to look back at his truck, saw the gunman climb into the cab, then something heavy slammed into the side of his head and he saw nothing more.

- T W O - - -

PAUL DESMOND CLIMBED OUT OF HIS CAR AND STOOD
looking at the tall, faceless building, its facade all dark
glass, reflecting the sky but changing its color. The
mounds of cumulus looked somehow muddied by
the opaque screen. He'd been in more such buildings
than he could remember, and just a glimpse of the
anonymous sweep of dark glass conjured visions of
their hive-like interiors. He could see acres of partitions,
padded in brightly colored burlap, swooned over by
decorators as if the rainbow splash compensated for
the dehumanization. It never bothered the bigwigs,
though, because they got to hang original paintings
on the wall, sit behind slabs of travertine for their
conferences while willowy blondes with legs a mile
long glided around them on their little cat feet, trays of

coffee and the latest in pastry in their neatly manicured hands.

Standing there looking up at the Northamerican Insurance building, he wondered why they needed him. Insurance fraud was not really his game. He liked more exotic work. You don't leave Czechoslovakia, and the only life you'd ever known, or expected to know, in the back of a peasant wagon just to find out whether somebody hid his TV in the garage before reporting a burglary.

But his taste for the exotic had taken him to places he now wished he'd never gone, years of reality eroding the boulder of his morality, reducing it, micron by micron, while he tried to stay alive in Vietnam and the Philippines, East Germany, and Cairo. He'd turned his back on the fatal attraction of intelligence work, but he sometimes wondered whether he'd waited too long. He had his own business now, Langley's creaky, Byzantine machinery far behind him. He was still a hired gun, but at least now he could choose the currency in which he got paid. And it was up to him whether the price was right. Maybe, he thought, insurance fraud is what I should have been doing all along.

It was a noisome thought, but he started toward the front of the building anyway. He stopped on the broad plaza, the scent of begonias from the too neat gardens on either side strong in the air, and stared at his reflection in the tinted glass behind which the lobby was just a wavering mirage of earth tones, further subdued by the dark windows. What he saw was distorted, a stick man in a business suit, Ichabod Crane wearing something from Brooks Brothers. His six-foot-two frame had been drawn like wire, the two hundred pounds he carried squeezed into a pin-striped pencil by the curved glass. He took a step, thought of John Cleese and his Ministry of Silly Walks, turned sidewise and stuck one leg out, bent it at the knee, and started to laugh.

"I have a silly walk, too." The voice was musical, feminine, and he was too startled to be embarrassed as he turned to see who had spoken.

Desmond found himself staring at a redhead not that much under six feet tall. Her suit was the businesswoman's version of his own, but it looked a lot better on her than his did on him. And it did little to conceal the figure it draped.

Her green eyes sparkled in the sunlight and her full lips trembled with amusement. "Sorry," she said. "I didn't mean to embarrass you. It's just that I've done the same thing."

"I'd like to see that," Desmond said, smiling.

"Okay." With that, she stuck one long, perfectly sculpted leg out in front of her, broke it at the knee, and swiveled her foot toward him. Desmond knew he should watch her reflection in the glass to get the full effect, but the leg was too nearly perfect, the distortion of the dark glass almost criminal.

She turned then without seeming to move and walked in that same disjointed gait for several paces before turning to wave to him and disappearing into the building.

Desmond shook his head, checked his reflection once more, and started for the lobby. By the time he had whirled through the revolving door, the redhead was long gone. He walked to the security desk, where a chubby man with a white walrus mustache pushed his peaked cap back on his ruddy forehead. "Help you?" he asked.

"I have an appointment with Valerie Harrison," Desmond told him.

The guard checked his phone list, dialed, and watched Desmond's face while he waited for an answer.

Desmond could tell when someone came on the line, because the guard nodded, turning his head just slightly to say, "Yes, I have a visitor for Miss Harrison." He covered the phone then, and his lips shaped the words, "Your name," before uncupping the receiver and repeating, "Paul Desmond." There was a slight pause, then the guard said, "Very good. I'll send him up." He replaced the phone.

"Sixteenth floor, Suite 1608," he said, nodding toward the bank of elevators across the polished marble floor.

"Thanks," Desmond said, turning toward the elevators. He crossed the floor, staring at the reflection of his shoe tips on the gleaming stone, cringing as he heard some sand crunch under his heels, and wondering at the damage to the faultless sheen.

One of the elevators was open and he stepped inside, punched a button marked "16," and moved to the rear, where he stood in one corner, his briefcase pinned against the elevator wall by his right knee.

The doors closed, and the car blasted off with a pneumatic wheeze. The car smelled of wood polish, an aggressive sweetness that made him crinkle his lips in distaste. He watched the numbers, and when the sixteenth-floor light went on, he stepped toward the door, leaning one hand out to brace himself for the sudden stop as the car slowed abruptly then glided upward the last few feet. The doors hissed open almost instantly, and he stepped out onto a dark green carpet, read a sign that sported numbers and a pair of arrows, and turned left for Suite 1608.

The wall on his right was glass, and beyond it, the maze of partitions was already teeming. Instinctively, he glanced at his watch, wondering whether he was late, but it was just a few minutes past nine. The wall on his right was solid, broken every few yards by a solid wooden door. On each, a brass plate listed the number and, less permanently, a slip-in identified the current occupant.

He found 1608 without difficulty, and the plate, sure enough, listed Valerie Harrison as its inhabitant. He knocked and heard a buzz in response. Grabbing the knob, he turned it and pushed inward to find himself in a waiting room. As he stepped through he noticed a TV camera mounted in the ceiling. Almost instinctively, he glanced at the receptionist's desk, saw the small monitor occupying one corner, and only then noticed the woman sitting in front of it.

She smiled pleasantly, flicking her hair back with one long-nailed hand. "Ms. Harrison will be with you in a moment, Mr. Desmond," she said, without really looking at him. She lowered her hand and began to clack at the keys of a computer keyboard.

Desmond found a seat on a leather sofa, leaned toward the end table to riffle through a stack of magazines, most of which seemed to be devoted to fine art and the collectibles market. There seemed to be specialty magazines for nearly every century of French furniture, Early American antiques, baseball cards, and virtually anything else that someone might choose to hoard.

He picked up one of the art magazines and leaned back to riffle through the pages. Along with the usual gossip, the slick pages were full of color, nearly every one featuring a photo of a painting or, more frequently, an ad for the kind of thing that could only be afforded by someone well enough off to collect canvases.

He started an article about Picasso's blue period, but the prose was wooden, overlarded with the kind of hyperbole critics use when they know their opinion is certain to be unchallenged because it's already everyone's opinion anyway. He spent a few moments flipping the pages to examine the photographs of representative canvases, keeping one eye on the clock behind the woman at the desk.

A door to the left of the desk, behind which he thought Ms. Harrison must be hard at work, remained stubbornly closed. He stared at it for a moment, as if he thought that would make it less formidable an obstacle, perhaps even make it swing open, but nothing happened, and he leaned back with his hands folded behind his neck.

His eyes had almost closed when a loud buzz snatched him back from the edge of oblivion. He sat up and looked at the woman at the desk, who pressed a button and said, "Yes, Ms. Harrison?"

A hidden speaker burred, and the woman nodded. She climbed out from behind her desk and walked to the door, standing there with one hand on the knob as she announced, "Ms. Harrison will see you now, Mr. Desmond."

She waited for him to get to his feet and grab his briefcase before opening the door and giving it a dainty shove. It swung open noiselessly, and she stepped aside to let him through. As he stepped past he caught a whiff of her perfume, something vaguely familiar that he couldn't name.

The door started to close behind him as he looked across the vast expanse of carpet, over the top of a magnificent walnut desk, and found himself staring at the redhead with the silly walk.

This time he *was* embarrassed. She grinned at him, letting the tip of her tongue just peek out between perfect teeth and trace the curve of her lower lip.

"So, Mr. Desmond, we meet again," she said.

"So it would appear."

"Well, since we both made fools of ourselves, I suppose neither of us gets an advantage."

"I wouldn't be so sure. The employer always has an edge to begin with. When the prospective hiree has behaved like a perfect idiot, one would think the advantage insuperable."

Valerie Harrison shook her head, her mounds of loose red curls trembling with the movement. "Not at all." Pointing to a leather chair beside the massive desk, she said, "Why don't you sit down?"

Desmond did as she suggested. "Perhaps we should get right to business while you're still in a charitable mood, Ms. Harrison. . . ."

She leaned back in her chair, but didn't look as comfortable as she apparently thought she did. It struck Desmond that she was aping something, some model not fully digested, as if she were new at her job, or had chosen someone to emulate, perhaps in one of those pointless seminars that seem to siphon off so much productive time and corporate capital to negligible effect.

"What do you know about art, Mr. Desmond?" she asked.

He grinned. "I know what I like."

"Nice try. But that's not what I mean."

"What *do* you mean, Ms. Harrison?"

She changed tack without warning. "Northamerican is the largest insurer of fine art and antiques in the country, did you know that?"

"As a matter of fact, I did. I took the trouble to check into the company after I received your call."

"Things have changed, gotten more urgent, since then."

"How?"

"I told you that we had incurred significant losses, through theft, and that we were interested in hiring you to recover as much of the stolen property as possible. But there has been another theft, and this time there has also been a murder."

"That is a police matter, Ms. Harrison."

She nodded. "I know. But we are more anxious than ever to retain your services. The police have their agenda, and we have ours. Needless to say, they do not precisely coincide."

"Tell me what happened."

"Three more canvases were stolen last night. They were flown in from Germany disguised as printed circuitry, but the truck which was to transport them from JFK to the Pratt Museum was found this morning in Long Island City. The driver, a man named Peter Flannery, was in the back of the truck. He'd been shot several times. The only things missing were three paintings."

Desmond sucked on a tooth. "Is there a possibility

he was involved in the thefts? That it blew up on him somehow?"

"The police suggested the same thing, of course. And anything's possible, but that wouldn't explain the other missing paintings, because the same shipping companies were not involved in all of the thefts. That was one of the things we hoped you would find out for us. I'm prepared to offer you a substantial fee."

"How much are we talking about, Ms. Harrison? The missing art, I mean?"

"Seventy-three million dollars. That, at least, is the insured value. The market is almost out of control, as you may know. But as long as paintings continue to move at auction the way they have, those prices will continue to increase."

"How many canvases are missing?"

"Nine, plus the three taken last night. Twelve altogether."

"That makes for a fairly hefty average price. More than six million dollars apiece."

"Most of that value is tied up in a few canvases. Four Monets and a Matisse."

"And you have no idea where they might be, who stole them, or how?"

"Not a clue. The police are baffled as well. They have a fine art task force because of the recent spate of thefts, but so far they have been unable to come up with anything. I don't need to tell you that seventy-three million dollars is a lot of money. More than we would care to pay. But we don't have much time before the first of the payments will become due. So there is some urgency involved."

"I have other clients, Ms. Harrison, as I'm sure you

know. I don't know how much time I can devote, at least initially."

"Time is money, or at least that's what my father used to say. I suppose it's true. In any case, we are prepared to act on that assumption. In addition to expenses, we will pay you a guarantee of two hundred thousand dollars, against one percent of the assessed value for each canvas recovered. If you locate them all, that will be nearly three quarters of a million dollars."

"Time, as you say, is money. Unfortunately, I have much more of the former than the latter. Accordingly, your price is quite attractive."

"Then you'll take the assignment?"

Desmond was noncommittal. "I'm not sure yet. Tell me everything you know. No point in my getting in over my head."

"Where shall I start?"

"The beginning would be a good place, I think. . . ."

- THREE- - -

RAY MILLER DIDN'T LOOK LIKE A COP. HIS HAIR WAS long, pulled back into a ponytail, and hung over the neck of his faded denim work shirt. The twinkle in his ear was from a diamond earring, and his gaunt frame looked more appropriate for an emaciated basketball player than an officer of the law. But his big-knuckled hands were strong; the forearms, visible up to the elbow where the rolled-up sleeves hid his biceps, were corded with muscle.

Leaning back in his chair, he fixed Desmond with a quizzical expression. "You mean to tell me," he said, shaking his head as if he couldn't quite grasp the concept, "that Northamerican has hired you to find a dozen paintings, and they are actually going to pay you good money to do something that we have been unable to do for free?"

Desmond smiled disarmingly. "That's about the size of it."

"Hell, it's their money, but I don't think you'll have any more luck than we've had. Unless you already know something more than we do."

"What's that supposed to mean?"

Miller didn't answer immediately. He fished a crumpled pack of Marlboro Lights from his pocket, pulled one from the pack, and staightened it between his long fingers before jamming it into his mouth. Repocketing the pack, he withdrew a cheap plastic lighter, lit the cigarette, and tucked the lighter away. His answer followed the first puff of smoke, almost as if he meant to disguise the words somehow. "It means maybe Northamerican has been holding out on us. Maybe they know more than they're willing to tell us."

"Why would they hold out on you?"

Miller smiled benignly. "Look, Mr. Desmond, I don't know how much you know about art collectors, museums, and all that. But . . ." He paused, waiting for Desmond to enlighten him, and when his visitor said nothing, he continued, "Some of these folks are queer ducks. I don't know why, and I don't care why. Maybe it's something to do with taxes, maybe it's got to do with not wanting anyone to know what they own. Hell, for all I know, maybe they don't even own the paintings in the first place. Half the time they probably don't. They take loans to buy a canvas, so technically it belongs to the lender anyhow."

"Fraud, is that what you're thinking?"

Miller sucked on the cigarette. "Why not? Look at it this way. You're rich as hell, but your money's tied up. Suddenly you need cash, lots of it, more than you can get your hands on in a hurry. You have this painting, it's insured, so . . ." He shrugged.

"But the money goes to the lender, not the owner, doesn't it?"

"Not as long as you make your payments on time. You put the money in the bank, do whatever it is you have to do, and nobody gets hurt. In the meantime, you have a bundle to play with, make more money."

"Nobody gets hurt, maybe, except Northamerican. So why would they hold out on you? If the paintings aren't found, they have to cough up."

"Don't expect me to shed any tears for an insurance company, Mr. Desmond. And as for them having to cough up, sometimes there are more important things than money. Maybe they're protecting a client because they have bigger fish to fry. Maybe there's some other business relationship between client and insurer that's worth protecting. I know that sounds cynical, and I don't even believe it myself. But this thing is so damn frustrating, I sometimes think maybe I'm looking in the wrong places for the wrong things. I start spinning webs and get caught in them myself."

"What have you learned so far—about the missing paintings, I mean?"

"Not much. As near as we can tell, not one of them has turned up on the black market."

"Black market? Artwork?"

"Like I said. The rich are different. They like to own things, and sometimes they aren't too particular about how they come by something. You like Monet, say, and there's nothing on the legitimate market, or at least nothing you can afford, then maybe you look elsewhere. A man happens to know where you can get hold of one. It'll cost, of course, but not as much as a legitimate sale."

"If you had to guess, where would you say the paintings were right now?"

"I'm not paid to guess, Mr. Desmond." Miller sucked on the weed again, let out a thin stream of smoke, then added, "But most likely they're sitting in some vault somewhere. It's too soon for some of them, although not all of them, to have made their way onto somebody's wall. But there hasn't been a demand for a buyback, ransom, whatever, so I have to believe that whoever took them did so either to keep them or to sell them."

"I gather we're not talking about the ordinary kind of fence, here."

Miller laughed outright. "Damn right we're not. Fact is, where you draw the line between a legitimate art dealer and a black-market gallery type is anything but clear. Reputation is everything with these people. Think about it. If somebody's asking you to lay out, say, two million dollars, you want to know that this man knows what he's talking about. You want, in other words, authenticity. But you don't sell Picassos out of the back of a station wagon, like some hot Corning Ware. So, some of the gallery owners live on the edge a little, let their expertise maybe suggest potential buyers. Nothing on paper, nothing you could prove in court. In fact, some of them might go a whole lot further, maybe even suggesting that such and such a canvas might have a real fan somewhere, you know what I mean. Word gets around and, bingo, such and such a painting disappears, sometimes for good."

"And do you know which gallery owners are closest to the line?"

"Sure I do, but I can't prove anything."

Desmond changed tack. "What about this latest theft? Any leads?"

"The German stuff?" Miller shook his head. "Not yet. Too recent. It takes a while for word to leak out. There's a lot of backbiting and spite work involved. Somebody gets pissed off at somebody else and starts dropping little hints that so-and-so just might have a Monet or two squirreled away in the closet. Sometimes they even send anonymous tips to the Crayon Patrol. That's what the rest of the department calls us. They're just jealous, I think, because we get more wine and cheese than they do. Anyhow, half the time we check into something like that, it turns out that somebody got into a snit and decided to make a little trouble. Usually, there's nothing to the tip. Mostly, it's grunt work like just about every other kind of police work. All that sweat doesn't suit our image with the upper classes, but that can't be helped."

"What about the murder?"

"The Flannery thing, you mean?"

Desmond nodded. "I understand from Valerie Harrison that it's the first time violence was involved."

"Maybe for her clients, but it sure as hell ain't the first time for us. Crime is crime, Mr. Desmond. When millions of dollars are at stake, there is always someone willing to cut out your heart. Whether he uses a machete or a palette knife is all a matter of degree, nothing more."

"Do you think it was an inside job?"

Miller shrugged. "If you're asking me whether I think Flannery was part of the problem, I don't know. We're looking into it, working with homicide. But so far, it doesn't look like it. Flannery was squeaky clean. Just what he seemed to be, a hardworking stiff who put in two shifts whenever he could to save money for his kids' college tuition. Besides, there were so many layers of insulation between him and the truth, he probably couldn't have helped if he wanted to. You look at his bank account, his life-style, what have you, and there's not a hint of unexplained money. If he was involved, he buried the profits in a coffee can. We haven't dug up his backyard, but if I had to guess, I'd say he was just an innocent victim. What we can't figure is why kill him, unless he knew one of the thieves. Maybe we'll never know. Naturally, that doesn't mean we can rule out involvement on his part, at least not until we have someplace better to look. But for the time being . . ."

"I'd like to work with you on this, if—"

Miller shook his head. "Look, I'll give you whatever information I can, but you have your agenda and I have mine. That means you'll think I'm dragging my feet and I'll think you have tunnel vision. That isn't the best kind of working relationship, so I think we'd be better off staying in touch but out of each other's way. If you want a look at the files on the paintings in question, give me a list, and I'll have them pulled. But for the time being, I think we'd best let it go at that. I'm open-minded, though, so if you dig up something you think might be of interest, let me know. And I'll do the same."

"You know best."

Miller chuckled. "Hell I do. If I knew best, I would have listened to my old man. He told me not to become a cop."

"Sometimes we do what we have to," Desmond suggested.

"Yeah, well, I still should have listened to him." Miller stubbed out his cigarette. Getting to his feet, he said, "Look, you want me to hook you up with Rich Allen, the guy who's working the Flannery killing, let me know."

"I suppose I should talk to him," Desmond agreed, getting up out of his chair. "And if you don't mind, I would like to look at the files you mentioned."

"No skin off my ass. You got the list?"

Desmond nodded, yanked his briefcase off the floor, and set it on the corner of Miller's desk. Opening it, he pulled out a pad, made a quick list with a mechanical pencil, and handed it to Miller.

The detective perused the list for a moment. "Big bucks," he said, pursing his lips. "No wonder Valerie wanted some outside help."

"I don't know how much help I'll be, but it's a job."

Miller grunted. "Some job. You find half of these, you can buy a place on the beach someplace and never work again." He looked at Desmond for a moment, his eyes narrowing slightly. "You any relation to that sax player?"

It was Desmond's turn to grunt. "Actually, no. I took his name when I became a citizen."

Miller looked interested now. "Where you from?"

"Czechoslovakia. I came over in 1968."

Miller nodded as if he understood. "How'd you get into this line of work?"

"It's a long story."

"I got to grab a sandwich. You're welcome to come along. I'm a good listener. I'll put in the list before we leave, and the files'll be ready when we get back. Save you a second trip, maybe."

Desmond thought about it, then deciding that Miller was, for whatever reason, trying to build a small bridge, he decided to accept the offer. "Sure. I'm buying, though."

Miller smiled. "Why do you think I invited you?"

"And you say the rich are devious." Desmond laughed.

"Hey, I'm a quick study. I watch how they do it and adapt to my own environment."

— FOUR — — —

DESMOND STRUGGLED WITH HIS BOW TIE. HE WAS
still in the bathroom, bent over the sink, his neck
stretched to the breaking point; his muttered curses
were taut and high-pitched.

"Having trouble, honey?"

Desmond cursed at the question, too. Audrey had a
way of making him feel as silly as he ought to feel.
Wearing a tuxedo was one of those occasions, and they
both knew it. In the mirror, he saw her appear in the
doorway behind him, her face radiant. He wasn't sure
whether it was expectation or amusement at his
expense, but they had been together long enough that
he suspected the latter.

"Damn monkey suit," he muttered.

Audrey chuckled. "You should see how funny you

look. Like a zebra that wants to be a giraffe. Why are you stretching your neck like that?"

"It's the only way I can see the goddamned tie."

"I told you to buy a clip-on."

She had, but he had refused. On those rare, but not rare enough, occasions when he had to wear a tux, he thought he should wear a tie actually knotted by human hands instead of some machine in Taiwan or mainland China. It was some sort of perverse respect for a set of conventions he mocked at every opportunity. But he was no less in their thrall for all of his contempt.

"I don't get it," he said. "I mean, will the paintings look better if I can't breathe and look like a decoration on a wedding cake? Why do they insist on this?"

Audrey approached, rested a hand on his shoulder. "Because," she informed him, "the idea of affairs like this is public display. You have to show everyone that you belong to the club. So you wear the uniform. Money has more than a little to do with it, too, I suspect. And lest we forget, you spent so much time burrowing through the world like a mole that public display is like sunlight to a vampire where you're concerned."

"You should have been a sociologist, instead of a painter."

"Painters *are* sociologists, Pavel. You know that as well as I do."

Desmond smiled at her use of his birth name. It meant she was sympathetic to him, for all her teasing. His fingers grappled with the slippery silk for a moment, then he pulled. "Voilà!" He stepped back and whirled like Fred Astaire.

Expecting plaudits, he was surprised to see Audrey's face dissolve in hysterics. "What's wrong?" he asked.

"Did you see it? I mean, did you really see it before you turned around?"

"Sort of. I was so excited to get it done, I wanted to share my joy with the woman I love."

"Thank you. But turn around. I'm not sure I'm ready for so much happiness. Turn around, and take a good look."

Desmond did as he was ordered. In the glass, his neck its normal length now, he could see the tie clearly. One wing was twice the size of the other. Together, they sat at a forty-five-degree angle. It looked altogether like some sort of mutant moth with broken wings. Desmond bit his lip. "No good, huh?" he asked.

In the mirror, he could see Audrey shaking her head. "No good at all, Paulie. No good at all. Turn around. I'll fix it."

Meekly, he turned, raised his chin like a little boy waiting for a bib, and felt the sudden release of pressure on his throat as Audrey untied the tie. She worked quickly, and when she was done, he didn't even bother to check her work in the mirror. "Perfect," he said.

"How do you know? You can't see it."

"I know who tied it. It's perfect."

"It is rather good."

"See?"

Audrey turned to leave. "Janine is here. I want to give her a few last-minute instructions."

"Where are the girls?"

"With Janine, of course. They prefer their baby sitter to their parents. It's natural."

"Were you like that at their age?"

"I'm still like that."

Desmond watched her leave the bedroom, then reached back to turn off the bathroom light. He wasn't even tempted to check the bow tie before the switch clicked.

Downstairs, he found his daughters in the den with Janine. Sally, the older of the two, was hunched over her Genesis controls, and some creature named Sonic, supposedly a hedgehog, was darting around through pipes and girders, accompanied by clanging bells. Maria, who professed contempt for video games, watched as if mesmerized. Janine was reading a two-week old issue of *People*.

"We'll be late, girls," Audrey said. "You go to bed when Janine tells you to, understood?"

Sally grunted and Maria bobbed her head wordlessly.

Desmond stood back and looked at his wife, proud and humbled at the same instant. She was magnificent for any age, but for a woman in her middle forties, she was something special. The figure was a little fuller than it had been at their first meeting, the cheeks just a little rounder. But whenever he looked at her, he saw the slender, jean-clad figure sprinting across the Berkeley campus, a tangle of red hair trailing behind her, braless breasts bouncing under her work shirt.

She felt his appraising gaze and looked at him sharply. "What are you thinking?" She knew the answer, and he knew she knew, but he gave the obligatory answer.

"Nothing."

"I'll bet." The gold flecks in her green eyes seemed to sparkle for a moment. It was an indication either that she was angry, or that she was thinking exactly what he was thinking. He wouldn't want to bet the farm on which it was.

"We'd better go," he said. "Folks at these wine and cheese bashes are adamant about punctuality."

Audrey laughed. "Wine and cheese? At the biggest opening in the Pratt's history? I don't think so."

"I thought all you artsy types do that, live on *vin et fromage,* or whatever."

Audrey pinched him hard enough to leave a bruise on his biceps. "Let's go, you Philistine! I want to get a look at this woman who gave you the tickets."

The ride to the city took nearly ninety minutes. It started in the pleasant rolling hills above the Hudson, where vineyards oozed like lava down toward the water. The green was thick, its smell pungent. Despite the heat, Desmond kept the windows open and the air-conditioning off. He and Audrey both preferred the smell of woods. Instead of taking the thruway, they used back roads for the first thirty miles or so, some solo Monk on the car stereo. To Desmond, it couldn't have been any closer to the America he'd been looking for so long ago now that it seemed like another lifetime. Beautiful scenery, great jazz, and the woman he cared about above all else on the planet in the seat beside him.

But it had been a long road. He still had agonizing nightmares, filled with the mechanized thunder of tank treads rolling into Wenceslaus Square in early '68. Prague Spring, they called it, as if everything that was happening, everything that was hoped for, could be lumped together in a single phrase. It was political anguish reduced to Madison Avenue hype. But for most people, that was all that remained of that long-ago time. For Desmond, though, it was different. It was a future that might have been crushed under those clanking treads, a life uprooted, a history cast off like a snakeskin, not by choice, but by necessity.

And what came next was, with the sole exception of Audrey, even worse. His engineering degrees, the time at MIT and Berkeley, thoughts of architecture, burying his heartache in the uncompromising discipline of science all seemed like some cruel prelude to two decades in the employ of American intelligence agencies. In some ways, he had been a natural—a Czech by birth, fluent in that language, as well as German and Russian, an emigré—no wonder the CIA found him attractive. The wonder, though, was that he had found the Company just as attractive.

He had learned much about himself in the course of the first ten years in Europe and all the Easts—Near, Middle, and Far—so much, in fact, that it took him nearly another decade in Langley to realize that what he had learned was that intelligence was not for him, not because he was not good at it—he was—but because it was twisting him into knots, slowly but surely. Audrey had endured the anguish, stood by him as no one else would have, and when he finally puzzled his way all the way through the maze, she was still there, surely the eighth wonder of any world.

That was ancient history now, but he knew what they said about those who ignored history. Looking out at the river, the east bank bathed in moonlight, slivers of that light lying on the water like so many swords, he knew he was lucky, luckier than he had a right to be, luckier than some good friends had been. He had managed to come through the meat grinder intact, scarred and scared, but not destroyed.

Running his own company, even though it seemed to suspend him in that murky twilight between his old world and the one he wanted for his wife and daughters, kept him alive, paid the bills. It was his compromise with the world, a one-man pact with reality that he honored every day, and that the world honored in the breach more often than not. He would do it because he had to, because he was fit for nothing else, really. But that was all right.

There was, after all, salvation—Thelonious Monk and Charlie Parker, John Coltrane and Miles Davis. The music of men who had waged their own private wars with the world and, win or lose, had made something lasting, left behind something that had not been there before. He was, in his love of jazz, more American than anyone he knew, or maybe more European than he thought, because he could not find the music on the radio, or in the malls. In a way, that was all right, too. Coming to America had been a kind of quest. Searching for the music was just a way to reenact it over and over again, make it ritual.

"Monk's Point" came on, and he leaned over to turn it up.

Audrey leaned back in the seat, then reached out to let a hand rest on his leg. "What's on your mind, Paul?" she asked.

"Nothing."

"Don't try to fool me. I know you too well, Pavel. When you turn the music up like that, it means you're thinking about something."

"Sometimes," he said, "it just means I'm thinking about the music."

"Not this time."

He patted her hand. "No, you're right. Not this time."

"Well?"

"Later, hon. Let's just relax and enjoy the drive."

"You're uneasy about this job, aren't you?"

"Not really."

"You could have fooled me."

"I don't think so. I fooled you once, and you've never let me forget it. No way I could do it again."

"You don't much like the kind of people we're going to be with this evening, do you?"

"Not much, no."

"I don't either, if it makes you feel better."

"I guess. What will really make me feel better, though, is to take off this damn straitjacket. I can't breathe."

"You're not supposed to."

"Oh. Now I feel better. I was worried I was doing something wrong."

- FIVE- - -

THE PRATT WAS A BEEHIVE AS THEY APPROACHED IT from Fifth Avenue. A huge banner, nearly three stories high and anchored to the front of the building, featured Monet-like water lilies. It fluttered in the warm breeze, its colors shimmering in the floodlights bathing the gleaming glass facade of the museum.

Seeing so many black ties, Desmond felt less foolish, but only slightly. It still struck him as cruel and unusual punishment to be shoehorned into a monkey suit. But Audrey didn't seem to mind, and he did his best to grin and bear it.

Desmond fished the invitation from his jacket pocket, handed it to the stiffly starched attendant, then took Audrey's elbow to steer her through the maze of velvet ropes.

"Quite a turnout," he mumbled.

"It's not often a show of this importance makes an appearance. Even in New York," Audrey said. "It's probably the biggest thing in ten years. It's quite a coup, you know. Some of these canvases haven't been seen by the public in this century."

"So I've been told. With any luck, you'll meet the man who pried them loose."

"What's Hemenway like?"

"Not much, as near as I can tell. But then, I only spoke to him for a few minutes and that was on the phone. I'll be bearding him in his lair tomorrow."

Audrey gave him a genteel elbow, and he grinned. "Oh, you mean what *is* he like, not what *does* he like, is that it?"

She scowled, but she was used to him, and he was used to her scowling, so they left the end of the maze, Desmond, feeling just a bit like a lab rat, wondering whether he had earned a little corn or an electric shock.

They joined the elegantly attired line at the foot of an escalator. "Feels sort of like the unemployment line in Bel Air, I'll bet," Desmond whispered.

A tall, silver-haired man ahead of him heard the crack and turned to grin at him. "Not well enough dressed for that." He laughed. "But the escalator makes social climbing so much less strenuous."

As they stepped onto the escalator they glanced toward the next level. Valerie Harrison was standing there, watching the arrivals. She wore a formfitting blue sheath that did nothing whatever to disguise her considerable endowments. When she spotted Desmond, she waved frantically.

Leaning close, Audrey whispered, "Who in the world is that? And why is she waving at you?"

"That's Valerie Harrison, from the insurance company."

"No wonder you took the job. My God, what a . . ."

"Body?" Desmond suggested. He took another elbow in the ribs for his effort. When he caught his breath, he whispered, "She's very pleasant, and besides, she's signing the checks, so be nice."

At the top of the escalator, Desmond stepped out of the line, followed by Audrey. After he'd introduced the women to each other, Valerie said, "Come on, no need for you to stand in line. Let's go to the reception room first, unless you're in a hurry to see the paintings."

"I could use a drink, actually," Desmond said.

Catching his eye, Audrey nodded. "So could I. . . ."

"Great! Follow me." Valerie headed toward a pair of gleaming walnut doors, opened the one on the right, and led the way into a carpeted room, humming with conversation.

There was a wet bar, and Desmond ordered a diet Coke. Audrey, since she wasn't driving, and since she felt the need for a little fortification, asked for a stinger, and Valerie ordered a seltzer.

"Quite a turnout tonight," Desmond said, taking a sip of his soda.

"It's a circus. It always is. Once we get through this, I'll feel a whole lot better."

"I'm surprised your job requires you to be here," Audrey said.

"It doesn't," Valerie answered. "But I can't stand the thought of sitting in an office, treating art as if it were nothing more than gold bars or stock certificates. If I had any guts, I'd be working in a gallery somewhere."

Audrey perked up, thinking that perhaps Valerie was more than a Euclidean treatise decked out in haute couture. "Are you an artist?" she asked.

Valerie shook her head. "Not anymore. I haven't painted in years. I have a degree in fine art, but when it was painfully clear I had to choose between painting and eating, I went back to school for an MBA. The fall was almost complete. Insurance was just the last bounce."

"I think I'll take a walk, see who else turned out for the opening," Desmond said. "If you see Mr. Hemenway, point him out, would you?"

"I can introduce you, if you like. He's right over there," Valerie said, pointing discreetly.

Desmond shook his head. "No, I'll just watch him tonight, get some idea on how the other half lives. I don't want to socialize too much. You never know who might turn up in a place like this."

"You don't really think you'll find the thieves here, do you?" Audrey asked.

Desmond placed a finger to his lips. "No, but I'd like to get a feel for the place. Mr. Hemenway was anything but cordial on the phone this morning. Made it sound like seeing me was a huge concession—to what, I have no idea. I'd like to nose around a little without his condescending assistance."

He left the women and worked his way toward the main gallery housing the exhibit. Familiar faces surrounded him, the movers and shakers out to keep their reputations burnished. Several glanced at him curiously, wondering whether they should know him and, if not, what he was doing there among them.

Desmond smiled at an actor, whose name he couldn't quite place, but the man was too busy eyeing the cleavage of the long blonde beside him.

He watched Hemenway for a few moments, in deep conversation with a smaller man whose tuxedo fit as poorly as Desmond imagined his own did. Hemenway kept one hand firmly on the other man's shoulder, as if trying to keep him from running away.

Once, the smaller man looked at Desmond and let his gaze linger a few seconds, prompting Hemenway to turn around. But the director of the museum did not know him, and turned back to his animated discussion. Desmond drifted away, looking at people as well as canvases.

He saw a couple of Astors and Whitneys, somebody from the *Times,* one of the Sulzbergers, but he wasn't sure which one, and at least half a dozen faces vaguely familiar from the silver screen. Once, he found himself staring into the vapid gaze of a local TV anchor, the face blank, almost stunned, as if he'd just heard something he couldn't believe. It took Desmond a few moments to realize it was the same expression the man wore on TV and, presumably, was the configuration of the man's features in repose.

Finally out in the main gallery, away from the tinkle of ice and the steady buzz of conversation, he felt as if he'd stepped out on a terrace into the fresh air.

A handful of people drifted from painting to painting, and Desmond took his time, letting his gut select canvases for special attention. One sequence of Monet haystacks, the rich orange, pink, blues, and purples marking the passage of sunlight from one corner of the world to another, was overwhelming. Desmond could almost smell the sweet decay of the damp hay and had to restrain himself from reaching out to run his fingers over the thickly textured pigment.

Entering another gallery, he heard angry voices and moved into the next gallery, where he saw a crowd of tuxedos and evening gowns milling behind yet another velvet rope. Several of the tuxedos were arguing with a pair of long-suffering museum guards, waving their invitations and pointing to their watches.

Desmond watched curiously, heard the click of hard leather heels on the floor behind him, and turned to see Clarence Hemenway hustling toward the disturbance.

The director nodded vaguely in Desmond's direction, his lips moving but without uttering sound, and hurried past. At the entrance, he raised his hands, until the crowd grew quiet. Then, with a grand flourish, he unhooked the rope and waved the throng on into the galleries.

The two guards looked at each other, then moved off to take their assigned positions for the duration. Desmond mingled quietly, examining several paintings that caught his fancy. Now and then, he was forced to stop his ears to avoid the nasal pronouncements from particularly opinionated vistors, but the art was more than compensation.

All the major Impressionists were represented, some by as many as two dozen works. And several of the second-tier practitioners of the manner had a room of their own. Once or twice, he caught a glimpse of Audrey, still talking with Valerie Harrison. As they drifted from one painting to another the two women turned more than a few heads, and Desmond was pleased that not all of the lust was directed at the taller of the two redheads.

The guards were strategically placed, and Desmond noted that the most expensive canvases were clearly visible from at least two different posts. The guards themselves seemed as interested in the crowd as they were in the paintings. They scanned faces, never letting their eyes linger too long in any one place.

Any abrupt movement brought a glance, a raised voice, a quick stare. They were not there to enforce decorum, but any commotion might be an indication that the paintings were in jeopardy. It was a thoroughly professional crew, from Rollins Security. Desmond knew Don Rollins, and thought that a visit with him might be a good idea and made a mental note to that effect as he drifted into another Monet room.

Like the other galleries, it was crowded. He spotted Audrey, by herself now, and moved over to join her. Slipping in behind her, he linked his arm in hers and planted a wet kiss on her bare shoulder.

She was startled, but didn't bother to turn. "No wonder you don't get invited to these things very often. You just don't know how to behave."

"How'd you know it was me?"

Audrey turned and gave him an angelic smile. "I didn't," she said. "But it would have have been true no matter who it was."

"Has it happened before?"

"At least half a dozen times."

"You seemed to hit it off with Ms. Harrison very nicely."

"She's very nice. And bright, too. We had a pleasant chat."

"I thought you'd like her."

"Did you—"

A sudden shout stopped her in midquestion. Heads turned toward the sound, and Desmond looked around trying to spot the source of the disturbance. Another shout, this one hard-edged, echoed from the high ceilings, and Desmond realized it had come from the next gallery.

He started to run as a woman's shriek sliced through the silence. There was another shout, full of the same guttural fury as the first two, and Desmond careened around a corner, nearly knocking over a platinum blonde and sending her drink in a bright rainbow all over the tuxedo of her companion.

The crowd was backing away from someone, but Desmond couldn't see who, or how many.

"He's got a knife!" someone shouted, and Desmond pulled two men aside just as a vaguely familiar man in an ill-fitting tuxedo dashed toward one of the Monet haystacks. He raised a hand over his head and the glitter of polished metal arced toward the canvas. The man grunted, slamming the blade into the center of the canvas and slicing toward one edge of the frame.

Someone grabbed Desmond by the arm. "Be careful," the woman said. "He's a lunatic."

Desmond shook off her arm and raced toward the man, who sliced in the other direction, then, hearing Desmond's footsteps, turned toward him, brandishing a heavy butcher knife with a ten-inch blade.

"Stay back," he snarled. "These are mine. I can do anything I want with them."

Without looking, he jabbed the knife at the tattered canvas behind him, striking the wall and slicing upward. The shriek of rending canvas filled the silence for a moment, then the man darted toward the next canvas.

A guard materialized at Desmond's shoulder. "I've

called the police," he said, "but we've got to stop him before he destroys another painting."

As if goaded by the guard, the small man darted to his left, slicing into and through a second haystack, ripping it from side to side right through the center.

"Mine!" he shouted. "This is mine. Genius, you see, genius! And worthless."

Desmond took a step forward. More guards were materializing, trying to get the patrons out of harm's way and to form a cordon around the cutlery-waving patron. The madman brandished the knife, waving it back and forth, waist-high. He was holding it the wrong way, and Desmond was comforted by the fact that he was clearly an inexperienced knife fighter.

"I think you'd better put the knife down," Desmond said, "before someone gets hurt."

"Fuck you. You're like all the rest of them. Bottom feeders. Bloodsuckers. You bastard!"

Desmond shook his head. He sensed rather than saw the guard moving to the right, and he slipped a little to the left, trying to keep the man's attention fixed on him.

"Why are you destroying these—"

"They're mine, I told you. I can do whatever I want with them."

"But you . . ."

The man turned then and ripped the canvas from near the top all the way to the bottom edge of the frame. The painting hung in four pyramidal tongues now, all four of them lolling toward the crowd. Paint chips littered the floor, and the wall behind the painting was deeply gouged by the furious assault of the butcher knife.

Desmond darted forward, getting the man's right arm in his grasp, twisting it behind his back. The guard moved in as Desmond jerked the pinioned arm and the knife clattered to the floor. The man tried to twist free, but Desmond rammed the arm up toward the opposite shoulder, and the man groaned, then stopped writhing. He turned then and spat, missing Desmond, then sank his teeth into Desmond's wrist.

The guard grabbed the man in a headlock and wrestled him to the ground, Desmond on top of the two of them. The man kicked his feet like a furious child, but was unable to free himself from their combined weight.

Desmond looked up in time to see several blue uniforms shoving their way through the crowd. Beyond them, he spotted Valerie Harrison, one hand to her mouth, a stunned look on her face. The police moved in, and Desmond handed his armlock to a burly patrolman. Two more cops took the man by his arms and cuffed him, then started to muscle him toward the exit.

Valerie Harrison rushed toward Desmond. "Are you all right?" she asked.

He nodded, glancing at his wrists and rubbing the white indentations left by the madman's teeth. "Yeah, I'm okay. I hope those weren't insured by your company."

"One was, yes, but—"

"Thank God for small favors," Desmond said, looking for Audrey.

— SIX— - -

DESMOND STOOD OUTSIDE OF THE PRATT MUSEUM. IT was raining, that muggy drizzle that can make New York summers almost sub-tropical. The air was thick, clung to the skin like invisible paste. But nobody seemed to mind. It was the relief that they had been praying for. He lit a cigarette and watched the patrons shuffling along on the line, and it reminded him of lines at a McDonald's. Art as fast food—"I'll have a big Mac, fries, and a gander at the Matisse."

A lot of blue-haired ladies, their slick raincoats dripping money and moisture, gossiped as the line moved along. Perfume was thick, even in the heavy air, and as Desmond puffed he watched a couple of scalpers work the line, trying to buy or sell tickets. One man, who looked more like a biker than an art lover, scored a pair of passes at twenty dollars, the printed price, and Desmond watched him move toward the end of the line. For a moment it looked as if he was going to take his place on the culture-loving serpent, but after a second's hesitation, he pushed on, started waving the tickets toward people approaching from Fifth Avenue.

An older man in a raincoat stopped and talked to the biker, then shook his head and moved on past. Curious, Desmond drifted toward the biker type, watched him wave the tickets again, and this time hook his quarry. Two well-dressed women, who looked enough alike, despite the difference in their ages, that Desmond thought they might be mother and daughter, bobbed their heads, listening to the biker's spiel. Desmond was close enough now to hear his patter. "Hottest ticket in town. Forty bucks is cheap ladies, for a show like this. I mean, how often does a major Impressionist retrospective blow through town, even the Apple?"

The younger woman tugged the older one's sleeve, but the mother was hooked now and unsnapped the clasp on her purse. Desmond was close enough to hear the click. The biker backed off, sensing that he had already made his sale. The rain trickled down his slender arms, seeming to follow the contours of a tattooed dragon on his left arm, then collecting in a small pool at his crooked elbow. The woman opened her wallet, removed a pair of newly minted twenties, snapped them each to make sure no bills clung together, and handed them over.

With a flourish, the art-loving Hell's Angel raised the tickets overhead, brought them down into the woman's palm with a smack, then raised the hand to his lips and smacked it again. "You won't regret it, ladies," he said. He noticed Desmond watching him, scowled, then moved back the way he'd come, probably looking to score some more tickets for resale.

Desmond pinched the light from his butt, tossed it into a trash can, then moved toward the business entrance to the museum. The Pratt was new, and already had a formidable reputation as the place to see art and to be seen seeing it. Inside, out of the rain, Desmond listened to his damp heels click on the polished stone floor as he walked down a long corridor.

He had an appointment with Clarence Hemenway and knew it wouldn't do to keep him waiting. The director of the Pratt, a man whose face popped up regularly in slick magazines like *New York, GQ,* and *Vanity Fair* as often as it did in *Art News,* was known to have a short fuse. According to a lengthy profile in the magazine section of the *Sunday Times,* Hemenway was the newest thing in big-ticket museums, a man who knew how to promote himself as well as his museum. He worked the society circuit like a medicine-show shill, but it had paid off handsomely, not just in gifts to the Pratt, art as well as cash, but in publicity.

Hemenway knew that profile was more important than substance, or so said the article, written by someone who clearly admired the director's achievement while holding his methods in something not unlike contempt. Hemenway came from a wealthy, but somewhat checkered background, and had spent more than a little time abroad. There were gaps in his résumé that he glossed over with self-deprecating humor, although Janet

Miranda, the writer, had hinted in her article that there was so much smoke there had to be at least a little fire.

Desmond knew the type. The world seemed to be full of them, nestled securely atop corporations and foundations, people who dismissed the notion of privilege but owed their prosperity to that concept more than to any accomplishment. He took a deep breath as he reached the reception area, found himself staring at the back of an androgynous head trying not to wonder about its owner's gender.

He cleared his throat and the androgyne turned to skewer him with mascaraed lasers. "Yes," she said, her tone already dismissive without knowing the man or his business. "Can I help you?"

"I have an appointment with Mr. Hemenway," Desmond said, trying to keep his tone pleasant. "I believe he's expecting me."

She tugged a calendar out from under a stack of magazines, flipped through its pages, and when she found the right day, looked up. "Your name?"

"Paul Desmond."

She nodded as if that was precisely what she was expecting. Her severe haircut, clearly done with a razor, made a helmet of her black hair, so shiny it resembled metal. "You're early, Mr. Desmond. Mr. Hemenway isn't here yet."

Desmond looked at his watch. His appointment was for eleven, and it was five past. She caught the significance of his glance and scowled. "Mr. Hemenway is fashionably late. He expects it of his appointments." Her tone was brittle, as if informing him for the hundredth time of something he should have known on his own.

"You can have a seat over there," she said, indicating a leather settee.

"Thank you." Desmond walked toward the settee and lowered himself to its soft cushions. He watched the woman work, wondering what exactly it was that she did. She was bent over some papers on her desk, and he imagined her lips curled in a sneer as she read.

At least, he thought, it's air-conditioned. He felt wilted as two-day-old salad, and reminded himself that this was one reason he didn't miss New York as much as his friends thought he should.

A large canvas, bold, amorphous swirls of color on raw linen, hung on the wall above the assistant's desk. It looked like it might be Haring or Basquiat, one of the graffiti wunderkinder who had parlayed limited vision into major careers. Tapping his foot, he stared down the long hall, wondering whether Hemenway would enter by that route or if he was out in the galleries, glad-handing some big-wig or other.

As if in answer to his question, the glass doors at the end of the corridor opened and rain-dampened street noise swirled in, a hiss of tires on wet pavement punctuated by a blaring horn.

Desmond recognized Hemenway immediately from his photo. The museum director was tanned and looked fit, even athletic, and larger than Desmond would have thought. Hemenway glanced at him without interest as he announced his presence to his assistant. "I'm here, Arlene," he said, stopping beside her chair and resting a hand on her shoulder.

The soft silk of her black blouse showed fingerprints when he lifted the hand. She gave him a smile. "Your eleven o'clock is here," she said, canting her head in Desmond's direction.

He turned then, seeming to notice Desmond for the first time. He nodded, then moved past the desk and on into his office. Desmond leaned forward on the edge of the settee, and Arlene held up a hand. "He'll buzz when he's ready for you," she said.

Desmond sat back, knowing that Hemenway was into effects and would let him cool his heels just long enough to make his point, which would be a hell of a lot more meaningful to Hemenway himself than it would be to Desmond.

Ten minutes later the intercom buzzed, and Arlene gave Desmond a supercilious glance, just to let him know that she, too, got the point. Desmond smiled pleasantly and walked toward the open door. Hemenway was at his desk, his Armani jacket draped carelessly over a high-backed chair that looked like it came from Ben Franklin's house. His sleeves were rolled to the elbow, showing off his tan to good effect, and his tie was loose enough to reveal the unbuttoned collar. The tie, Desmond noticed, must have cost somewhere in the vicinity of a hundred dollars, and he had the sneaking suspicion that Hemenway would like to have left the price tag on, just to make sure everyone knew to the penny.

"What can I do for you, Mr. Desmond?" His voice was almost oily with self-assurance, the kind of pipes that self-improvement gurus used in their infomercials, rich and resonant and smug almost beyond belief. He knew why Desmond was there, and they both knew it, but Desmond was willing to play along, at least to a point.

"As I told you on the phone, Valerie Harrison suggested I talk to you about security for several paintings to be included in your next show. A recent series of art thefts is some cause for concern on the part of Northamerican. And I might add that last night's little psychodrama has done nothing to allay that concern."

Hemenway bobbed his head knowingly. His modishly long brown hair glistened in the artificial light. His black eyes looked like glass against the deep tan, and Desmond wondered whether they might not be contact lenses.

"Valerie worries too much," Hemenway said. "But I suppose that's what she's paid to do. What would you like to know?"

"For openers, I'd like to know who on your staff knew to expect the three German Expressionist canvases that were stolen the night before last."

"I've been all through that with the police, Mr. Desmond. I told their Lieutenant Muller everything I know, which was precious little indeed. No one on our staff knew enough about the transportation of those canvases. I didn't know myself. That was by design, by the way. We wanted to forestall the possibility of any trouble. Publicity is a strange thing. You can't get enough of the good kind, and you can't get rid of the bad soon enough."

Desmond ignored the mispronunciation of Ray Miller's name, which he presumed to be deliberate, another foray into condescension. "There are nearly three dozen canvases in the Impressionist retrospective that are insured by Northamerican, as I'm sure you are aware."

"Actually, I'm not. The museum, of course, has its own insurance, but owners often take out their own insurance, just to make certain. I am not usually privy to which canvases are insured by whom. Naturally, that information is on record here, but not the sort of detail I bother with."

"Not interested?"

"Actually, no. I have a head full of details, as I'm sure you can appreciate. Running an institution of this size is no easy task. The glut of trivia would choke a whale, and the more of it I can ignore, the better I like it. And I don't really have a need to know, in any case."

"Suppose something were to happen to a canvas?"

"Such as?"

"Theft, for example."

"And?"

"What procedure would be followed."

Hemenway smiled. "In the unlikely event one of our paintings were stolen, we would, naturally, call the police. We have our own security people, and they would be notified. Insurance would cover the loss, of course, but not really. Mere dollars, even in astronomical numbers, are no substitute for a work of genius. How much money would make up for the loss of the *Mona Lisa*, do you suppose, Mr. Desmond?"

Desmond shrugged. "It depends, I suppose."

"On what?"

"On what the *Mona Lisa* means to you. I've never seen it, so I don't have an opinion. I've seen reproductions of it, of course, but it's not to my taste, and I suppose that disqualifies me from even answering your question."

"Not really. It's a question with no answer, actually. No amount of money can make up for the loss of such a thing. Once it is gone, there is no bringing it back. It cannot be redone. That's the thing that most people fail to understand about art. Each work is one of a kind, *sui generis.* If Beethoven had written only eight symphonies, it would not have mattered if Brahms had written another. It would be welcome, to be sure, but it would not make up for the loss of Beethoven's Ninth."

"That's one way of looking at things, I suppose."

"It's the *only* way, Mr. Desmond. Let me set your mind at ease on that score. The only way."

Desmond nodded, a vague movement of his head that seemed to satisfy Hemenway that his point had been taken at face value. "What do you make of last night's incident?"

"I don't have an opinion. There are many disturbed people in this world, and art, like anything of value, is likely to become a focus for some obsession or other. I don't imagine this latest event is in any way different. People have attacked sculpture and paintings in virtually every major museum in the world, with the possible exception of the Hermitage, although I'm not sure we would have heard about such an event in any case. Not until lately, at any rate."

"Are you concerned about a possible repetition? Have you made arrangements for additional security?"

"Of course, both. But I thought you were concerned with recovering stolen art rather than protecting canvases safely in our hands."

"Technically, that's true. But it seems to me that it's in everyone's interest that we keep my quarry to an even dozen. Besides, the more I know about your practices, the more ideas I might have about what went wrong. I want to see the whole chain, one link at a time."

"To identify the weak one?"

Desmond nodded. "Yes. Or the crooked one."

"I don't see—"

Desmond cut him off. "Look, Mr. Hemenway. Whoever made off with those paintings did not get lucky. This was not serendipitous theft. The people who stole those paintings knew exactly what they wanted, and they knew exactly where it would be and when. That much, I think, is beyond dispute."

"It would certainly seem so."

"That means that they had information from the inside. There may be a pattern that will point in the right direction. Right now, the only thing all twelve paintings had in common was the fact that they were insured by Northamerican. But that is an artificial circumstance."

"I don't quite follow. . . ."

"Other paintings have probably been stolen as well. I don't know about those, because Northamerican doesn't care about them. But if I can see the larger picture, I might get a clearer understanding. So, the more I know about things on your end, the better the chances of spotting something. I will, of course, talk to the shippers as well. I have already spoken to the police. But I want to broaden my data base, if you'll forgive the analogy. I want every bit of information, without regard to apparent relevance. Only then can I sift through the mountain of detail for the molehill of significance."

Hemenway sighed. "All right. I'll have our chief

security officer give you a tour. I still don't see how it will help, but I suppose you know better than I about such things."

"Oh, I do, Mr. Hemenway. I do."

— SEVEN —

DESMOND STUDIED THE GRAY FACE OF BELLEVUE
Hospital the way a climber scrutinizes the Matterhorn.
Inside the solid stone, housed like exotic fauna, could
be found every coiled inversion of human thought,
men and women tied in knots by their genes, by their
histories, or by the city itself. And one of these human
puzzles, Derrick Jones, was of particular interest, but
Desmond wasn't quite sure he was up to it.

Ray Miller had told him that Derrick Jones was the
name of the lunatic who had attacked the canvases the
night before, or at least that was what the madman
claimed. Miller was still checking it out. Other than
the man's alleged name, not much was known about
him. Miller said Jones claimed to be an artist, but that
too, had yet to be verified, and the ravings of a madman
were not high on Ray Miller's priority list. He would

check it out, of course, but then he had a thousand other things to check out, and when he would do so was anybody's guess. But Desmond couldn't wait for the twelfth of never.

He wondered why he was even going to bother. Used to conspiracy, to the alternate faces reality donned like throwaway masks, he was convinced that something about the events of the preceding night meant more than they seemed. Valerie Harrison was not so sure, but Desmond had to go with his gut. He knew that Hemenway had been talking to "Jones" before the attack. And yet an hour ago, Hemenway hadn't let on that he knew the man.

Desmond entered the hospital slowly, wondering whether he would walk out again without difficulty. He didn't like hospitals of any kind, but mental hospitals were the worst. Once inside, he looked at everyone with suspicion, and knew that mistrust was returned by everyone else, staff and patients alike. He felt as if he were being watched, as if someone on staff might clap a hand on his shoulder at any moment and ask him why he was not in his room. Sanity was so fragile, so elusive, and ultimately, so subjective, that no one could demonstrate on demand the legitimacy of his own tenuous grip.

Once inside, he felt the hair on the back of his neck begin to rise, but he ignored it, walked to the desk, and asked to see Derrick Jones. The man behind the desk, bigger than Bubba Smith and about as likely to smile, asked him to sign in. "You family?" he asked, spinning the register around and clapping a ballpoint on a chain into the gutter.

"No, professional interest," Desmond said. Glancing

up, he saw that the attendant was looking at him closely, and he looked away, watching his hand struggle to form a signature that looked vaguely like the one he usually fashioned. To his own eye it looked like a forgery, and for a moment he wondered who he was, if maybe he was already delusional. He shivered, like a dog just out of the rain, then finished signing with a confidence he did not feel.

"You a doctor?" Bubba asked.

Desmond shook his head. "No. An investigator. I was there last night when Mr. Jones earned his admission here."

Defying all expectation, Bubba laughed. His smile was positively radiant. "Tore hell out of some paintings, didn't he?" He laughed again, as if it were a good joke, and Desmond almost joined him.

"Yeah, he did that," he said.

"Well, now he gets to finger-paint for his own self. We keep him long enough, maybe he can come up with something to replace what he fucked up." Once more he laughed. He scribbled a pass, then slid it across the countertop. "Fourth floor. That's a security floor. So if you're packing, leave it at the checkroom, next to the elevators."

Desmond realized that routine here was not like routine anywhere he had ever been. Grabbing the pass, he thanked the attendant and headed for the elevator.

The corridor was dimly lit, the walls cold, and the air scented with the sour tang of artificial pine. The elevator couldn't come soon enough, and when he stepped inside, he turned quickly, as if afraid he had been followed. But the car was empty, as he knew it would be, and it staggered up, its cables creaking, its gears moaning with reluctance, then shuddered to a halt. When the doors opened again, the car was a few inches short and Desmond had to step up to the floor. The doors closed too soon and banged his ankle. Tugging his foot between the black rubber bumpers, he felt as if he had narrowly escaped the gums of ancient, greedy jaws.

This hall was, if anything, even gloomier than the first-floor corridor. He found the receiving desk and, beyond it, a heavy wire mesh with a metal door. On the other side of the mesh, he could see a long row of doors, some of them open, held back against the wall with rubber doorstops. Others were closed. All of them, instead of windows, had rectangles of the same heavy mesh. It looked more like a prison than a hospital, an impression heightened by the uniformed cop sitting in an alcove behind the receiving desk.

The cop was chewing on a sandwich, and he nodded at Desmond. "Help you?" he asked.

"I'm here to see a patient named Derrick Jones," Desmond informed him.

"Flip is inside. He'll be back in a coupla minutes."

"Flip?"

"The ward director. Looks like Flip Wilson, only about three times as large. How he got his name, I guess. Never asked."

Before Desmond could thank the cop, he saw a hulking figure in starched greens, bulging over the upper torso and razor sharp from the waist down. He was on the other side of the door, but even through the mesh, Desmond saw the remarkable resemblance the cop had mentioned.

Flip opened the door, then locked it from the outside,

a heavy key ring jangling against the metal frame. He tossed the keys on the desk, then looked at Desmond. "Afternoon . . ." He paused, waiting for Desmond to explain his presence.

"Here to see Derrick Jones . . .?"

"Got a pass?"

Desmond nodded, handed him the stiff paper, and waited.

"Man likes to cut things," Flip said. "Got him restrained."

"Things or people?" Desmond asked.

Flip grunted. "Don't care to find out if he makes such a fine distinction."

"Can I see him?"

"Sure thing." Flip grabbed the keys again and worked the lock. He stepped through the open door, waited for Desmond, then pulled it closed behind him, locking it with a sharp twist of a thick wrist. "Got to stay with you," he said.

"Fine."

Desmond followed the floor chief halfway down the corridor. Jones was in one of the rooms whose door had been left open. When Desmond stepped inside, he could see why. Jones was lying on a heavy metal-framed bed, thick leather straps holding his arms and legs in place.

The madman looked at Desmond curiously for a moment, almost smiling, then twisted his lips into eerie grin. "One meatball," he said.

"Pardon me?" Desmond asked.

"One meatball, I said."

Desmond nodded as if it made sense, then, with a look at Flip, added, "You get no bread with one meatball."

"Celery stalks at midnight," Jones replied.

"Like those old tunes, do you, Mr. Jones?"

Jones just grinned. He looked smaller than Desmond remembered him, even frail. His age was indeterminate; somewhere over forty was as fine as Desmond could cut it. The hair, unruly and overlong, was salt-and-pepper. He was the perfect image of a fruit loop. But the blue eyes sparkled with humor and intelligence.

"I was wondering if I could ask you a few questions," Desmond said.

"Ask me now."

"Monk?"

"Worry later . . ."

"Monk," Desmond concluded, nodding. "You're a jazz fan, I gather."

"Shoot."

"Those paintings you destroyed last night, Mr. Jones. Do you remember that? At the museum?"

Jones stared hard at him, but said nothing. Desmond waited for a few moments, and when it was apparent that Jones was not about to answer, he said, "You say those paintings are yours, if I understood you correctly. Is that right?"

"Why are you here?" Jones asked. "You were the one wrapped me up last night. I recognize you now. The court recognizes the . . . you a cop?"

Desmond shook his head. "No. I work for an insurance company. Actually, I work for myself, but I have a contract with Northamerican Insurance."

"Those paintings weren't insured. They're mine, and I didn't take out no insurance on them. Take out some insurance, Jimmy Reed."

Desmond tried not to let the free association interfere.

"How could they be yours, Mr. Jones. They were part of an Impressionist retrospective. They were Claude Monet's work. Surely you know that?"

Jones shook his head. "The Tiger's Revenge."

"I'm sorry . . . ?"

"Claude Balls, man. Where you been? The Yellow Stream. I. P. Daly."

Desmond sensed a slight change in Jones, as if the man were watching him even more closely, trying to measure him somehow, but using a scale that Desmond could not fathom. "Why do you insist those paintings were yours?"

"Why do you insist they are insured by Northamerican?"

"As a matter of fact, one of them was."

"Then why are you here, man? Why you bust in on me and destroy the blessed serenity of my surroundings with your gray-flannel rudeness? Leave me be. I ain't mad at you, pretty baby, don't you be mad at me."

"Mr. Jones, I—"

"Van Gogh's ear, man. You know what I'm saying? Van Gogh's ear. Should have used a fucking razor. Cuts quicker, cleaner. Damn Ginsu ain't worth a tinker's dam."

Desmond looked at Flip, who leaned against the wall just inside the door, his massive arms folded across a barrel chest. He was watching Desmond with amusement. "Crazy as a motherfucker is our Mr. Jones."

"Something is happening, and you don't know what it is, do you, Mr. Jones?" Jones shouted.

"'Ballad of a Thin Man,'" Desmond said. "Dylan."

"Things are not what they seem. Things are not what they appear to be. Things just are, man. They just fucking are. You know what I'm saying?"

"Should I?" Desmond asked.

Jones snorted. "Don't call me, I'll call you. Uncle Sam wants you. Everybody wants to be my baby. Seek and ye shall fucking find."

Flip was getting impatient. "How much more of this shit you got to hear, man?" he asked.

Desmond shrugged. "I guess I'm finished."

"Finished, you ain't even started. I am a mystery inside a riddle wrapped in an enigma, man. Come see me when you can. Not if I see you first."

- EIGHT - - -

ANGEL WAS AT THE WHEEL AS THEY PULLED THROUGH the elaborate wrought-iron gate. The guard stood to one side to let the van pass, his finger never far from the trigger of his AR-15. The guard's uniform was familiar, a slightly upscale version of the one Angel himself had worn in El Salvador. But those days were long ago now. Gone, but no matter how hard Angel tried, not forgotten. It was good working for the Colonel again, but it kept the memories alive, and Angel had memories he would just as soon not have.

Angel stopped the van once through the gate, watched the ornate black metal grating close behind him, then hopped out. He knew the guard, a man named Diego, who had also worked for the Colonel in El Salvador. Angel walked to the kiosk, waited for Diego to step inside, then leaned his head in.

"Que pasa?" Diego asked.

"I want to use the phone, amigo," Angel said.

"I already called the house. The Colonel is expecting you."

"I want to talk to him myself."

Diego shrugged, snatched the cordless from its cradle, and handed it to Angel. Pressing the intercom, Angel turned away, not because he didn't want Diego to hear what he had to say, but because he didn't want Diego to see his face when he heard the Colonel's voice. Things had gone well in one respcet, but not so well in another. No one knew that better than Angel. While he waited for someone to pick up he stared at the van, saw Luis puffing nervously on a cigarette, the little orange glow winking, a feather of smoke seeping through the window, open just a crack to keep the conditioned air inside.

It was because of Luis that he had to make this call. The Colonel already knew that, of course, as he seemed to know everything, but still, it seemed better to use the phone. He could always try to ram the van through the gate again, maybe disappear into Miami, where every campesino had a cousin who knew somebody who could give you work and keep your secret. It was not as safe as New York, but then it was warmer than New York and it was New York that had caused all the trouble. The Colonel probably knew that, too, understood it. But would he forgive it? That was the question. Maybe what they had in the back of the van would make a difference. Maybe the Colonel would be so happy about it that he would forget how angry he was at Luis.

Someone finally picked up, and Angel sighed. It was

not the Colonel. The voice on the other end was strange, sounded like a woman, but not one he knew. She told him she would put the Colonel on, and Angel looked through the thick shrubbery toward the house. He could only see the third story, where lights were on, but only just. Angel had never been up on the third floor, and he wondered if that was where the Colonel was now. He watched the windows, thinking maybe to see the familiar silhouette on the filmy curtains, but nothing moved.

"Angel, why are you making me wait?" The voice exploded in his ear, and Angel jerked the receiver away for a moment. He heard Diego laughing at him, but didn't turn around.

"I just wanted to let you know that we are here. And that everything is all right."

"No, Angel, everything is *not* all right. You know that, my friend."

"*Sí.* I know that. But we are here, and we have the packages."

"Then bring them to the house, pronto, Angel. With a name like that, you should have wings. You should fly when I call you. Don't you know that?"

"*Sí,* Colonel."

"Then fly, my friend. Now!"

"*Sí,* Colonel, I will fly."

Angel heard the whisper of dead air as the Colonel hung up, and he turned to see Diego watching him closely. "Trouble, my friend?" Diego asked. Angel wondered whether the neutral tone of the question concealed a certain secret pleasure at his discomfort, but decided that it didn't matter. Were their roles reversed, Angel would wear an inward smile, too.

Working for the Colonel was not easy. But it was always good to see someone else squirm, not because you took pleasure in his discomfort, but because it meant that you were not the one who had to endure the Colonel's wrath. You knew, though, that your turn would come around again, as surely as a horse on a carousel. It was all a matter of time.

Angel handed Diego the phone and smiled. "There is always trouble somewhere, amigo." He walked back to the van and climbed in. Turning in the driver's seat, he rapped his knuckles on the partition behind him. In a loud voice, he said, "Raul, get ready. We are going to the house now."

Raul's muffled acknowledgment was all but drowned by the roar of the engine as Angel stepped on the gas and released the clutch. It had been a long drive, and he was tired. It was almost worth enduring the scathing to come for the chance to slide between cool sheets and close his eyes. They had driven straight through from New York, taking turns at the wheel, but it was not possible to sleep in the van, and the tiny white pills he took, like those the truckers used, made him nervous, edgy. His skin felt as if a thousand ants were scurrying around beneath it, racing along the veins like tiny tunnels.

The van rolled toward the house, its tires hissing on the wet pavement. Cascades of water from the lawn sprinklers rattled against the roof and the doors, splattered the windshield, and painted it with tiny jewels. Passing through a thick patch of flowering shrubs, he felt for a moment as if he were back in El Salvador, where the lowland jungle, its leaves thick with dust, shuddered under a hot wind as the trucks thundered past. That seemed so long ago, too, but it changed everything once and for all, made him see what was not there.

He could see the house now, a sprawling Spanish-style villa that, according to household gossip, once belonged to a very famous movie star who had committed suicide by cutting her wrists and drowning herself in the huge swimming pool in the courtyard. Angel didn't believe it because he knew movie stars lived in California, not Florida. But no matter how you looked at it, it was some house.

Angel backed the van up to the service entrance, leaving just enough room for the van doors to open, then jumped out of the cab. Luis climbed out of the passenger seat, lighting another cigarette. He was nervous, and Angel could see the tremors in his partner's cheek, just under the left eye.

The service-entrance door opened, and Angel nodded to Juanito, the houseboy, who stood in the doorway. Opening the van, he waited for Raul to shove the first of the three large packages to the edge of the van floor, then grabbed it. Raul crab-walked forward, grunting when he stepped to the ground. The package was bulky but not heavy, but Raul always grunted when he worked, no matter how easy the particular task might be.

Inside, they walked down the stairs to the basement, leaned the package against the wall, and climbed the stairs again. It took them ten minutes to get all three of the packages inside. Angel did not know what was in any of them. He had been told only what the packages would look like, and where to find them. It had been a piece of cake getting them.

When the third package was out of the van, Luis closed its doors and followed Angel and Raul down the stairs to the basement after closing the service-entrance door. The three men stood under the harsh lights of the basement, Luis sucking greedily on yet another cigarette.

They heard the Colonel coming, and Luis started to shiver a little bit. Angel clapped him on the shoulder. "It'll be all right, amigo. The Colonel is a man who understands how the world is. You'll see."

Luis nodded, but the movement of his head was so tentative, it was obvious he didn't believe Angel for a moment. When the Colonel entered the basement, wearing a long silk robe of the deepest red, with gold thread woven through the shimmering cloth, he looked at the three men in silence for a long moment. His leather-soled slippers clapped on the cement floor as he crossed the huge room.

The Colonel was taller than Angel and the others, and slender, where they were chunky, but he had the same black hair and blacker eyes. His skin had the same olive cast, but where they were coarse-skinned, his was smooth, the difference a product of their difference in caste, a product of privilege. And the Colonel's Spanish was more polished, more genteel. There could be no mistaking who was in charge.

"You have the three packages?"

Angel nodded. "*Sí*, Colonel, as I told you."

The Colonel didn't smile. He didn't say thank you. He simply brushed past the three men to where the three packages leaned against the wall. From the recesses of his robe, he pulled a switchblade, clicked it open so unexpectedly that Luis jumped. The

Colonel turned to look at him, shaking his head at such a display of anxiety, but said nothing. Instead, he used the switchblade to slice through the brown paper covering the first package. Tearing the heavy paper aside, he sliced through the heat-sealed plastic bands that bound a large flat cardboard box to a thin wooden pallet, then cut the tape binding one end of the box.

Carefully turning the box on its side, he knelt, a knobby knee peeking out from the red cloth of his robe. He opened the tongue on the carton and reached inside. Angel could see the bubble wrap inside, a strip of masking tape holding it closed. The Colonel tugged the contents into the open, sliced the tape, and peeled back the bubble wrap.

The Colonel stood then, stepped back, his hands shaking. His head nodded as if in answer to an unspoken question. "Beautiful, so beautiful." He wasn't talking to his men, and they knew it.

Angel looked at the painting, unmoved, wondering why he had gone to such trouble to obtain it. It had cost a man's life, though no one could have anticipated that, but that was, after all, a small matter. Three years with the death squads in El Salvador had taught him that there is precious little on the planet that was not worth a human life, the cheapest of all commodities.

The Colonel turned then and looked Angel in the eye. "Do you know what this is?" he asked.

Angel shook his head. "No, Colonel."

"Look at it, Angelito, look at it closely."

Angel did as he was told, moving closer, until he was standing alongside the Colonel. Try as he might, he could not see what had the Colonel so excited. "It . . . it looks like nude women."

"It is, *pendejo*, it is. It is called *Bathing Girls.* It was painted by August Macke in 1913. It is one of the finest German Expressionist canvases in the world. Magnificent!"

"Very pretty, Colonel," Angel said, not sure it was the right thing to say. And when the Colonel turned with a scornful expression, Angel knew that it hadn't been.

"Open the next one for me, Angel. I want to stand back. I will look away, and you will tell me when you have the painting out."

"*Sí*, Colonel."

Angel drew his own knife and set to on the second package. His hands were shaking as he worked on the wrapping, and it took him long enough that the Colonel snapped, "Hurry up, Angel. Hurry up."

But the bubble wrap finally slid out of the carton, and that part, at least, went smoothly. Inside was another painting. Like the first, it meant little to Angel, but he made sure it was right side up, then said, "It's ready, Colonel."

He stood there, feeling like an idiot, one hand balancing the painting by a corner of its frame. He watched the Colonel's face as it changed expression a dozen times. Angel had seen the look a thousand times before, usually on one of the men watching one of the bikini-clad blondes who frequented the Colonel's pool parties. It was somewhere between outright lust and abject surrender, a response to beauty that, in this case, Angel did not see.

"Egon Schiele, you are a madman!" the Colonel

whispered, "But a genius, too." He moved forward and knelt before the canvas. "Self-seer, that is what I am, too. You have painted *me,* Egon. *Me.*"

He backed away, getting to his feet again, and tilted his head.

"Shall I open the other one, Colonel?"

The Colonel shook his head. "I know what it is. It is the Beckmann, *Young Men by the Sea,* lots of naked boys, Angel. You prefer the women with no clothes, eh?"

Angel laughed uncertainly.

"I will look at it later, savor the anticipation." The Colonel paused to look at the three men. "This business of the trucker is *muy malo.* I don't like it."

Angel spread his hands, trying to explain. "It couldn't be helped, Colonel. Luis, he . . . the man worked with him. He knew Luis, and—"

The Colonel bobbed his head. "I know, I know. You told me. Let's go outside, shall we? It's such a beautiful night."

Angel sucked in his breath. He looked at Luis, who seemed relieved. It was not going to be so bad now. They followed the Colonel upstairs and out into the courtyard. Under the moonlight, the pool looked as if it were full of liquid silver. The Colonel sat down at a table and nodded for his men to join him. Angel sat on the Colonel's right hand, as always. Luis sat across from the Colonel, his back to the pool, and Raul took the remaining chair.

"I know you don't have any idea what those paintings are worth, and you would not believe it if I told you," he said. "But that doesn't matter. I have them now, and that is all that matters."

He looked to the houseboy, who hovered nearby. "Bring us some wine, Juanito. Pronto!" He watched the houseboy disappear into the house. He sat there looking at the sky while he waited. Angel was beginning to fidget again. It didn't feel right. He looked at Luis, who still seemed relieved. Raul, as usual, looked impassive, his features slightly Indian, immobile as bronze.

Juanito reappeared with a tray, an open bottle of wine at the center of four goblets. He set the tray down on a nearby table, poured four glasses, and set one in front of each of the men.

The Colonel sipped his wine, then waited for his employees to do likewise. When all three had tasted the wine, he took a deep breath. "You did well to get the packages," he said.

"Thank you, Colonel," Angel answered.

Then the Colonel shook his head. "But this business of the truck driver, that was very bad. It will make things very difficult. Because of that, things are spinning out of control now. It will be very difficult for a while."

"I am sorry, Colonel. But it couldn't be helped."

"I know," the Colonel said. "I know." He raised his glass, took another sip, then set it down. His hands were in his lap for a moment, then the right came up. Angel almost missed the small silver revolver in the Colonel's hand, until a glint of moonlight caught his eye. The Colonel fired twice, hitting Luis in the right eye and the center of the forehead. He stood up then, leaned across the table, and shoved Luis back off his chair and into the pool.

Shaking his head, the Colonel looked at Angel. "He should have known better."

"*Sí*, Colonel," Angel said, watching the small automatic disappear into a pocket of the Colonel's robe. "He should have known better."

– NINE – – –

DESMOND SAT IN HIS STUDY, A STACK OF REFERENCE books on his desk. Through the window, he could see his daughters playing Wiffle ball. As usual, Sally was hitting everything that came near the plate, sending the other kids into hedges and over the fence. The neighborhood boys were in awe of her. She ran faster, threw harder, and hit far better than they did. Something about these incontrovertible facts seemed wrong to them, and they kept coming back, day after day, trying to find out what it was. Desmond could tell by the baffled knit of their brows that this mystery haunted them. Girls weren't supposed to be that good. But Sally was that good, and better. If only they could discover why, maybe they could beat her. But Desmond knew they didn't have a chance.

He had the sound on low because his study door was open. The haunting sound of Tony Scott's music surrounded him like a cloud. *Music for Zen Meditation,* it was called, Scott's clarinet acompanied by koto and shakuhachi, improvisations on Japanese melodies, a match made in a bluer heaven than that overhead.

Flipping through the books, he was trying to find some mention of Derrick Jones. Something about the strange man had captured his fancy. Jones had been taunting him, playing with him, tossing out teasing hints, he was certain of that. But what had he been hinting at?

It was not credible that Jones was precisely what he claimed to be, the man who had painted two of Monet's canvases. That had to be some kind of delusion. But if Jones were an artist, then maybe there was some other meaning in what he had shouted as he wielded the butcher knife. Then again, maybe Jones was exactly what he seemed to be, one more pretzel-brained misfit, drifting through life like a loose balloon, his string trailing behind him, looking for someplace to get tangled up. And for Derrick Jones, maybe that place had been the galleries of the Pratt Museum of Modern Art.

A call to Ray Miller had yielded just what Desmond had expected—nothing. Jones was on the back burner for the moment, Miller said. And no one was likely to move him up on the hit parade anytime soon, because Clarence Hemenway was disinclined to press charges. As far as the police were concerned, Derrick Jones, or whoever he was, was just another big-city fruitcake.

Valerie Harrison had never heard of Jones, had

never seen him before the outburst, and as far as she knew, there was no reason why he might have it in for Northamerican Insurance. The fact that only one of the two paintings had been insured by them seemed to suggest randomness, the kind of Brownian motion all too commonplace in modern life, where people who have never met encounter one another in life-and-death collisions: a walk to the neighborhood McDonald's just as a disaffected postal worker vents his frustration through the muzzle of an assualt rifle, a trip on the thruway reaching an underpass just as two bored teenagers decide to toss a ten-pound rock on the next passing car, a stroll down Broadway not knowing that a brick older than your grandfather is finally going to relax its tenuous grip nad fall ninety feet to bury itself in your skull.

The thirst for meaning doesn't let us accept that random lethality without a struggle, but the bumper sticker is right: shit happens. And it just might be that Derrick Jones is nothing more than the latest example.

He heard Audrey come in from her studio and got to his feet, kneading the taut muscles at the back of his neck. Sticking his head into the hall, he waited for her to come upstairs, and when she didn't, he called to her.

"Got a minute?"

"Be right there." He walked over to the window and stood leaning on the sill. Sally was batting again, and a hulking kid from across the street was doing his damnedest to throw smoke past her. But the harder he threw the Wiffle ball, the more rebellious it became, and Sally walked on four pitches, flipping the bat end over end like Reggie on her way to first.

Desmond turned when Audrey knocked on the open door.

"Come on in," he said. "Just watching Sluggo kick some macho ass."

Audrey stood beside him, letting one arm encircle his waist. "I know what you're thinking," she said.

"What's that?"

"You're thinking how unfair it is there are no women in major-league baseball."

Desmond laughed. "Something like that. Hell, there are kids in the big leagues who are not as big as Sal will be, and they probably don't field any better than she will. There must be thousands of girls like her, too."

"She's really good, isn't she?"

He nodded. "Yeah, she is. And you know why?"

"Your genes?"

Desmond laughed. "I don't think Czechoslovakians have baseball in their genes, Audie. She's good because she loves it. She just flat loves it. I've never seen a kid who loved it half as much as she does. She'd play twenty-four hours a day, if we let her."

"Sometimes I think we do. You do, anyway. I worry every time I travel that you two are out on the lawn until four A.M. playing catch or whatever it is you do. But you didn't call me in here to talk about baseball. Or did you?"

Desmond shook his head. "No, I didn't. I was hoping you could help me with something."

Audrey gave him one of her knowing smiles. "If I can, of course . . . "

"How would I go about finding out if someone was an artist?"

"You might try asking him or her. That would be the easiset way, I should think."

Desmond snorted. "Right. Why didn't I think of that?"

"Who are you talking about?"

"The gate-crasher from the other night."

"That lunatic? You think he's an artist? Why, because he claimed he did those canvases? A sad, strange little man, for sure, but that doesn't make him an artist. Surely, you don't believe him."

"Why shouldn't I?"

"He's a madman."

"He has both ears."

"That's different."

"Why?"

Audrey hesitated for a moment. "All right, maybe it isn't different, but . . . "

"But what? Just play along with me on this. He says his name is Derrick Jones. The police are still looking into that, but let's just say that's he's telling the truth on both counts. His name is, in fact, Derrick Jones, and he's a painter. How could I prove it? Where would I go to learn more about him?"

"You could start with the New York State Council on the Arts, I suppose. They have a directory of members. But some of the spookier artists I know are social misfits of one kind or another, certainly not joiners. It wouldn't mean anything if he weren't listed."

"And if he's not the clubby type? Is there some other way?"

"I can make a few phone calls, I suppose. I mean, how many Derrick Joneses can there be? If I find one who's a painter, then maybe he's telling the truth. But we should at least be able to check further, in any case. Let me see what I can do. If you learn anything more than his name in the meantime, let me know. The more I have to go on, the quicker I can work."

Desmond patted her rump. "Thanks, I appreciate it. I know you have your own work to do, but this thing is chewing at me. I can't escape the feeling that it's all tied together somehow—the stolen paintings, Jones, the hijacking. . . . I think he's the key, and everybody else thinks I'm crazy."

"Not me. I *know* you're crazy. But it doesn't mean you're not right." She disengaged herself, and Desmond watched her leave, wondering how she stayed so slim. It looked as if she hadn't gained an ounce in the twenty years he'd known her, and if she had, it must be correcting a tiny flaw he'd never noticed.

He went back to his desk and started on the next reference volume, an encyclopedia of twentieth-century art and artists. He turned first to the index, found no fewer than eleven artists named Jones, but no Derrick. There wasn't even a D. Jones.

He turned to the entry on Monet, as much out of despair as curiosity, and started to read. Five pages later he knew more about Impressionism than he needed, and had no more insight into Derrick Jones than when he'd begun.

Closing the book, he glanced toward the window in time to see the Wiffle ball clear the fence again. He didn't have to watch the runner to know who'd hit it. The phone rang, and he snatched at it eagerly, grateful for anything to get his mind off the blank wall. It was Ray Miller.

"Desmond, you'll never guess what I just found out."

"Then I guess I shouldn't try, Lieutenant."

Miller snorted. "Our man Derrick, he wasn't shitting us. He's an honest-to-God painter. Or at least he has a loft, down in TriBeCa, Greenwich Street, to be exact. I'll probably be stopping by there later this evening. You might want to meet me there."

"Any chance I can get in sooner than that?"

"Two—one, you can join the department, get assigned to the case, and convince a judge to give you a warrant, which will take a lot of time, so don't even try."

"And two?"

"Seems Mr. Jones has a roommate. Weird name, K-A-L-I, sounds Asian. I don't know if Kali is male or female, but if he or she is home, I suppose you might be invited in. Unless, of course, Kali is in on last night's little passion play. Not sure I'd want to find out without backup. Especially if Derrick's Ginsu was part of a set. Know what I mean?"

"What time are you planning on getting there?"

"About six, six-thirty. Maybe a little later. Lots of paperwork, and all that. Anyway, thought you might like to know."

"I appreciate the tip, Lieutenant. And yes, I would like to be there when you go in. I'll get there at six." He hung up the phone, wondering if he was about to get a break or just a larger perspective on a puzzle that would be no less baffling.

Audrey was in the doorway when he turned around, a pad in her hand. She smiled. "You were right. Derrick Jones, your Derrick Jones, is an artist. He's Welsh by birth, but he's been here a long time, so for all practical purposes, he's homegrown, as an artist and as a lunatic."

"Where'd you get this information?"

"I protect my sources."

"I know. Where'd you get it?"

"I called Tim Avery, a friend in TriBeCa, an art director for Warner Records. He's been around a long time, and done just about everything on the commercial side, but he stays plugged into the other side, too."

"Jones or your friend?"

"Both, I guess, and leave my grammar alone. Anyway, Tim used to use Jones now and then for album covers. Says he's talented, maybe even a genius, but flaky and unreliable. The work, when it came in, was brilliant, but it got to be more trouble than it was worth using him."

Desmond patted the desk. "Sit down here, tell me all about him."

Audrey sauntered across the open floor, exaggerating the swing of her hips, and took the seat Desmond had indicated. Looking at the pad, she continued. "Tim hasn't seen him in a few years. I asked him if he'd heard about the incident at the Pratt, and he said he'd seen something in the *Times*. But the story hadn't mentioned Jones by name."

"Was he surprised when you told him it was Jones?"

"Yeah, a little. He said Jones was unpredictable, but he never had the sense that he was unbalanced. Just sure of himself, convinced of his own genius."

"Did you ask Tim if he thought Jones was capable of forging a Monet?"

"As a matter of fact, I did."

"Well?"

"Tim said that stylistically for sure. He didn't know whether Jones had the expertise to do any more than that, but he remembered a cover Jones did for an avant band called the Waterlilies. Jones did it as a Monet. Warner almost got sued for unauthorized use of a copyrighted work, until their lawyers got involved and Jones explained what he'd done."

"Which was?"

Audrey shrugged. "Just painted something in Monet's style. It wasn't a reproduction of an existing work. But Tim said the effect was uncanny."

"Thank you, darlin'," Desmond said, patting her thigh. "Thank you very much."

"There's more."

"I'll have to hear it later. I've got to go to the city this evening. But if you could dig a little more, I'd be most grateful."

"How grateful?"

"How grateful do I have to be to stay in your good graces?"

She winked.

"That grateful, huh?"

-TEN- - -

DERRICK JONES STOOD BEHIND THE METAL GRATING, his fingers curled through the mesh, his nose pressed up against it, staring at the man in the dark gray suit on the other side.

"Who sent you?" Jones asked.

"Come on, Derrick, you know the answer to that." The man nodded to the attendant, who jangled his keys and unlocked the door. As it swung open Jones swung with it, his feet braced on a metal bar reinforcing the bottom.

The man in the suit shook his head. Turning to the attendant, he muttered, "Maybe you ought to keep him, after all."

The attendant laughed. "You take him. We got plenty more where he came from."

"Makes you wonder what the world's coming to, doesn't it."

"Long since wondering, myself. I got it all figured out. You keep this gate for a few years, you'll get it figured out, too."

The man in the suit stepped up behind Jones and peeled his fingers away from the mesh one by one, then pulled him backward. Jones ran to the attendant and leaped in the air. Instinctively, the attendant caught him, letting his wind out in a suprised whoosh. He let go then, and Jones fell to the floor, curled into a fetal ball, and peered up at the man in the suit through a fan of fingers.

"Sucker's heavier than he looks," the attendant said.

The man in the suit smoothed his silver hair. The gesture revealed a heavy banded gold watch on his left wrist, and a cuff link set with what had to be a ruby. It was too red to be anything else. His silk tie dangled free of his suit coat as he bent down to tap Jones on the shoulder. "Derrick, come on, we have to go now."

Jones shook his head violently. "Don't want to."

But the man in the suit was in no mood for obstreperous behavior. He grabbed Jones by one ear and twisted, pulling upward in the same motion. Jones seemed to realize that he had two choices—follow the ear or lose it. He rose awkwardly, lost his balance, and yelped with pain when the man in the suit did not let go.

"I had to work as hard as I care to, to get you out of here, Derrick. I don't want to work any harder now that I've done it. Come along, and be good." The man's deep voice betrayed his exasperation. He sounded like an irritated schoolmaster.

Jones stood unsteadily, looking longingly back through the grated door as the attendant closed and locked it.

"Are you hungry, Derrick?" the man asked. "I'm sure the food here was less appealing than you are accustomed to. Let's go get you something to eat."

Jones rubbed his ear and nodded in resignation. "You buying?" he asked.

The man nodded. "Naturally."

"All right, then," Jones said.

They walked to the elevator. The man in the suit, having no further use for the attendant, did not bother to say good-bye. The way he wrinkled his nose, it was evident that he found his current surroundings extremely distasteful. He stood at the elevator, one hand on the button, which he stabbed repeatedly, as if the car would sense his urgency.

When it opened, Jones took a step back, but the man was too quick for him, grabbed him by the biceps, and tugged him into the car. Only when the door had closed did he let go.

They fell with a swaying creak, the musty stink of industrial cleaner swirling around them. The tiled floor of the elevator was sticky beneath his expensive Italian loafers, and the man was careful not to let his suit jacket come into contact with the dull wooden walls of the car, as if he feared some sort of contamination.

Walton Henry, of Johnson, Henry and Rifkin, did not run errands like this for every client, but sometimes the client had enough influence, and was willing to pay enough, that he broke with custom and did as the client asked. He had been head of the firm for eleven years now, and it was the first time he could remember, since his accession, that he had been to Bellevue. There was always something new under the sun, no matter what the bard said. He smiled at the thought as the door opened on the ground floor and he stepped out into the lobby. Through the glass doors across the lobby, he could see his limo waiting, Jules standing by the rear door, ready to jerk it open as soon as he spotted his employer.

Seeing one of the perks of his position so conspicuously in attendance soothed Henry's inflamed nerves a bit, and he took a deep breath before grabbing Derrick Jones by the arm again and hustling him toward the door. Jules opend the backdoor of the limo, and Henry shoved the smaller man inside, then climbed in after him.

Jules took his place at the wheel, then canted his head toward the rear, waiting for instructions.

"Find us a coffee shop, Jules, one of those Greek places with gyros."

Jules nodded, then closed the soundproof panel, sealing himself into the driver's compartment. Walton Henry looked at Derrick Jones as the limo pulled into traffic. "So, you've really done it this time, Derrick," he said.

Jones shrugged. "I guess."

"I don't know how much longer you can expect leniency in these matters."

"I don't want leniency, Walton."

"What do you want, then?" Henry sighed.

"Recognition. I want my rightful place in the canon of twentieth-century art. I want my own work in the Pratt, MOMA, the Guggenheim. That's what I want. I don't suppose you can understand that, though. Think of it as wanting to be on the Supreme Court. It's a decent analogue."

"You are paid very well for your work. Very well indeed."

"But nobody knows it's mine. Money just isn't enough, I guess."

"It had better be, Derrick. I had to twist more than a few arms to get you released, you know. I prevailed on Mr. Hemenway not to press charges. The police were accommodating. But I don't know how much more I can do for you."

"I never asked you for anything, Walton."

Before the lawyer could respond, the limo swerved into a parking lot on the West Side. Henry lowered the tinted glass beside him and looked outside.

"Where the hell are we, anyway?" Jones asked.

"Somewhere around Hudson Street, I should think, from the look of things." Henry opened his door and climbed out, waiting on the broken asphalt of the parking lot for Jones to follow him. When the artist closed the door, Henry turned to examine the place Jules had chosen for their meal. It was an old-fashioned diner, all chrome and glass. Through the window, Henry could just make out the tops of plastic booth benches. Not the kind of place he preferred to dine, but it would serve his purpose.

He led the way up the short flight of steps into the diner and headed for a booth, Jones in trail and a waitress bringing up the rear, slapping a pair of plastic-coated menus against her thigh.

She arranged their place settings, then moved off when Henry ordered two cups of coffee.

The two men sat there quietly, Jones not wanting to talk, Henry not knowing what to say. When the waitress returned with their coffees, Henry ordered a hamburger and Jones asked for a gyro.

"We have to figure out how we're going to make this up to you know who, Derrick. He's quite upset, as I'm sure you can imagine."

"I don't give a fuck if he's upset. He's got plenty of reason to be satisfied with what I've done for him. He doesn't deserve the work I've done for him."

"Perhaps, Derrick, you overestimate the value of your services."

"You don't get anywhere in this world if you don't. Nobody knows that better than a lawyer, Walton. Am I right?"

Henry laughed at the barb. Tugging on his left ear, he nodded slightly, his blue eyes sparkling. He liked Jones, even though he didn't understand him. There was a part of him that was very much like Derrick Jones, and he had taken great pains over the years to keep reminding himself of that similarity. "You're right, Derrick. But that doesn't change the facts. There are some people in this world who do not have a sense of humor. Especially about things that matter to them. And it was not very wise of you to tell the world that you were the artist of the paintings you destroyed."

"They were mine. Why shouldn't I say so?"

"No one believes you."

"You do."

"That's different. And you had better hope that no one else does. Because you will be in a world of trouble, if you're not already. You don't seem to understand just how serious this is. You have put a number of people in jeopardy by your behavior. And they are not at all forgiving, Derrick. Believe me when I tell you."

The waitress brought their orders, and when she had gone, Jones picked up his gyro. He took a huge bite, ignoring the sauce running down over his fingers while he chewed. Swallowing noisily, he let the sandwich drop to his plate. "He sent you to get me out, didn't he? Told you to get me out or else. He owns you, just like he owns me, doesn't he?" Jones asked. "He flat out owns you. All your fancy clothes, your big car, the place in the Hamptons, Aspen, all that goes up in smoke if he lights a match, doesn't it?"

Henry shrugged. "I wouldn't say that he owns me, no. He has a claim on my services, of course, but that's not the same thing."

"You're splitting hairs, Walton. That's what lawyers do, but we're not talking lawyer-client, here, we're talking man to man, two slaves trying to figure out how to handle massa. And we both know who massa is. But unlike you, I know I can handle him. I still have that much going for me."

"You can't handle him, Derrick. You have to know that. You just can't handle him."

"I can try."

"You can get yourself hurt, even killed."

"He doesn't scare me."

"You can be responsible for unspeakable harm befalling the lovely Kali. He has a very short temper, and he is not particular about whom he sends on his errands. They are not always as careful as they ought to be. Think about that before you do anything foolish."

"Is that why you got me out, to threaten us? What is

that on your fee schedule, Walton, five hundred an hour? Six?"

Walton shrugged. "We are dealing in realities, Derrick. You know as well as I do that he has a violent temper, that he is not above using anyone and anything to get what he wants. How many times, how many ways, do I have to say it?"

"He's gotten all he's going to get from me. You can tell him that."

"I don't think so."

"You don't think he has, or you don't think you will?"

"Both . . ."

Jones picked up his gyro and took another bite, smiling wolfishly around the pieces of lamb and tomato as he chewed. "Eat your hamburger, Walton. Find out how most of us live."

"No, I don't think so, Derrick. I'm not hungry. And I have work to do."

Jones grinned broadly now. "Then you go on. I can get home from here."

"Part of the arrangement is that you will seek psychiatric help, Derrick."

"I don't need a shrink."

"That's not for me to decide. But it is part of the arrangement. You would not be here, otherwise. That he is willing to go that far means you still have some value to him, Derrick. But if I were you, I would not overestimate that value." He fished a card from his pocket and slid it across the table. "Call Dr. Calderon. He's expecting to hear from you this afternoon."

Jones bobbed his head. "Sure. Sure I will. I'll do

that. Maybe I can find out what my dreams mean."

"Call him." Henry got to his feet, reached into his pocket for his wallet, and took out a twenty. He dropped the bill on the table and started to walk away, then stopped. Without looking back, he said, "If you don't, I won't be responsible for what happens, Derrick."

— ELEVEN — — —

TRIBECA WAS THE NEWEST ARTISTS' WARREN. THE Village had long since been too pricey and too Philistine for those who took their art seriously or wanted others to do so. SoHo had fallen by the wayside when yuppies discovered the benefits of loft living and priced the painters out of the market. It wouldn't be long before TriBeCa went the same route. Already, the exodus had begun to Long Island City's warehouse district and, gulp, New Jersey, where Hoboken and even Jersey City were preferable to paying city prices.

As he parked his car on Greenwich Street and walked toward the address Ray Miller had given him, Desmond couldn't help but wonder whether Derrick Jones was well-heeled or had been in that first adventurous handful who had discovered the old stone buildings of the triangle below Canal, which gave the region its name, and managed to get a foothold before the Wall Street and Hollywood types started turning their pockets inside out to live with the night creatures who made arty ghettos so much more interesting than East Sixty-eighth Street or Central Park West.

Already, the inroads of commerce were manifest. Spiffy new stores with overly clever names like Say Cheese (a photo gallery) and Shear Lunacy (an avant hair salon), lined boths sides of the street. Desmond had a friend who swore it would be time to move to Sweden when a mortuary named Death and Stuff opened for business. From the looks of Greenwich Street, it wouldn't be long now.

He found the address easily enough. It was an eight-story limestone building in one of the hybrid architectural styles that were so common south of Fourteenth Street. Judging from the lintel stone, it had once housed some sort of textile firm, but it had been reworked into a fashionably seedy address. Inside the vestibule, which smelled faintly of linseed oil and urine, there was even an intercom, and a quick survey of the nameplates revealed one marked *D. Jones/Kali*. There were eight buzzers, and he figured each level was a floor-through.

It was still a few minutes before six, and Desmond walked back outside to give Ray Miller a chance to show. Chances were better than even that access was via a freight elevator, either tricked out to look like something from a French film, or rendered as low tech as possible to preserve an artificial semblance of the building's past. Either way, it was more than likely that the inner door would be locked.

Lighting a cigarette, he crossed the street to a bar decorated with flowers in macramé planters. Lipstick plants, spider plants, anything that would droop, seemed to be acceptable to the decorator. Inside, he sat at a rickety table. It rocked back and forth as he rested his weight against it, and he took a matchbook from the table and inserted it under one leg to provide some stability.

The waiter, who identified himself as Roy, took his order, and Desmond watched the front of the building across the street. When his diet Coke arrived, he sipped it idly. There was still no sign of Miller, and it was now five after six. He wondered how long he should wait before either giving up and going home or, more likely, having a stab at talking to Kali on his own.

The Coke was watery, something he should have expected when he paid $2.50 for it. More than likely, the rent on the bar was three times what it should be and in six months some other bar with some other window dressing would take its place. But the prices would stay the same, and the diet Coke would be just as watery.

At six-thirty, the last ice crunching between his teeth, Desmond got up and walked outside. There was still no trace of Miller, and rather than waste a trip into the city, Desmond was determined to get something for his expenditure of gas and tolls. He knew there was the danger of tainting evidence, but he didn't give a damn. He was more interested in recovering seventy three million dollars' worth of stolen art, and if Jones would help him—a prospect that was remote at best, he was willing to chance it.

Crossing the street, he reentered the vestibule. With his finger poised over the intercom button, he decided to try the knob on the inner door. It was, after all, New York, and locks and latches took even more abuse than cops. The door swung open, and he stepped into the hall beyond.

The tang of linseed oil and mineral spirits was even stronger. He was getting the impression that more than one artist called the building home. To his surprise, there was a new elevator, and it was open. He stepped in, pushed the button for eight, and waited for the car to move. But nothing happened. Looking more closely, he realized it was one of those key-operated jobs, and he stepped out into the hall again. Moving toward the back of the building, he found a shaft for the freight elevator, but the car was somewhere up above. Craning into the dimness, and peering through the accordion gate, he could make out the cables dangling like industrial-strength Spanish moss.

He walked toward the back, wondering whether he might find fire stairs and, if he did, whether it would be worth an eight-flight hike to find out Kali wasn't home. He could, of course, just walk back to the intercom and buzz, but since he had no authority, he wasn't sure that was the wisest course.

With a shrug, he started up the steps. They were relatively clean, smelled faintly of pine cleaner, and reasonably well lit by New York standards. He reached the eighth floor sooner than he'd thought and later than he wished, and found himself in a narrow corridor that ran the length of the building back to front. Walking toward Greenwich Street, he found a door with a brass nameplate engraved with the initials *D.J.*

He pushed a brass button in the doorframe and heard the angry snarl of a buzzer echoing from deep inside. He listened for some indication that someone was inside and, when he heard nothing, pushed the button again. Taking a deep breath, he waited again. The scrape of metal on metal drew his eyes back to the door.

"Who is it?"

It was a woman's voice, probably Kali. It was more musical than he expected, though he had no reason to expect anything at all.

"My name is Paul Desmond," he said. "Are you Kali?"

"Derrick said you'd come by."

He heard the latch click, and the door swung open without a sound. The doorway was empty, and his instincts flashed into overload. A woman he had never met was opening the door to a perfect stranger in the heart of New York. Why had Jones said he'd come by? How had he known? And if it was what he wanted, why hadn't Jones given him the address? The questions were too many and too confusing to sort through in the split seconds available.

"Well, don't just stand there, come in!" Kali snapped.

Desmond wished he'd thought to bring his gun, but it was too late now. Resting one hand on the door-frame, he took a tentative step over the threshold.

"Come on, come on, it's not a lion's den, for Christ's sake."

Desmond stepped all the way in and felt the door brush past him on its way closed. It banged shut as he turned. Kali was taller than he'd expected, and considerably younger. But it was her hair that caught his attention; a woven rope of dark bronze draped over one shoulder, it reached almost to her knees. Her eyes were blue, and darted nervously, despite the warm smile on her handsome face.

She smoothed the front of her T-shirt, which bore a likeness of Tim Hardin and the legend *Old-Time Smugglin' Man.*

"You know who I am, then?" Desmond asked.

"Not really. But DJ said you'd most likely come by, so . . . I mean, it's not like I open the door to every asshole who finds his way to the doorbell, you know."

Desmond swept his eyes through the vast interior of the dimly lit loft. He saw paintings everywhere—one end seemed to be devoted to a studio, and canvases in various stages of undress leaned against every available wall, sometimes five and six deep. The living space was much smaller, and much more orderly, but even here canvases hung on the wall, butted end to end.

"Nice place," Desmond said.

"You like tea, Mr. Desmond? I already have the water on."

He shook his head. "No, thanks."

"All kinds of herbal shit. Anything you want."

"No, thanks."

"Well, follow me while I make my own." She was barefoot, and her long legs moved gracefully as she headed toward the living space, threading her way among a handful of canvases lying flat on the floor. Over her shoulder she said, "DJ is not the neatest guy you've ever met." She turned to make sure he didn't accidentally trample a painting in the dim light.

In the kitchen area, where the light was better, Desmond could tell that Derrick Jones, whatever he was, had access to money. The kitchen was modern, its appliances state-of-the-art. The cabinetry alone was worth a good twenty thousand dollars. Looking around while Kali finished making her tea, he examined the furniture, which was obviously expensive, despite its lived-in look. Unlike some lofts he'd seen, this one had been been carefully thought out, clearly an architect's effort rather than the slapdash solution of an impoverished painter.

Tea in hand, Kali took him by the arm and pulled him toward a pair of leather sofas, dropping down and folding her jean-clad legs beneath her, then tugging him down beside her. "What can I do for you, Mr. Desmond?" she asked, sipping the greenish fluid in her cup.

Desmond shrugged. "I'm not sure, really."

"Then why are you here?"

"I guess I'm curious."

"About DJ?"

He nodded. "I was at the Pratt the other night, and—"

"So was I. You were one of the men who jumped on him, weren't you? I almost didn't recognize you without your tuxedo."

Desmond laughed. "I didn't recognize myself in it, to tell you the truth." She laughed, too, a musical sound like that of a large recorder, throaty, almost woody in its resonance. "Tell me about Mr. Jones."

Kali laughed. "Nobody calls him that. He's not the 'Mister' type, in case you hadn't noticed."

"All right, then, tell me about DJ."

"What's to tell? He's a great artist, only nobody knows it. I mean nobody with cash, which amounts to the same thing, I guess. These days, anyway."

"This place doesn't look like he's exactly a starving artist."

"You're assuming it's his."

"Isn't it?"

She tilted her head in a "who knows?" dismissal of his question.

"How long have you known him?"

"Ten, twelve years. We've lived together off and on for much of it. I was studying art and picked up some money modeling. That's how I met him. We hit it off, and the rest is history."

"You're being somewhat vague, Kali."

"Life is vague, Mr. Desmond. Smoke abounds, as DJ likes to say. And it's a waste of time trying to see through it."

"I'd like to ask you a few questions, if I might."

"What sort of questions?"

"About DJ's work."

"You'd better ask him. I can't talk about his work. He doesn't like it."

"I already went to see him. He was, shall we say, less than forthcoming. Maybe the hospital isn't the best place to talk, but I got the impression he didn't really want to say anything anyway."

"He wants to talk to you. He told me that."

"You visited him, did you?"

"No, he came by this afternoon."

"Came by? You mean he's out of the hospital, already?"

"Yeah. He said to tell you he'll be in touch."

Desmond leaned back on the sofa, more confused than ever. "Maybe I'll have that tea, after all."

- TWELVE- - -

THE PHONE WOKE HIM. DESMOND TURNED TO LOOK AT the illuminated dial of the clock as he reached for the receiver. He felt Audrey stirring beside him and snatched the phone up before it could ring again.

"Hello?" His throat was dry, his voice a froggy croak, barely recognizable even to him. He thought it might be Ray Miller with a belated apology for his failure to show at Jones's loft.

The voice on the other end betrayed its own uncertainty. "Is this Paul Desmond?"

Trying to keep his voice low, Desmond answered, "Yes. Who is this, and why the hell are you calling me at this time of night? It's nearly three o'clock in the morning."

"Is this the Paul Desmond who works for Northamerican Insurance?"

Desmond was losing his patience now. "Yes. Hold on a minute."

Getting up, he brought the cordless phone with him and walked to his office. Once inside, the door closed behind him, he said, "All right, who is this?"

"It could be anybody, couldn't it?" The man on the other end chuckled. "But if you think about it, you'll know."

"Jones, is that you?"

Another chuckle. "Very good. See, it didn't take you long to wake up."

"What do you want?"

"The question is, what do *you* want? And do I have it. That's another question. I think I know the answer to that first one. And if I'm right, the answer to the second is yes."

"Jones, I don't like riddles. And I don't like lunatics waking me out of a sound sleep."

"Hey, we all have things we don't like. For instance, I can't stand black velvet. I hate ABBA. I loathe Wayne Newton. But they're here, you know. Nothing I can do but live my life in spite of such petty grievances. You got a strange line of work, Mr. Desmond. You ought to be more tolerant of anomalies. Routine is the enemy of discovery. Sounds like William Blake, don't it? But it isn't. That's me."

"Jones, you better tall me something to keep me on the line, and you'd better do it quick."

"Monet ring a bell?"

"Of course . . ."

"Manet?"

"Is this art history by phone or do you have something more. Anybody can drop names."

"How long will it take you to get here?"

"Where are you?"

"You've been here."

"Your loft?"

"Bingo!"

"Why should I come there at all?"

"Because you're looking for something. Maybe I know where it is."

"You'll have to do better than that."

"I can. But I need to make sure of a few things first. See, I don't know whether I can trust you or not. You don't know whether you can trust me, either. That might make it look like a wash, but the thing of it is, you got to look deeper, Desmond. It's you who's looking for something. I'm not. You want to find it, you got to roll the dice. Maybe I'm blowing smoke, maybe not. You don't come, you won't know, will you?"

"I'll be there."

Desmond dressed as quickly as he could, left a scribbled note for Audrey, and headed for Manhattan. The ride down the thruway was quick and easy in the middle of the night. Switching to the Palisades Parkway, he watched the ghost of the George Washington Bridge, its cables outlined in lights that did not glitter so much as float in the haze.

Taking the Henry Hudson as far south as he could, he switched to Twelfth Avenue, then drifted east to pick up Broadway for a while. Night people drifted through the muggy streets like phantasms. All purple hair and leather, sunglasses and chains, they walked with heads down, boots kicking at trash on the sidewalk. The air was thick as soup, filled with the stink of the slime that coated the inside of garbage cans.

In the oppressive heat, the hookers wore even less than usual, which was already less than the law allowed, and their waves were limp. Like wilted flowers, they drooped in the doorways, barely bothering to glance at the few passing cars. For them, too, it was too damn hot.

Desmond found Greenwich Street deserted. He parked in front of the loft building and climbed out. Dressed in jeans and work shirt, he didn't look nearly as out of place as he had on his last visit. Pushing open the lobby door, he pressed the buzzer for the eighth floor, and an angry burr filled the vestibule as he pushed the door open and walked to the elevator.

Once upstairs, he stopped the elevator to gather his thoughts. He wasn't worried about his safety, not really. But unlike last time, this time he had the Browning. He didn't know enough for anybody to be afraid of him. At least not yet. But having the automatic on his hip was a little insurance. If Jones was neither hallucinating nor pulling his leg, all that might change, but only time would resolve that uncertainty.

He listened for a moment, wondering what he expected to hear and wondering, too, what it was that Jones had to tell him. Knowing that he was just stalling, he pulled the stop button out, let the car drift the last few feet, and pressed toward the door before it opened.

The hall was split almost halfway down by a rhombus of light from an open door. "That you, Desmond?" Jones's voice echoed in the empty passageway.

"Yeah." A shadow split the rhombus, then Derrick Jones peered around the doorframe, his head tilted ninety degrees. He grinned when he spotted Desmond. "Damn if you don't look casual as all get out. See an ad for that shit in *GQ*, did you?"

Desmond laughed in spite of himself. "It's what the sleepy suburbanite wears on urgent midnight visits to Babylon."

"Babylon is right, mon," Jones said. "Sodom and Begorrah, too."

"You mean Gomorrah, don't you?"

"Spent some time in Dublin, I did." He stepped back to allow Desmond to enter the loft, then slammed the door so hard the echo thundered along the hall and back as if someone were bowling with boulders. Turning to Desmond, Jones asked, "Drink?"

"Diet Coke?"

"Probably got one. Come on in." Jones led the way into the living area, pointed Desmond to a sofa, and continued on to the kitchen. Over his shoulder he said, "You know Kali." It wasn't a question, and he didn't wait for an answer before opening the refrigerator.

Kali was curled in a ball, her head resting on an arm of another sofa, but her eyes were open. She smiled and waved a hand, but said nothing.

Jones was back with a beer in one hand and a can of diet Pepsi in the other. He tossed the soda to Desmond and dropped onto the sofa beside Kali.

Desmond opened the can, covering the top in case it spurted, then took a sip. "Now, what's so urgent?"

"Urgent? I don't know that I said it was urgent. Just that I knew something you didn't, something you'd probably like to know."

"And what is that?"

Jones looked at Kali, who screwed her face up as if to say, *Here we go again.* She sat up, twirled her long braid around her fingers, then let it land in her lap as it uncoiled like a snake. "Maybe Mr. Desmond doesn't want to sit here and watch you make a fool of yourself, DJ," she suggested. "Maybe you should just tell him what you want to tell him so he can go home and get some sleep."

Jones laughed. "He's in New York now. Nobody sleeps this time of night in New York. Nobody worth knowing, anyhow." He looked at Desmond, his head cocked, a crooked grin on his face. He looked younger than Desmond had thought him to be. Maybe it was the light, or maybe it was his childlike demeanor. He tucked his legs up under him, took a sip of his beer, and said, "All right. Let's play twenty questions."

Desmond thought about getting up, but knew he had to give Jones a little more rope. "Okay," he said.

"Why would anyone steal a painting?"

"To sell it, presumably. And presumably at considerably less than its assessed value."

"That's one reason."

"Is there another?"

"I'm asking the questions, Des," Jones snapped, almost pettish. "What else can you do with a stolen painting?"

"Ransom it, I suppose."

Jones clucked, his disgust almost palpable, as if he were trying to discuss relativity with the village idiot. "Come on, come on, come *on.*"

"I suppose you could also keep it."

Jones beamed, nodding his head enthusiastically. "Now you're cooking," he said.

"It's my turn, Mr. Jones. Do you know where the stolen paintings are?"

Jones shrugged. "Maybe I do."

"Either you do or you don't."

"It's not that simple."

"Just how simple is it, then?"

Jones wagged a finger. "Nah, nah, nah. Not so fast. We are talking very ticklish stuff here, Mr. Desmond. You might be dumb as a brick, for all I know. I'm not sure how much I ought to tell you."

"I'm not sure how much you know."

"Try me."

"Does the same person have all twelve of the paintings?"

Jones shrugged. Instead of answering the question, he changed the subject. "Wait here a minute." He got up nimbly, a cross between a sprightly leprechaun and a Buddhist monk as he rose without using his hands. He stood on the sofa for a moment, did a pirouette, then jumped to the floor. "Wait here a minute," he said again.

He headed toward the studio portion of the loft and disappeared into the shadows. Desmond sipped his soda, watching Kali, who looked as if she had drifted out beyond the orbit of Mars. Her eyes had a faraway look, and her mouth was slack. She seemed altogether unaware of his presence. He wondered if she was on something, decided she probably was, and that it was none of his business.

Jones was making a racket out of Desmond's line of sight. And when he finally reappeared, he was holding a canvas, its back to Desmond. He stood a few yards away, set the canvas on the floor, and spun it around with a whistled fanfare. Desmond caught the aroma of some sort of solvent, benzene or toluene, something organic. Before he could place it, Jones distracted him.

"You ever see this before?"

Desmond nodded. "It's Monet's *Madame Monet in a Red Cape*. One of the paintings I'm looking for." Desmond leaped to his feet. "Where in hell did you get it?"

Jones crinkled his face into a gnomic smile, produced a BIC, and flicked it. Desmond leaped toward him, but Jones was too quick. The flame flickered as the lighter brushed the center of the painting, and the canvas was a sheet of flame, igniting with a dull thump.

Jones started to laugh. There was an hysterical edge to it, and Desmond wondered if he could stop. He looked at Kali as if for an explanation, but she was still moonwalking, oblivious to the sheet of flame and the stinking black smoke.

He turned back just as Jones let the stretcher fall to the floor, the canvas just charred tatters hanging in blackened strips now. Smiling, he asked, "So, do I have your attention, Mr. Desmond? Or do I have to use a two-by-four, the way the farmer did on the mule?"

"You have my attention."

"Good. I'll be in touch. You better go home and get some sleep. And don't worry. Things are not what they seem."

"But . . ."

Jones shook his head. "Not now, Mr. Desmond. Not now. Not yet. I have a few things to take care of, first.

I'll let you know when I'm ready."

"If you know half of what I think you know, Jones, you better be careful how long you keep playing idiot games. If you don't believe me, ask Pete Flannery."

"Who the fuck is Pete Flannery?"

"Look it up," Desmond snapped, heading for the door. "Start with the obituary column."

- T H I R T E E N - - -

CLARENCE HEMENWAY SAT DOWN CAREFULLY, straightening the creases in his pants legs with nervous fingers. As he leaned back, the sofa whispered to him and the smell of leather swirled around him. He leaned over to set his scotch and soda on a ceramic coaster. The glass scraped against the hard surface with a sound like grinding teeth.

He rubbed his neck, feeling the beginning of stubble. The rasp of skin on whisker offended his fingertips and his sense of himself. "I'm not sure this is a good idea, Willie," he said.

He picked up his drink and took a long swallow, feeling the ice against his teeth, letting the scotch sear him on the way down.

Willie leaned against the doorframe across from the sofa. His cream-colored suit was a more casual cut, and three times as expensive as the one Hemenway wore. Under it, he wore a brightly colored shirt, open three or four buttons. The glitter of a heavy gold medallion nestled in the rainbow V against a tanned and hairless chest. He ran a hand through the mound of blow-dried black hair that made his head seem abnormally large, the black eyes in the deep tan tiny as birds' eyes. He grinned, his teeth white as new piano keys.

"I don't think, amigo, that you should tell me what is a good idea, okay? Let's get that straight right now. We got to talk, you and me. *That* is a good idea."

Hemenway shrugged. "You're the boss."

Willie laughed. "Don't put it that way, amigo. You make it sound like you don't get nothing out of this business, you know? But it ain't like that. You get plenty."

"I get headaches, that's what I get."

"Don't you tell me about no fucking headaches. You don't know what headaches are, you know that? I know about headaches, thanks to you."

Hemenway sighed. "What do you want, Willie? Why am I here? Why did I have to fly twelve hundred miles just to listen to you when there are fifty million telephones between New York and here? Tell me that."

"You got to come because I don't trust no fucking telephone and because I don't like New York. You know that. How many times I told you that? A thousand? I don't like New York. The less I have to be there, the happier I am."

Hemenway licked his lips. "So what do you want to tell me?"

"I don't like this business, this nut case flipping out in your museum."

"You think I do? You think I planned it, do you?"

"It's a bad business, Clarence, you know that?"

Hemenway sighed again. "I know it, yes, of course I do. But these things happen. There was no way to know. You understand that as well as I do."

"Then since we couldn't know it would happen, we have to deal with it. Is that what you are telling me?"

"Pretty much."

"So, how do we handle it? What are we going to do about it?"

"I don't think we have to do anything. It won't happen again."

"Did you talk to him?"

"No. But—"

"Then how do you know it won't happen again?"

"It won't, that's all. Don't worry about it."

"So, I don't worry about it and I pretend that it never happened. And what if it does? What then?"

"I told you it won't. Trust me."

"I don't trust nobody, amigo. You know that. I really think you got to take this more seriously than you been taking it. And now there's this man Desmond nosing around. What about him?"

"What would you do if you were in my position?"

Willie snorted. He walked to the far end of the leather sofa, sat down, and grabbed his own drink from the table matching the one at the other end. He tossed it off in one swallow, clicked the glass down with a sharp crack, and said, "You don't want to know that. Trust me."

Hemenway laughed. "I don't trust nobody, Willie. You know that."

Willie looked at him sharply for a moment, before his lips curled into a grin. "First of all, if I hear you right, you're telling me you don't trust *me,* and this I don't like to hear. Secondly, you don't say nobody, you say anybody, which makes me think that maybe you are making fun of me, Clarence. Is that what you're doing? Making fun of me?"

"No, of course not."

"Good. Because if you were making fun of me . . ." He let the thought die, its silent ghost hanging there in the air between them for a long moment, before he changed the subject. "Where is Jones now?"

"Probably at his loft."

"You're sure he's out of the hospital?'

Hemenway nodded. "I'm sure. It's been taken care of."

"Good. But there's still the matter of this Desmond. We have to do something about him, I think."

"That's not a good idea. Already the police are asking questions about this truck driver. We can't afford to have them asking more."

Willie stroked his chin, his lips pursed. "That was *muy malo.* But it has been fixed."

"What happened?"

Willie slammed his fist into the arm of the sofa. "You don't ask me what happened, Clarence. You don't do that. I don't like it."

"I have to know. Suppose the police—"

"The less you know the better. You know what you have to know. We are talking about things that you don't understand. But I understand them very well."

"But I don't—" The harsh jangle of a telephone interrupted him. Willie looked annoyed, then stalked out of the room. Hemenway leaned back on the sofa and looked out at the brilliant sunshine. The house seemed suddenly to surround him like a prison, despite the light.

He had been telling the truth when he told Willie he didn't trust him. But that hadn't dawned on him until Willie left the room. Sitting there alone, he found himself wondering what Willie would do if he crossed him. He knew the man well, he thought, but there was a dark center to him, a place that he held close, and the public man seemed to revolve around it like a cloud of incandescent gas swirling around a black hole.

And whenever he thought about the dark, heavy center, he knew that he didn't want to get too close, lest he be sucked in and disappear. As it was, he felt like chattel, running whenever Willie called, not even bothering to ask how high when Willie said jump, just gathering his legs beneath him and reaching for the sky. And no matter how high he leaped, it was never high enough. One look at the disdain in Willie's black eyes was enough to tell him that. And Willie seemed to delight in humiliating him, to press buttons no one else knew were there. The truth was, he was in thrall, as much as he wanted to deny it.

He looked at the paintings on the walls—marvelous works, masterpieces, really—but there was no warmth to them, not because the works themselves lacked warmth, but because the house was a cold, lifeless place. It was always filled with people, parties going on at all hours, people materializing as if out of thin air, then disappearing just as abruptly. But there were never enough visitors to dispel the chill. At first, he had thought it was the air-conditioning, that Willie, for reasons known only to himself, set it high and kept it there. But now he knew better. Now he understood that the cold was a reflection of Willie himself. The black eyes were cold, and either impossibly deep or as shallow as the reflecting skin of a mirror. Either way, Willie kept himself closed off, imposing himself on the world around him without revealing anything of what he thought or felt.

Clarence Hemenway had seen such men before, known a few of them better than he would have wished. They were users, like Willie, brutal men who would cut your throat as soon as look at you, crush you like an acorn under a hunter's boot, and leave the wreckage on the ground to rot. He didn't kid himself that the resemblance was only superficial. He had seen too much to believe that, seen only too clearly just how brutal Willie could be when it suited him, out of need or simple pleasure.

There had been a time he thought he could be like Willie, cruising through the world like a great white shark, a throwback, relying on primal instincts fifty million years old to take what he wanted. But time had disabused him of that fancy notion. He had learned that he was not like Willie at all, that he was here for the pleasure and at the sufferance of men like Willie. He was too easily cowed. All his bravado was window dressing, smoke to hide the trembling coward inside him.

He wanted to run. But there was no way he could get away, not now, not yet. Getting himself free of

Willie would not be a simple thing. It was, however, a thing he knew he had to do before it was too late. He didn't know how much time he had, but it wasn't much. The world now seemed like a giant machine, poised to crush him. Already, the engine was running, the flywheel was spinning, the gears grinding into motion.

Listening to the subdued mutter of Willie's voice from the adjacent room, he was reminded of another, simpler time when he would sit on the porch on a late summer afternoon, watching the clouds slowly coalesce into a thunderhead, the gathering storm slowly darkening the sky, the rumble of thunder far off, barely audible at first, more like a trembling of the air than an actual sound. But he could tell when it was coming, and he watched it, fascinated, immobilized by that fascination that was almost terror. Eventually, the first splash of rain would darken the cement steps, rattle through the leaves of the ancient elm in the yard, washing away a week's dust.

When it rained, it seemed as if it would rain forever. But when it was over, everything seemed shiny and new. The sun would come out, the leaves would glisten in the returning sunlight, drops of water sparkling like diamonds. The geraniums in a planter on the edge of the porch seemed to catch fire. But it wasn't in his nature to savor that time. It was the storm itself he held on to. As the thunder would crash and the lightning slash like swords across the black sky, he would sit there, feeling the chilly wind out of the west, the splatter of cold rain on his cheeks and bare knees. He would tremble like the elm leaves, his whole body racked by a shaking he could not control.

It would have been a simple thing to get up and go inside, close the door to shut out the roar, but he never did. He was transfixed, immobile as a fly in a web, watching the approach of its weaver.

Knowing Willie was like that. He was as immobile now as he had been then, as incapable of getting up and walking away. It seemed sometimes as if that were his fate, to watch the inexorable advance of his own destruction, a destruction he courted as much as he feared it.

His reverie was broken by the sharply raised voice in the next room. At first, the words were just a jangle rattling off the cold walls, but gradually he started to undertand what Willie was saying. He leaned forward to hear more clearly.

"I don't care. I will kill you, do you understand?" Willie was screaming. "I will cut your heart out and feed it to the dogs. I will . . ." The shouting ended in an apoplectic splutter, then the phone crashed against its cradle. A moment later bells jangled as the phone came cartwheeling through the open doorway, trailing its wire as if pursued by a serpent.

Almost immediately, Willie followed the wire and stood in the doorway, and it seemed as if the room grew suddenly dark. Hemenway didn't ask who had been on the other end. He didn't want to know.

But Willie didn't care. "That was your Mr. Jones," he said. "He threatened me, and, my friend, he threatened you."

Hemenway felt his body begin to collapse. When he spoke, his voice was soft, almost a whisper. "What are we going to do?"

"I don't know about you, amigo, but I know what I will do."

"What?"

"I am going to cut off his balls and eat them."

"Where is he?"

"I don't know. But I will find him. One way or another, I will find him."

— F O U R T E E N — - -

DERRICK JONES STOOD IN FRONT OF A HUGE CANVAS.
The glare of the overhead lights was giving him a
headache, and worse than that, it was blurring the
vision in his skull, making it hard to focus on what he
wanted to do.

Kali was watching television, and every once in a
while her laugh cut through the screaming frustration
in his head, snapping him back to where he was, and
why. He wanted to shout at her to be quiet, but that
would just lead to a fight, and as good as it would
make him feel, it wouldn't help him cover the raw
canvas in front of him. And he knew better than
anyone that it was this current failure that was making
him so edgy.

The blankness of the linen, a smear of paint here and
there, stretched like a beige tundra to every horizon. It

seemed to taunt him, daring him to try to obscure the blankness with something meaningful. And Jones wasn't sure he could. I talk a good game, he thought, but when the bell rings, I stay in the corner.

He looked at the window and at the lights beyond the smeared glass. Slamming the palette against the canvas, he stood with his arms folded until it began to slide away, leaving bands of color behind, thick as clotted blood. He wanted to stalk away, but something held him in place. He was a prisoner to the inexorable workings of gravity and knew he could not leave until the palette finally lost its desperate battle to cling somehow to a surface that did not want to be encumbered.

Finally, with the sucking sound of an open chest wound, the last tendrils of pigment gave way and the palette hit the floor edge on, the tame click a feeble signal that the battle had at last ended.

Turning away from the smeared paint, the marred line, he walked to the window and leaned on the dusty sill. On the wood, he noticed tiny, faint smears of color, memorials of other tortured respites when the city had drawn him away from work that was not going well. He cranked the handle until the louvered panel swung all the way back against the brick wall. He leaned out into the night, Kali's laughter now just a distant tinkle. Far below, the streetlights looked like balls of pale light, and beneath them, the twin beams of a passing car's head lamps picked out the glitter of a bumper, a piece of tinfoil in the gutter, some broken glass.

That was what it was all about, he thought—light and what you do with it. He'd learned that from

Monet and Seurat, from Mary Cassatt and even from Matisse. Light was everything; control it, and you were master of the canvas. Tonight, though, he was master of nothing. Emptiness was in charge.

He knew he shouldn't have made that phone call, knew that he was walking the thinnest of wires, and that it might part without warning. But that wasn't enough for Derrick Jones. It never was. He had to tap-dance, stretch the wire to its limit. The phone call had reopened a door now barely held closed by Walton Henry. But maybe it was time to get it over with, kick the first domino and see how many would fall. Besides, he told himself, Walton Henry did not control Willie. If anything, it was the other way around. And Willie was an unpredictable bear trap. The yawning jaws trembled at the least provocation—the passage of a fly, a change in the temperature, the spring coiled, waiting. And sooner or later, they would close. Better to get it over with. If you lived to hear the echo of the clashing steel, so much the better. But even if you didn't, at least the enervating tension would be gone.

He found himself wondering about the man who called himself Paul Desmond. That it was a false name he had no doubt. Why was another matter. For some reason he could not name, Jones felt the inclination to trust him. But deep inside was a tiny, nagging voice warning him that he could and should trust no one. He had opened Pandora's box and a thousand things he could not name had already been set loose in the world, some flying out with the fluttering immediacy of bats and others leaping out like scared rabbits and heading for every corner. But there were still others, creeping slowly like shapeless, wet things from under rocks, and it was these night things that were the most dangerous. He had set in motion something that could very easily swallow him, and he felt for a moment like a man who stands below the trickling spillway of a dam, waiting for the fuse to reach the charge he's planted.

Even Paul Desmond, whoever he was, might not be able to save him. But that didn't matter. He had lit the fuse before he'd ever heard of Paul Desmond. If anything, the man with the barest hint of an accent might be a lucky straw that could save him, but he knew better than to count on it.

Looking out at the roofs of the shorter buildings that stretched toward the river and the hazy myth of New Jersey beyond the polluted waters of the Hudson, he wished that he could fly, that he could just pitch forward, right now, spread his arms, and sail like a hawk. Sometimes, when the painting was going well, it felt like that. He felt free then, unanchored, as if he could soar to the moon if he wanted to. But not tonight. Tonight he was a man who had a millstone around his neck, and if he pitched forward through the open window, he would fall so fast and so far he would see the light of day in China.

Pulling his head back in only reluctantly, he walked back to look at the canvas, and when it looked no different, except for the tendonous strings of hardening paint as expansively blank as when he'd walked away, he turned his back on it. There was always tomorrow. If tomorrow were allowed to come.

He stood with his arms folded, watching Kali for a moment. She seemed rapt, as if whatever were on the screen were magic, and he envied her her silly laugh, the way it consumed her, the way it shook her body, made her breasts tremble, and seemed to come from so deep inside her. He wanted to laugh like that, and wondered if there had ever been a time when he could have.

He started toward her, when the buzzer snarled behind him. Kali looked at him, used the remote to turn off the sound, and said, "Well, are you going to answer it?"

He shook his head. "No. I'm not expecting anybody. Are you?"

"No. But you must have heard of unexpected company."

"If it's unexpected, it ain't company, honey. Not now. It's trouble. Get your sneakers on."

She looked at him like he was crazy. "What for?"

"We're going for a walk."

"Now?"

He leaped toward her as the buzzer rasped a second time. "Now! Come on, hurry up, Kali."

She bent to retrieve her sneakers, but Jones couldn't wait for her to put them on. Grabbing her arm, he hauled her from the sofa and dragged her toward the open window.

"What's wrong? What are you doing?" She tried to pull free, but he squeezed tightly, sinking his fingers into the soft flesh above her elbow.

At the window, he whispered, "Climb out!"

"Are you crazy?"

"There's a wide ledge. Climb out, I'm telling you. It's our only chance."

"No."

He climbed up onto the window ledge just as the doorbell rang.

"I'm going to see who it is," Kali said.

"Don't open that door!" Jones hissed. "Please, get on the ledge."

Someone pounded on the door with what sounded like a hammer. "Mr. Jones, are you there?"

The voice had an Hispanic accent, and Kali looked at him, bewildered now. "Who is it?" she whispered. "Are you in some kind of trouble I don't know about?"

Jones smiled. "You could say that, yes. The fact is, *everybody's* in some kind of trouble you don't know about."

"What kind of trouble? Can't you—"

But he shook off her question. "You can't fix it, Kali. Nobody can fix it." She lifted one leg to the windowsill, and he held on to her while she hauled the other leg up. "Put on your sneakers, quick!"

Derrick jammed one sneaker on, and as she started to tie it the dorr rattled under another assault. Jones jammed her other foot into its sneaker and tied it himself. As soon as both were knotted, he hauled her out the window. The ledge was nearly three feet wide, and at its edge ran a low wall of stone, capped by terra-cotta tile.

He didn't know where it went, but at the moment there was no alternative. "There's probably a fire escape somewhere. If there is, use it. Get out of here as quickly as you can."

"Where should I go?"

"Go to Gail's. Stay there. I'll call you as soon as I can."

"What are you going to do?"

"I'll think of something." He leaned close to peck her on the cheek, then cupped one breast in both hands and squeezed. "For luck." He grinned.

He waved her toward the back of the building, then reached back for the handle of the louver and turned it until he could no longer exert any pressure on it. The window was still open nearly a foot, but it was the best he could do. Maybe they wouldn't think to check outside.

He moved away from the window just as the door flew open, the jamb splintering under a heavy impact, slivers of wood scattering across the floor.

He could hear men talking, three of them, at least. "Señor Jones? You here?"

"He's not here."

"He better be here."

All three had accents, and Jones licked his lips as he listened. Things were starting to move now, faster than he thought. And he hadn't counted on them coming after him this way, not this soon. He stayed just beyond the window, trying to hear what they were saying, but they had stopped talking. Now and then one of them muttered a curse, but nothing more.

Glass broke, then more, and he realized they were trashing the place, determined to punish him as best they could. They were sending him a message, letting him know what to expect when they got their hands on him.

One of the men came near the window, and Derrick could see his shadow spill onto the black asphalt of the ledge. The window began to move, and Derrick backed away, expecting someone to poke his head outside, but nothing happened. The window stopped moving and the shadow moved away.

He could hear the rip and tear of canvas now as the intruders vented their anger on a canvas. He moved along the ledge, toward the rear of the building. For a split second he found himself hoping it was the big, empty one that had given him so much grief, but he knew better.

At the next window, he lay down to crawl past, hoping he could stay below the sill. He couldn't see Kali in the darkness, but couldn't risk calling to her. When he had safely passed the window, he scrambled to his feet. He wanted to peer inside, see if he recognized any of the men, and to see what they were doing, but he couldn't take the chance they might spot him. The sooner they left, the better, and if he stayed out of sight, they would probably leave sooner rather than later.

At the back of the building, the ledge grew broader, and the entire back wall of the loft was glass. He stopped at the corner, looking for Kali, but there was still no sign of her. Retracing his steps, he stopped at a ladder that led down the side of the building and peered over. Far below, he could just barely see her. He turned his back and reached for the first rung, lowering himself as quickly as he could.

Just as his head dropped to the level of the terra cotta, he saw another ladder, one that led to the top of a cupola where two skylights were mounted, and he scrambled back to the roof. He sprinted to the ladder and climbed up, not stopping to question what he was doing, not even thinking about it. He was an automaton, moving as if in obedience to electronic signals, drawn to the peril below like a moth to a candle flame.

When he reached the top of the cupola, he crept onto its slanted roof and peered through one of the skylights. Far below, he could see three men. They were still venting their rage, tearing the furniture apart, tossing drawers and contents in angry rainbows. The clunk and clatter of the carnage drifted up all around him through open windows on the sides of the building. Mesmerized, he dropped to all fours, then lay flat, his arms folded under his chin, and watched.

By the time the men had finished their vandalism, he was asleep.

- FIFTEEN- - -

THE JASON HANDSWORTH GALLERY LOOKED MORE
expensive than Desmond had imagined. When Audrey
told him that Handsworth might be able to help him,
Desmond had expected to find some seedy storefront
on Hudson Street, full of left-handed gloves passing as
found art, cobwebs in the windows, and streaky hand-
writing pleading WASH ME on the grimy glass. He had
revised his expectations upward when Audrey told him
the Handsworth Gallery was on Madison Avenue in
the Seventies. But now, standing on the sidewalk,
peering in at a Frank Stella geometric on the wall, he
knew that he had fallen short by several orders of
magnitude.

Desmond felt out of place on Madison to begin
with, and as he pushed open the door and felt the first
cool breeze, tinged with incense, waft out into the

oppressive heat, he knew he was entering deep waters. But Valerie Harrison had thought it might be useful to talk to Handsworth, and Desmond couldn't disagree. When Valerie agreed to join him and offered to make the arrangements, there was no way to put it off. So, here he was.

A receptionist asked his name and buzzed back for the owner, then told him Handsworth would be out in a few moments. In the meantime, she told him, he should feel free to look around.

The muted lighting inside was calculated to show off the artwork to its best advantage, and Desmond found his eyes drawn to canvas after canvas as he wandered through the maze of walls and movable partitions. The current show was devoted to the work of someone named Donato. The canvases were striking, their muted colors full of a kind of brooding intensity. They were mostly female nudes, their bodies lush, but their eyes dark, suggesting that their minds were elsewhere. He found a placard that told him the painter's first name was Louis and he wondered what Audrey would think if he brought one home unannounced. But then he saw the price tag on another canvas, a portrait of a wild man wearing a crown of bones, his unkempt beard full of birds and fish, and he thought twice. Twenty grand was way out of his range.

Desmond was still contemplating the Lear-like monarch when someone called his name. He turned to find someone he took to be Jason Handsworth, arms folded across his chest, appraising his appraisal. "You like Donato's work?" Handsworth asked.

"Very much. I'm not sure I'd want to meet this fellow in a dark alley, but . . ."

Handsworth laughed. "He's harmless enough. Supposed to be a poet, a friend of the artist." Then he stuck out a hand. "Jason Handsworth."

Desmond responded with his own name and a handshake. Handsworth took him by the elbow, a maneuver that was well practiced. "Valerie is already here. Why don't we go on back to my office? We can talk there."

"Fine. I appreciate you're willingness to see me on such short notice."

"If it will help me get a few of Audrey's canvases in here, I'd talk to the devil himself." Handsworth laughed, and it seemed genuine. "Your wife is far more gifted than she realizes. But I suppose you already know that."

They entered a long corridor, its white walls broken every few feet by a large canvas, and Handsowrth finally led the way into a spacious office. The rear wall was glass and overlooked a sunken garden. Valerie Harrison was sitting in a chair in the corner, a catalog on her lap. She smiled when Desmond entered, and he waved hello.

Desmond walked to the window and stared down at a fountain in the center of a garden. Brick terraces intersected one another at odd angles, creating nooks where white wicker furniture offered the chance to sit by oneself. The terraces were heavily planted, studded with sculpture, both stone and bronze, and several tall trees filled the garden with shade.

Handsworth dropped into a chair. "That's what keeps me sane," he said. "You wouldn't believe how manic my business can get."

Desmond laughed. "I'm starting to get some idea. As a matter of fact, it is one of its more recent manic moments that brings us here."

"Have a seat, Paul."

And when Desmond dropped into a chair that allowed him to study the garden, Handsworth went to a refrigerator. "Sparkling water?"

Desmond shook his head. Handsworth opened the refrigerator, pulled out a bottle of Perrier, bent to see what else it might contain. "Coke? Ginger ale? Diet Pepsi?"

Desmond settled for a diet Pepsi, and when Valerie declined another Perrier, and Handsworth was seated, Perrier in hand, Desmond got right to the point. "Have you ever heard of Derrick Jones?"

Handsworth nodded slowly. "I see. So *that's* why you're here. . . ." He sipped his Perrier from the bottle, set it on a coaster on his desk. "I was at the Pratt the other night when it happened. And yes, I know him. Not very well, but probably as well as anyone can. Strange fellow."

"How talented is he?"

"Very. Perhaps not as talented as he thinks he is, but a lot more talented than many artists who are . . . better known . . . more successful. . . ." Handsworth shrugged. "I don't know quite how to quantify it. But he can paint, I'll give him that."

Desmond took a sip of his diet Pepsi and watched a red-winged blackbird land on the edge of the fountain, bob its head several times, making tiny ripples on the surface of the pool. He looked at Valerie before asking his next question. "Is there any possibility he painted those canvases that he destroyed at the Pratt?"

Handsworth laughed loudly. "No. None whatever."

"You're sure about that?"

"Absolutely. I mean, we're talking about paintings worth millions of dollars. Miss Harrison can testify to that, I'm sure. Regardless of who owns them, they are too valuable to be cavalier about them. They are under lock and key twenty-four hours a day, three hundred and sixty-five and a quarter days a year. Those paintings have pedigrees as surely as the Bourbons and Hohenzollerns. The chain of possession is unbroken and thoroughly documented. In more recent decades, the paperwork is almost stifling. Every transfer, every exhibition, almost every casual glance, is recorded. It's out of the question that Derrick Jones could have painted them, no matter what he claims."

Valerie was nodding in agreement, her face somewhere between a smile of satisfaction and relief.

But Desmond was not inclined to give up so readily. "Surely, Jones would know that. So why would he claim he did them?"

"He's mad. I don't think that's open to argument. I suspect he's feeling neglected, underappreciated, bitter. Who knows, maybe he'll be able to sell a few canvases now, fallout from the notoriety. It's happened before. It'll happen again, I'm sure."

Desmond chewed on his lower lip, as if debating whether or not to ask another question. Handsworth sipped his Perrier, waiting, and when Desmond said nothing, he asked, "What's on your mind, Paul?"

"I was just thinking. Hoping you're wrong."

"Why's that?"

"Valerie may have told you I've been retained by

Northamerican to recover a number of canvases that have been stolen."

"Yes, I know. But I don't see the connection."

"I was in his loft the other night, and Jones showed me a canvas, Monet's *Madame Monet in a Red Cape*."

"I doubt that very much. It belongs to the Hamburg Museum of Art. I'm sure it's very securely fixed to their gallery walls." Handsworth smiled as if that sealed the fate of Desmond's theory.

It was Valerie's turn to trowel a little mortar on the masonry of the tomb. "If he has that painting, I'm sure it would have shown up on the list of stolen canvases I compiled, Paul. It was exhibited in Barcelona only last year. If it had been stolen, Jason or I would know it. And even assuming he has that painting, it's worth milions. Why would he keep it in a loft?"

"He doesn't have it anymore."

"I don't understand. . . ."

"He destroyed it, doused it with solvent of some kind and set it on fire, right in front of me. He claimed it was a copy, one he had painted, and I was kind of hoping he was telling the truth. Not just about that painting but about the two paintings he destroyed at the Pratt."

Handsworth shook his head. "I don't think so, Paul. I really don't. I mean, I find it beyond credibility. There are ways to find out, of course. Not with the *Red Cape,* but with the canvases from the Pratt exhibition."

"I've already discussed that with Valerie. She thinks I'm crazy, but that's because she thinks Derrick Jones is crazy."

"Isn't he?" Valerie demanded.

Desmond laughed. "I know I'm not, and I have a funny feeling that he's not, either."

"But I don't understand," Handsworth insisted. "How could he have arranged for his forgeries to be substituted? And even assuming he could have done that, why go to all that trouble just to announce it to the world? What would be the point?"

"Hell, I don't know. Valerie asked me the same question. You probably know more about that sort of thing than I do anyway. By a long shot. The psychology of the neglected artist, all that sort of thing."

"Look, Paul, if you create a forgery, you do it primarily to fool somebody into thinking it's the real thing. It's very difficult to do, and there's no real way to know how often it succeeds, because if it *does,* nobody knows. What I'm saying is, if you pull it off, you keep your mouth shut about it, and you stay up late reading your bank statement. If Derrick Jones has been able to forge a couple of Monet's, how did they get into the show at the Pratt? And where are the originals?"

"Where would you look for them?"

Handsworth finished his Perrier, then set the bottle down carefully. He looked at Valerie Harrison for a moment, almost apologetically, as if what he was about to say might somehow offend her. "There's a black market for stolen art, of course. That's no secret. The originals could be sold, probably for a lot less than current value, maybe ten cents on the dollar, maybe fifty cents, it all depends on how many potential buyers you have, and how badly they want the work in question. This presumes, of course, that the buyer is willing to acquire the work with no intention to exhibit it, or even to disclose the fact of ownership."

"So Jones could be telling the truth?"

"Anything's possible, but—"

"Tell me everything you know about Derrick Jones."

Handsworth rotated in his chair and spoke looking out at the garden. "He's been around a long time. He used to hang with Kline and Pollack. He started out as an Abstract Expressionist. Was pretty good. Made a few of the shows. But he seemed to fall off the truck somehow, got left behind. There were all sorts of rumors— drugs, mostly, booze, the usual. The artist as tragic figure, his own worst enemy. He had a couple of one-man shows in the early seventies. By then, he was almost anathema in the galleries. He can be very difficult. His work wasn't selling, and the consensus seemed to be that he was more trouble than he was worth."

"Did he have the skill to forge a Monet?"

"That's a hard question to answer." Handsworth hummed into the Perrier bottle for a long moment, tapping its lip on his teeth. Finally, he nodded. "Yes, I think he did have the skill. But that doesn't mean I think he actually did it."

"Do you know anyone who knows him personally? Someone who's been in touch with him lately?"

Handsworth shook his head. "Not really. I suppose I can ask around, but I can't promise anything. As good a painter as he was, Derrick was always better at arson. He never crossed a bridge he didn't burn."

"Suppose I brought you a Monet and wanted to have you authenticate it for me, how would you go about it?"

"Depends on whether it's a known canvas. Then it's pretty easy. If it's something unknown, then it gets more complicated. The well-known works, there's usually a paper trail, which is the first thing we look at. Who owns it, where'd it come from, how much was paid, all the way back to Claude's studio, most of the time. If you're satisfied with the paper trail, then you look at the canvas itself. Subject, technique, chemistry, all that. There are pretty sophisticated lab tests. You don't usually bother with them, unless you have some reason to suspect forgery. When you're dealing with a well-known work, and both buyer and seller are known quantities, the lab route can be touchy. It ruffles feathers, as I'm sure you can understand. Nobody likes to have his honesty challenged. If it's a previously unknown work by a well-regarded artist, the lab route is more likely, but only just."

"If I find out that the paintings Jones destroyed are fakes, will you be willing to help me find the originals?"

"I don't see how I could possibly help, but I'll certainly do what I can."

"What I'll need is guidance on the black market, who might be likely to want a Monet, a Picasso, whatever. If you're not willing to name names, okay. I don't expect you to sacrifice your business relationships or scare off potential clients. But anything you can do will be a help. Maybe you can steer me to somebody who would be willing to point a finger."

Desmond finished his soda, got to his feet, and walked to the window again. Behind him, Handsworth said, "Now you have a better idea why that garden's there."

When Desmond turned back to the room, Valerie Harrison looked less certain about his thesis. The smile was gone. "If you're right, Paul, you realize that Northamerican may have been paying for other art, allegedly stolen or damaged beyond repair, when it was merely a forgery that was involved. People could substitute a forgery for the original, keep the original safe, and have its value in the bank, out of Northamerican's pockets."

Desmond smiled. "So what do you think? Is it worth another few days, just to be sure?"

She nodded. "And I think I'll want to put a little pressure on Clarence Hemenway. Maybe you're right. Maybe we really should authenticate the two canvases damaged at the Pratt."

— SIXTEEN— — —

CROSSROADS LOOKED LIKE EVERY OTHER CLUB
trying to hang on by its fingernails. Like most jazz
clubs and blues joints, it inhabited the decaying edges
of the city, where rents were, if not cheap, at least
manageable, and where the streets after dark were
full of shadows and strange smells. Desmond parked
in an empty lot, felt in his pocket for the Browning
automatic he hated to carry, and climbed out of his
two-year-old Buick.

He locked the car and stepped out of the lot onto
a cracked pavement. Papers lay in the gutter, too
tired to move with the weak breeze. He saw the
alternate-side-of-the-street parking signs and shook
his head. The theory was that the streets would be
cleaned on alternate days, but it had been weeks
since the last street cleaner had passed this way, and

more than likely, he hadn't bothered to put his brush down even then.

Desmond tried not to speculate on what Kali wanted. That she had called at all surprised him, and that she had suggested they meet struck him as odd, possibly even provocative. The deeper he scratched the genteel surface of the art world, the more convinced he became that Derrick Jones was a desperate man and, like most men in such a state, had resorted to desperate measures.

The biggest human being he had seen in six months stood outside the club, giving every would-be patron a quick once-over with a baleful eye. Clearly the bouncer, he seemed more a muscle-bound Cerberus ready to rip out your heart and feed it to you. Desmond stopped to read the poster for the week's act, Magic Slim and the Tear Drops, and congratulated Kali on her taste in music, assuming she knew or cared who was on stage.

Desmond paid the admission price, a steep saw-buck, and Cerberus opened the door for him. As he started down the steps Desmond felt the powerful throb of the bass, the hallmark of a great Chicago blues band. And the farther he descended, the more powerful the rhythm seemed. As Desmond reached the carpeted floor Magic Slim's buzz saw started to slice through the thick air that smelled of beer and sweat, and a moment later Slim launched into the lyrics, informing anyone who cared to listen that he didn't want no rough-dried woman.

It took a few moments for Desmond's eyes to adjust to the gloom, and as he moved down a narrow passage painted flat black, a blue glow filled the gloom ahead of him. He reached the entrance to the main room and found himself staring at thirty tables, two thirds of which were empty. But the partial house didn't seem to faze Slim, who tore into a slashing solo as if he were playing for fifty thousand people.

Desmond took a seat at a table near the back wall of the club, which was rough brick painted black. He put his pack of Marlboros on the table and fished a lighter out of his pocket, pulling a cigarette from the pack without picking it up. As he flicked the lighter a waitress in jeans and a black turtleneck materialized out of the gloom. Desmond glanced up as she hovered over him, ordered a diet Coke, and watched her disappear again.

Now that he could see reasonably well, he scanned the patrons, looking for Kali, but there was no sign of her. At least the music was fine, and he leaned back, soaking up the blues and wondering whether he had been led by the nose. Slim finished the first number, sharpened his low E, and bobbed his head. Without a moment's hesitation, the rhythm section kicked into a medium shuffle, and Slim settled into a scorching solo, his thick fingers tearing at the strings by the fistful. The Strat looked like a toy in his huge hands, and he seemed intent on gutting the guitar, bending two or three strings at a time.

The waitress was back, but Desmond barely noticed her. She set the drink in front of him and he reached for his wallet.

"It's on the house," she said, taking a seat beside him. He leaned toward her, trying to hear what she'd said, and only then noticed the thick braid dangling over her shoulder.

"Kali?"

"I didn't know you liked the blues," she said. "I guess I picked a good place for us to meet, huh?"

"What's going on?"

She shook her head. "After the set," she said.

He noticed that she had brought a drink for herself, and leaned forward to sip it through a straw without lifting the glass from the table. She turned to watch the band, and Desmond decided to play it her way for the time being. She had showed up, and that was already more than he had expected. It wouldn't do to push her too hard and scare her off.

Slim finished the instrumental and moved seamlessly into a slow blues punctuated by searing runs on the Strat, the tortured eloquence of his emotional vocals barely intelligible. Desmond sipped his own soda from the glass, staring at the back of Kali's head, as if he were trying to divine some secret trapped in her skull.

When the set was over, the lights came up, or at least another bank of blue floods came up, and it was possible to see reasonably well. Kali stood up, grabbed her soda, and then snatched at Desmond's hand to pull him to his feet.

"Come on in the back," she said. "A friend of mine owns this place. We can talk in her office."

Without waiting for an argument, she led him through a hole in the wall down another dark passage, toward a lighted rectangle at the far end.

He followed cautiously, his hand still grasped in hers, her fingers squeezing as if the two of them were on their way through a fun house and she feared they might be separated.

Once in the office, Kali seemed to relax a bit, and closed the door. It was cluttered, its walls covered with posters and promotional photos for half the living legends of the blues and more than a few of the departed. He recognized Muddy Waters and Howling Wolf, Little Walter and Magic Sam. Son Seals was there, so was Lonnie Brooks. Jimmy Johnson was tacked to a poster advertising Kenny Neal. Centered, in what looked very much like the place of honor, a notion Desmond approved, was a framed photograph of the quintessential blues guitarist. The autograph, its left-hander slant quite noticeable, said, *To Gail, a friend of the blues. Best Wishes, Otis Rush.*

Kali set her nearly empty drink on a cluttered desk and faced him, folding her arms across her chest. He hadn't realized how well built she was, and he felt embarrassed at noticing the rush of soft flesh pushed up through the deep V of her half-unbuttoned work shirt. She glanced at her cleavage, then smiled. Chastely then, she buttoned another button. "Sorry," she said.

Desmond, desperate to change the subject, asked, "What was so important, Kali?"

"Derrick's in real trouble. I just know he is. He won't tell me anything, but I know something is wrong."

"What happened?"

"Men came to the loft last night. Latinos. They broke in, and—"

"You said Latinos. Where were they from?"

"I don't know. Cuba, Puerto Rico. I don't know."

"And Derrick didn't give any indication?"

"No."

"Is Derrick all right?"

She nodded. "I think so."

"Where is he? I want to talk to him. I think I know what's going on, but I don't have all the pieces in order yet. Maybe I don't even have all of them. But if I'm right, Derrick has opened a can of huge worms."

"I don't understand."

"Kali, the less you know the better. Trust me, you don't need to know. But I have to see him. You sure you don't have any idea where he is?"

She shook her head. "I swear I don't know. We got separated last night."

"Tell me what happened."

Kali took a deep breath, then sank into a ratty armchair beside the desk. Breathlessly, she described the late-night assault on the loft, waving off questions each time Desmond tried to interrupt. When she was finished, she tented her hands and folded them over her brow, digging the fingertips into either temple.

"Where is he now?" Desmond asked.

"I *told* you. I don't know."

"What do you mean, you don't know? You must have some idea. Think, Kali, it's really important."

"I . . . we got separated last night, like I said. He told me to come here. But he didn't follow me off the roof, and . . . but he called me this morning. He said he was all right, but that it would be better for me if he stayed away from me for a while."

"Who were those men?"

"I don't know."

"Did Derrick know them?"

"I don't know. I don't know if he even saw them. But he seemed like he was expecting them. I mean, not them, necessarily, but someone. He was nervous all night. He kept trying to work, and he couldn't concentrate. That's the way he gets when he's worried about something. And as soon as the buzzer rang, he started pushing me out of the loft, like he knew who it was."

"He didn't mention any names?"

She shook her head. "None. At least I don't think so. I'm trying to remember, but it all happened so fast, I just don't . . . I can't remember."

"That painting he burned . . . the other night, when I was there. Did he paint that?"

She nodded. "Yes."

"You're sure?"

"Yes. He does that all the time. He's always copying things. Rembrandt, Picasso, Miró. Anybody. He does it for fun. He's always done it. He can copy something, or he can paint something else and you'd swear it was a Braque or a Van Gogh."

"Does he sell them? The copies, I mean?"

"I don't know. I guess so."

"Think, Kali. It's important."

"I don't know. There are papers at the loft—letters, bills, things like that. Maybe you can find out if he sells them, and who he sells them to."

"Does he have an agent?"

She shook her head. "He says agents are just bloodsuckers. They take half the money and don't do a damn thing to earn it."

"Are you staying at the loft?"

She chewed on her lower lip for a moment. "No. He

told me it wasn't safe. He told me to stay away from the loft until I heard from him that it was okay to go back."

"Where are you staying?"

"At a friend's. Gail, the woman who owns this place. I'm staying with her for a few days."

"Is the loft open?"

She shrugged. "I suppose so. They broke in the door, but I don't know whether DJ had it fixed or not. He didn't say and I didn't think to ask."

"These copies he makes, are there more of them at the loft?"

"Probably. There's hundreds of paintings there, and in another studio he has."

"Another studio? Where is it?"

"I don't know. I just know he has another place. Sometimes, when he's got a big commission, he stays there for days at a time. He even sleeps there."

"And you don't know where it is?"

She shook her head. "No. I asked him to take me there a couple times, but he always got pissed off, so I quit asking."

"Do you have a key to the back door of the loft?"

She nodded. "Yes, but, I . . ."

"Give it to me."

"I don't know if I—"

"Kali, this is getting out of hand. If Derrick is involved in what I think he's involved in, we are talking about life and death. One man has already been murdered, and from what you told me about last night, you and Derrick might have been next on the list."

She rubbed her temples again, then reached into a

drawer of the desk, pulled out her purse, and fished a key ring from it. She removed two keys, handed them over. "The silver one is the backdoor. The other one, the small one, is for the mailbox."

Desmond tucked the keys into his pocket. "Is there anyplace you can go, out of the city?"

She shook her head. "No."

"Besides Gail, who knows where you're staying?"

"Just Derrick."

"Don't tell anybody else. And make sure Gail knows not to tell anyone. Not a soul."

She looked at him then as if she was just beginning to understand. Her lips trembled, and for a moment Desmond thought she was going to cry. But she took a deep breath.

"Can you drive me home?" she asked.

The whine of guitar being tuned at full volume slashed through the walls, and Desmond nodded his head. "Yes, of course. We're not going anywhere unless you promise to call me if you hear from Derrick."

She nodded her head, then let her chin sink to her chest, and this time she didn't try to stop the tears. "I promise," she whispered.

- SEVENTEEN- - -

RAY MILLER WAVED A PAPER OVER HIS HEAD, A BROAD
smile on his face. "Here 'tis, Mr. Desmond."

"The warrant?"

Miller nodded. He ran a hand through his long hair,
succeeded only in moving the tangles around a bit,
and gave up. "It was like getting blood out of a turnip
getting this. I hope you appreciate all the trouble I've
gone to."

"If I'm right, you'll be more than pleased," Desmond
told him. "According to what Kali told me, we might
get our hands on enough to solve both our problems."

Miller laughed. "Problems, I got no problems. What

I got is a job, one that's impossible to do, that brings me into contact with enough fruitcakes for a dozen Christmases. But problems, no, I don't think I have any of those. Except for my backhand."

"Tennis?"

Miller shook his head. "Tennis is for wimps. Racquetball. That's a man's sport. Especially when you play with cold-eyed killers like I do." He pushed into the lobby of the loft building and waited for Desmond to join him. "I got to admit that this is the first time I ever executed a search warrant with a god-damned key in my hand. Don't seem right, somehow. It's no fun unless you can take a fire ax to the front door."

"From what Kali told me, most of the damage has already been done." Desmond led the way to the elevator, and Miller stepped in after him. As the car climbed he drummed his palms on the wall of the elevator. Desmond recognized a few licks from Joe Morello's solo on "Calcutta Blues."

"You're a Morello fan, are you?"

Miller was taken off guard for a moment. "What? Oh, yeah. Best drummer I ever heard. Should've gotten a lot more attention than he did. Being white worked against him, I guess. Crow Jim, and all that. But I think he's as good as Roach and Blakey and Philly Joe. By the way, I've been meaning to ask you . . . you're no relation to—"

Desmond knew what was coming and interrupted. "No. You asked me before, remember?"

Miller shrugged. "Oh, that's right."

*   *   *

The elevator stopped on the top floor, and Desmond stepped out into the hall. He bounced the key on his palm and walked down the hall. The front door had been replaced, and there was a heavy steel plate covering it, angle irons bolted into the jamb. It would take more than a burly shoulder to get through it next time. "Looks like Mr. Jones has been busy," Desmond said.

At the rear door, similarly reinforced, he inserted the key, hoping it still worked, and breathed a sigh of relief when the latch clicked. He shoved the door open and stepped into the loft, moving aside to let Miller follow him inside.

"Christ," the lieutenant whispered. "Look at this place. What a mess!"

"And we have to go through it piece by piece," Desmond said.

"And what, exactly, do you hope to find, Paul?"

Desmond shrugged. "Not sure. Probably not the stolen paintings, but maybe something to steer us in the right direction. Like I told you, he burned one right in front of me, then swore it was a fake."

"And you believed him? He's loony. Believe him and you believe the Warren Report, too, I guess."

Desmond shook his head. "No, I don't believe the Warren Report. But for some reason I can't explain, I believe Derrick Jones. I have to, because if I'm wrong, then seventy-three million dollars' worth of modern masterpieces are being destroyed canvas by canvas."

"Hey, you seen one haystack you seen 'em all. That's how I figure it."

Desmond knew that Miller was affecting an indifference he didn't feel. And it wasn't exactly a surprise.

It's hard to make your living when your stock in trade is the worst facets of human behavior and still pretend that rose-colored glasses cure all social ills. And there was the matter of perspective. When you see a corpse a day for two years, a few stolen paintings don't seem such a tragedy.

Desmond clicked on the lights, and the loft was suddenly blindingly bright. The two men moved in opposite directions and started looking through the stacks of canvases against the walls.

In the first fifteen minutes, Desmond found three Monets, a Picasso, and two Stellas. He pulled them aside and kept sorting. Miller called to him a few moments later. "Here's something looks like a Hopper."

When Desmond turned, Miller was holding a huge canvas away from the wall. Miller was right, it looked like the genuine item, from where Desmond was. And as he moved closer he saw nothing that suggested otherwise. But he knew it couldn't be genuine. Even if it had been stolen, Jones would not have been so cavalier in his storage. Or would he? Maybe he really was crazy, and it was just that simple.

Many of the canvases were only partials, some little more than pencil or charcoal sketches on raw linen. Others looked as if they were in the process of being painted over, new layers of paint partially obscuring a previous rendering, sometimes the same scene, sometimes in a style a world removed from that of the underpainting.

They had been there for less than an hour when Miller shoved a stack of canvases against the wall, sighed loudly, and lit a cigarette. "I got to tell you, Paul, if just ten percent of these things are the real thing, we're looking at enough to start a major museum."

"They can't be genuine. They just can't be," Desmond said.

"I don't think so either, but then I keep thinking, if little Derrick is a nut case, maybe some of them *are* real. I mean, I wouldn't leave them around like sheets of plywood, but I'm not crazy. I keep asking myself what a crazy man would do with a five-million-dollar painting that didn't belong to him, and I keep coming up with the same goddamned answer—I don't *know* what he'd do."

"He has another studio somewhere, but Kali doesn't know where it is. Or at least she claims she doesn't know."

"You think maybe that's where the stolen stuff is?"

"I don't know what to think. Something tells me that Jones doesn't have the real paintings. Unless I miss my guess, he knows where they are, and he was paid to copy them to cover the thefts."

"Then why did he gut those two at the Pratt?"

Desmond lit his own cigarette and answered through a plume of blue smoke. "I don't know. Maybe they weren't paying him enough for the copies. Maybe they tried to beat him out of his fee. Maybe they pissed him off. Maybe he just thought it was about time he started getting some recognition for his talent. What better PR stunt than to stage a coming-out party in front of half the art crowd in New York?"

"I'll tell you one thing—we have to get the lab

boys down here, let them start checking a few things out."

"Have you done that on the Monets?"

Miller shook his head. "Hemenway—you've met him, right?—is balking. He says he wants the paintings restored by the museum staff. He won't let them out of his hands. But suppose they're fakes, like Jones says?"

"I'll go you one better. Suppose he *knows* they're fakes?"

Miller dragged another Monet from a stack of canvases before answering. He leaned it against the stack of paintings they had been gathering, sat on the floor cross-legged, and rubbed his cheek. "Are you suggesting that Clarence Hemenway is involved in the thefts and, by extension, the murder of Peter Flannery? You can't be serious."

Desmond didn't hesitate. "I'm not suggesting anything, just speculating. I'd like to know more about Hemenway. Maybe he owes somebody, and this was his way out of the hole. Maybe he's got a retirement account in a Swiss or Caymans bank. I don't know what it is about him, but he rubbed me the wrong way. He seemed nervous when I talked to him. And that night at the Pratt, I saw him talking to Jones, and it sure didn't look like they had just met. He knows Jones, I'm sure of it."

"So what? These arty types all know one another. Hell, there are times when I think they all sleep in the same bed, like one big Appalachian family. It's like they're inbred in way, you know? Probably have hemophilia, like European royalty. But that's not a crime—it's just the way they are. They're just more comfortable with their own kind."

"But Derrick Jones is not one of them."

"No, but he's a painter. They tolerate geeks and fruitcakes because they produce the art. You want the paintings, you have to put up with beards, halitosis, and BO. You buy the artist a drink, give him a toot of coke, and make sure he's got plenty of paint and canvas, then you sit back and wait until he's done wrestling with his muse. Then you give him a few bucks and a pat on the head, like the family dog, while you see how much you can squeeze out of the jet set for the new work." Miller lit another cigarette and watched the smoke soar toward the ceiling, leaning his head back until it rested against a tall cardboard carton. His body language seemed to suggest that the conversation was finished.

But Desmond was not about to let go of one of the few loose threads he'd been able to find. "Have you done a background check on Hemenway?"

"You don't do that, not with the blue bloods. Everybody knows they have money troubles and marital troubles. But they all use the same three lawyers and it gets worked out nice and friendly like. Besides, if I start poking around like that, I get my nose chopped off. Somebody calls somebody in the mayor's office, he makes a call to the commissioner, and the next thing I know I'm writing parking tickets in Red Hook. And I hate Red Hook."

"I still think it's worth looking into."

"You can't have it both ways, Paul. You can't have our weasely little artiste a criminal mastermind and blame it on Hemenway, too."

"Why not? Why couldn't they be in it together?"

Miller stubbed out the cigarette impatiently. "In what, for Christ's sake? Give me some sort of outline, at least. I'm not good at improvising."

"I don't have one."

"I didn't think so."

Miller started to get up, lost his balance for a moment, and leaned on the carton. The side gave way under his weight and tore right down to the floor, spilling papers all over while Miller landed on his stomach with a grunt.

"You all right?" Desmond asked.

"Just injured my pride, is all." Miller laughed. Shaking his head, he tried to sweep the papers back into the box, but there were too many of them, and they kept cascading out before he was half-finished.

"Maybe we should look at those papers," Desmond suggested.

"Why, you think maybe Derrick left a confession?"

"Who knows? If I'm right, he already confessed in front of hundreds of people. What could it hurt?"

Miller gestured toward the box. "Be my guest. I'm going to have a look at the rest of the place. I think we have enough paintings for the lab. I want to call in, see what else they might want. If I'm lucky, maybe I can even get them to send a team over so they can gather their own samples. Who the fuck knows what they might want?"

Desmond started to look through the papers, calling over his shoulder, "Your warrant covers anything we might find, right?"

"You bet," Miller shouted, his voice echoing from the high ceiling.

Desmond took off his jacket and settled in. It was

going to take a long time, but he had precious little else to do. "See if there's some soda in the refrigerator, will you, Ray?" he called.

- EIGHTEEN- - -

RAY MILLER HUNG UP THE PHONE AND WALKED BACK toward Desmond, who was sitting on the floor cursorily shuffling some of the papers from the spilled carton. "I have to go to the office, Paul," he said. "I should be back in a couple of hours."

"Trouble?"

Miller snorted. "Trouble? No. Just paperwork. Bullshit like that. I have to write up a request for the lab before they'll even consider something like this. If everything goes smoothly, I'll be back as soon as I can. If I hit a snag, I'll give you a call here. You can decide whether you want to hang around or not."

Miller walked to the door and opened it. "You keep an eye out, Paul. Whoever tossed this place just might come back. Especially if they're still looking for Mr. Jones. You have a weapon?"

Desmond patted his hip. "Yeah. Right here."

"You know how to use it, do you?"

Desmond smiled. "I think I can handle it. It's not exactly rocket science." He didn't tell Miller that he still held several records at the annual competition Langley sponsored at Camp Peary.

Miller snapped off a casual salute and twirled out the door like Seinfeld's friend Kramer. The door banged closed, echoing in the vastness of the loft.

Desmond hauled mounds of paper to one of the sofas in the living area. The furniture had been trashed, most of it broken. Even the sofa on which he dumped the mountain of paper had been slashed. But it didn't look to Desmond as if the men who had broken in were trying to find something they suspected hidden somewhere in the loft. The violent upheaval looked more like the product of rage, as if, in not finding Derrick Jones at home, they were determined to leave him no home to return to.

When Ray Miller had headed downtown, he was lugging a couple of canvases, hoping the visual aids might interest the lab boys in solving a puzzle that, for a change, did not involve a corpse. If he had any luck, there was the chance that they might know a hell of a lot more by morning.

Before settling down to the papers, Desmond got on the phone to call Audrey and tell her not to expect him home until the following day. And he asked her to find out as much about art forgery as she could manage in the next twenty-four hours.

Setting a couple of empty cardboard boxes on the floor beside the arm of the sofa, he cleared a spot for himself and sat down, an ashtray on the floor, and started to sort through the papers. He had no idea what he was looking for, but he hoped that when he was finished, he would have a little better idea of what Derrick Jones was like and, just maybe, enough evidence to prove or disprove his suspicion that Jones was the key to the missing art.

The papers were a hodgepodge. Apparently, Jones was one of those squirrels who saved everything. There were receipts from everywhere—McDonald's to Bloomingdales; letters, some of them bearing postmarks twenty years before; dozens of small rectangles reading *Inspected by #35* or *#42*, or *Louise,* retained as if they were clues to some mystery only Jones knew existed; table napkins, some with phone numbers or addresses, long since bled to blurs by moisture, some with sketches in pencil or marker. If it was made of paper, the midden contained at least one example of it—even paper bags and labels soaked free of cans or bottles. There were pages torn from magazines, and most of the time Desmond perused them without a clue as to why Jones had saved them. But he couldn't allow himself to get discouraged.

He wondered whether there might not be some rhyme or reason in the accumulation, one that was so simple he overlooked it, or so obscure he'd need a guide to find his way to it. But the best guide was Derrick Jones, and for the moment he was missing in action, no more a presence than Judge Crater or Glenn Miller.

After two hours he had several small heaps of papers. The letters he kept together, thinking to read them once he had gone through the mess. Anything with a phone number or an address, whether or not it had a name—and most of them didn't—he put in a second pile. Another contained those pieces of paper that contained names. Sometimes you get a picture of someone just by looking at whom he knows. And since Jones was hiding out, any name, any address, any phone number might be a clue to his present whereabouts.

The phone rang, the electronic chirping of the cordless making Desmond jump out of his skin. It was buried somewhere on the sofa, and it rang three more times before he was able to put his hands on it.

Pushing the button marked PHONE he listened without saying anything, hoping to hear Derrick Jones on the other end. But the irritated barking was Ray Miller. "Damn it, Paul, say something!"

"Ray?"

"You expected maybe David Letterman?"

"Well . . . ?"

"You want the good news first or the bad news?"

"Give me the bad news."

"I ain't coming back tonight."

Desmond sighed audibly. Miller hastened to add, "Before you slit your wrists, the good news is the lab boys will come by tomorrow and pick up a few things. They'll run some tests. They kind of liked the canvases I brought in. I think it piqued their curiosity. Now all we have to do is keep them curious."

"You coming with them?"

"Yeah, probably ten, ten-thirty. I'll need the key, though. Can you get it to me, or should I come by for it?"

"I'm staying in the city overnight. I'll meet you here in the morning."

"See you then."

As Desmond hung up he felt depressed. That the lab was interested was good news, but it seemed so feeble somehow. He wanted answers to bigger questions, and they were not going to be found at the other end of a microscope. Maybe Kali could help, Desmond thought, but he wasn't sure she would agree. But he had nothing to lose by trying. He pulled a notebook from his pocket, found the number she had given him, and picked up the phone. He punched in the number and held the receiver to his ear, listening to the distant crackle in the void, full of chirps and an answering whistle, like a signal from a missing space probe.

It rang a long time, and when someone finally answered, the voice on the other end was tentative. But it was Kali, and she agreed to come to the loft. Desmond didn't want her out alone and told her to stay where she was, he would come get her. She seemed relieved, as if the prospect of venturing out alone were more than she could bear.

Gail's apartment was ten minutes away, on Hudson Street, and Kali was ready when he got there. As they left Gail's building Kali checked up and down the street, as if she expected to see someone come charging out of the shadows with a gun in one hand and a meat cleaver in the other. But Desmond tugged and she stumbled to the waiting car.

Once the car was moving, she seemed to relax a little. "I think someone has been watching me," she said.

Desmond looked at her sharply, but said nothing. He hoped she was wrong, but knew that his reassurance would ring hollow. He didn't know, couldn't really, and there was no point in pretending otherwise.

He parked in front of the building again and opened the door for Kali, then hustled her into the vestibule. She seemed nervous and kept looking over her shoulder back into the street. "Did you see someone, Kali?" he asked.

She shook her head. "No, but I keep feeling these eyes on me, you know? It feels like there's bugs on my skin. Everything tingles. I guess it's just nerves, but I can't help it."

"Don't apologize. It's perfectly normal."

She laughed. "You know something? That's the first time in years anybody's called me normal." She slipped an arm through his, and squeezed.

"So I lied."

That made her laugh harder, but as they moved into the hall she cast one more anxious look past Desmond and out into the darkness.

As they waited for the elevator Kali shivered. "This place gives me the creeps. I keep asking DJ if we can move, but he say's there's no way. He says he can't afford it."

"Is the loft his?"

Kali didn't answer, and Desmond realized it was at least the second time that she had avoided the question of ownership. But he didn't want to push it. He needed her cooperation, and he couldn't take the risk of making her think of him as an adversary.

When the elevator stopped on the top floor, Kali was reluctant to leave the car, but Desmond tugged her into the hall. "There's no one here, Kali. Come on, it'll be all right."

She took a deep breath and followed him to the rear door. Desmond opened it quickly and turned on the lights before stepping inside. He went in first, and Kali lingered on the sill, as if uncertain whether she wanted to come in. But he gave her a reassuring smile, and she sucked it up one more time, shrugged her shoulders, and entered the loft.

She stood there looking around as Desmond closed the door. "They really made a mess of this place, didn't they?" She paused for a moment, then added, "Or did you do this?"

Desmond shook his head. He led her to the sofa and showed her what he had done with the papers. "What are you looking for?"

"I don't know. Anything that might help, I guess."

"You believe DJ, don't you? That he did those paintings from the museum?"

"Yeah, I do."

"Will it make a difference if he did? Legally, I mean."

"It doesn't really matter. The museum is not pressing charges."

"Does that mean they believe him?"

"No, I don't think so. I'm not quite sure what it means. The most innocent explanation is that they view the event as one more regrettable instance of human frailty, a deranged man doing what deranged men do."

"But DJ isn't deranged."

"That's what you and I believe, but I'm not sure whether anyone else believes it."

"I don't see how I can help you. I mean—"

"Look, more than anything else, I need to know where Derrick is. You say you don't know, and I guess I believe you. But there must be some clue in all this mess, a name, maybe an address. If you were trying to find him, where would you look?"

She shook her head. "I don't know. I mean, I never thought about it. He was always here or at the other loft, the one I told you about. He's never left me alone like this before."

"Think about it, Kali. What about friends? You have Gail. Does Derrick have someone like that, someone he could trust with his life?"

"I don't think so. I mean, he's kind of difficult. He didn't really have many friends. Over the years we've been together, he's managed to alienate just about all of them. And there weren't very many to begin with."

"Do me a favor, look through these papers, see if anything rings a bell. I don't care how remote the possibility. Anything you even think you remember might be just what I'm looking for."

Kali took a deep breath, sat down on the floor, and started to sift through the letters, looking at the return addresses. But envelope after envelope sped through her hands, like a new deck in cardshark's hands. They flashed through with a steady *slap, slap, slap* on the stack. And when she was done, she shook her head. "Nothing looks familiar."

He showed her the stack of papers with phone numbers, and she ticked them off one by one. But only two meant anything at all. One was a number Gail had before a series of obscene calls forced her to switch to an unlisted one. The other was her gynecologist.

"What about the other loft?" Desmond asked. "Did he have a phone there? He must have . . . what was the number?"

She shook her head. "He had a phone, but he wouldn't give me the number."

Desmond stood up to walk off his frustration. He kicked the mass of papers still to be sorted through and walked toward the rear of the loft. He stopped at one of the tall windows and leaned on the sill.

His foot scraped on something on the floor, and he looked down to see what it was. The corner of a business card protruded from under the baseboard heater. Curious, Desmond bent to rerieve it. As his fingers closed around the stiff cardboard, the window blew out over his head, showering broken glass all over his back. Instinctively, he dropped to the floor.

Kali had heard the noise and stood up to start toward him. "What happened? Are you allright?"

"Get down," Desmond shouted. "Now!" He started to scramble toward her, saw that she was frozen, and reached out to grab her by the belt. She seemed confused and tried to pull away, but Desmond dragged her to the floor. Another pane of glass blew out, its pieces clattering onto the polished wood behind him. And this time he could see the webbing of cracks surrounding a bullet hole in the far wall.

Pulling her back toward the wall, he said, "Stay right here, all right, Kali?"

Without waiting for an answer, he snaked along the base of the wall, away from the window. In the studio area of the loft he stopped under the fuse box and flattened himself against the wall as he straightened up. For an instant he was visible through the shattered window, but his fingers closed over the master switch and he jerked it down, plunging the loft into utter darkness as he sank to the floor. At almost the same moment he heard the slap of a slug burying itself in the plaster just above his head and, at the same instant, another cascade of broken glass.

Desmond saw a silhouette pass one of the windows, but not clearly enough to make out whether it was man or woman, let alone finer distinctions. He pulled the Browning and lay flat, waiting for the shooter's next move. Holding his breath, he watched the next window, and he saw the figure stop, as if uncertain what to do next. The figure raised its arm and brought it down again, and a pane of glass exploded into the loft. Desmond aimed and fired.

He took out the pane beneath the broken one. Someone yelped in pain, a man's voice, but that was all, a single unintelligible yowl. The silhouette was gone, and Desmond scrambled to his feet. Racing toward the window, he kept the Browning as steady as he could, but when he reached the shattered glass and looked out, he saw nothing.

Desmond ran back toward the living area and cranked open a window. Climbing out, he whispered to Kali. "Stay put."

Working his way carefully along the ledge, he reached a point just outside the window through which he'd fired. A smear of blood glinted on the sill, but there was no other sign that anyone had been there. He moved along the wall until he found the fire-escape ladder.

Leaning over, he saw a shadowy figure far below, more than halfway down. Even as he watched, the figure dropped the last fifteen feet and staggered to the mouth of the alley, where a dark sedan was waiting. The rear door of the car opened and clsoed without light, and Desmond saw nothing more as the car peeled out and disappeared.

He went back to the window and crawled in. "Kali, are you all right?"

Then Kali screamed, a long, shuddering wail that sliced through him like a razor, laying every nerve open to the night.

– NINETEEN– – –

RAY MILLER RAN HIS HAND OVER THE LEATHER SOFA
and whistled. Desmond glanced at Valerie Harrison,
half expecting her to be annoyed, but she grinned in
amusement.

"You can take it home if you like, Lieutenant," she
said.

Miller shook his head. "I'd be afraid the cat would
claw it to ribbons."

Valerie seemed surprised. "You have a cat? You
don't strike me as a cat person."

"Actually, no, I don't. But someday I might be
able to afford one. Then what would I do with the
sofa?"

Valerie exploded in laughter, leaving Desmond and
Jason Handsworth to stare at her in bafflement. When
she recovered, she said, "Maybe we should get down

to business. Mr. Desmond, this meeting was your idea, so why don't you start?"

Desmond sipped his soda, cleared his throat, and began. "Let me just briefly summarize where we are so that Ray and Jason will have the background."

Quickly, he outlined the missing art, the circumstances that led him to suspect that Derrick Jones was somehow connected, the shooting incident of the night before, and his belief that things were at once more complicated and simpler than they had seemed. When he was finished, he looked at Handsworth and Miller, expecting questions, but none was forthcoming.

"All right," he continued, "let me explain why I wanted this meeting. I think that Derrick Jones has, in fact, forged a number of modern masterpieces—far more, in fact, than the number insured by Northamerican. One thing we need to do is get a list of similar paintings reported stolen in the last few years." He looked at Valerie. "You would know better than I how to go about that, and how far back you should go. I would think at least as far back as the first theft reported to Northamerican, Valerie. And maybe longer."

"I still don't see the connection. The paintings I hired you to find have definitely been stolen. It seems to me that you're off on a tangent, Paul."

Desmond nodded. "I know that. And I'm not certain I'm not off the track. But Derrick Jones showed me a canvas that is on the list of stolen paintings."

Valerie leaned forward. "I still don't know what to make of that, Paul."

Desmond shook his head. "No. Me either. Or why

he burned it. I don't know whether he wanted to shock me, destroy evidence, or maybe convince me there was more going on than I suspected. He's a devious little bastard, and smart as a whip. But so far, whatever game he's playing, he's the only one who knows the rules. Anyway, when he burned it, he also suggested it was not the original. He implied it was a copy."

"And you believe him," Miller said, not certain whether to laugh or not. "You actually took the word of a madman?"

"I did. Because the alternative was unthinkable. I don't know what he *wanted* me to believe, though. You have the remains, and I assume that you still have the other paintings we took from Jones's loft."

Miller nodded. "Yeah, we still have them. They're at the lab. The crew was there this morning and they took a whole truckload of stuff for analysis."

Desmond looked at Handsworth. "This is where you come in, Jason, if you're willing."

Handsworth looked puzzled. "I don't see how."

"I think we need a complete examination of the paintings Lieutenant Miller and I found in the loft. Some of them are only partially finished, but all appear to be copies of modern work by significant artists. Some of them even appear to be the originals, but neither Ray nor I is qualified to make that judgment. The fact is that I suspect the police lab is not equipped to make the kind of examination that needs to be made of those canvases. I presume you know of a laboratory that has the sophistication and the specialized equipment."

"Sure. If they're forgeries, it shouldn't take too long

to determine it. But that won't help you find the missing paintings."

"No, not directly. But it will give us a clearer picture of what we're dealing with. My guess is that Jones was not just forging these paintings on a whim, he was doing it on commission. I'm convinced he had a buyer before he ever stretched a canvas. Kali as much as said that, although I don't think she knows for certain. She claims that Jones has a separate studio where he does a lot of work, and that she's never been there. If we can find that studio, we will have a better idea. But I'm not sure we can."

Valerie was still not convinced. "If Derrick Jones was forging artworks for someone, why does he still have the canvases?"

Desmond shrugged. "I don't know. I can make a few guesses, but I don't know enough yet to know how close they might be."

"Let me hear your guesses," Valerie said.

Miller chimed in. "Yeah. I don't have time to read, and this is better than a paperback mystery anyhow."

"For one thing, I believe Jones is a perfectionist. I think the partial canvases were left unfinished because he wasn't satisfied with them. He put them aside and started over."

"Who bought the ones he did finish?" Miller asked.

"I don't know. Not yet. But if we find whoever it was who did the shooting last night, we'll be a lot closer to him . . . or her."

"But what is the connection to the stolen work?" Valerie asked, still far from convinced.

"That's more speculative," Desmond explained. "But I have a feeling that what Jones did was make forgeries that were substituted for the originals whenever that was possible."

"That's preposterous," Handsworth exploded. "How could he do that? He just couldn't."

"Not by himself he couldn't, no. But he *did* say that the two canvases he slashed at the Pratt were forgeries."

"He's a lunatic," Handsworth insisted.

Desmond looked to Valerie for support. It was not lost on her that one of the damaged paintings had been insured by her company.

"Look, Jason," Desmond pleaded, "it's not like forgery hasn't been successfully carried out before."

Valerie nodded. "It's as old as art itself," she put in. "You know that, Jason."

Desmond continued, "During the Roman Empire, they were forging sculpture and other artifacts from Greek civilization. They were highly prized by the Romans, and there weren't enough to go around, so some enterprising artisans decided to fill the vacuum."

"And there's the example of Elmyr de Hory," Miller added. "He pretty much hoodwinked half the collectors in the world for thirty years. And more than a few museums. The way I hear it, there are still a lot of his paintings in collections. Some are even known to be forgeries, but the owners have reputations at stake. Hell, de Hory wasn't even prosecuted, because nobody wanted to get on the stand and admit that de Hory had made a fool of him."

"That's right," Desmond said. "And he had an easier time of it, because he specialized in modern work, which isn't as hard to fake."

Handsworth nodded. "I know, I know. Don't remind me. When I first started out in this business, I worked for Roland Larkin. He had a gallery in Chicago, the most prestigious in the Midwest, and he had more than a dozen de Hory forgeries in inventory at one time. In fact, forgery has been been given a little respectability lately. The Minneapolis Institute of Art had a show fifteen or twenty years ago. Everything from Greek vases to Picasso, and just about every step in between. Since then, people have started to collect forgeries, knowing they're fakes, and paying good money for them."

"Hans van Meegeren is another example," Valerie reminded them. "He specialized in the Dutch masters—Vermeer, Ter Borch, Rembrandt—which was hard as hell to pull off, because the older work develops cracks, called craquelure, which have to be there. Their absence is a dead giveaway. Some forgers just paint them on the surface, but that's fairly easy to spot. Some of the more creative forgers have developed special methods of aging. They use old canvas, duplicate pigment composition from the appropriate period, at least when they can. You name it. Van Meegeren even used badger-hair brushes like Vermeer, to simulate the stroke and texture as nearly as possible."

She stopped and looked at Desmond for a long time. It seemed that the silence would go on forever, as if no one wanted to agree with Desmond's hypothesis, but had no reason not to credit the possibility.

Finally, Miller said, "So, you want me to bring the confiscated materials and canvases to a laboratory suggested by Mr. Handsworth?"

"What have we got to lose?" Desmond asked. "Look, if I'm right, then we are onto something a lot bigger than simple art theft."

"And murder, don't forget," Miller reminded him.

"Right, and murder. We may be onto a ring that steals *and* forges. And there's no telling just how successful they might be, or how long they've been in operation. There's no reason to believe that Derrick Jones is the only one involved, either. Everyone agrees that he couldn't pull off the thefts without help, so at the very least, he has accomplices of some sort. But I think it might be more involved that that. I think he might have sponsors, people in a position to identify those works to be forged and/or stolen, in a position to facilitate the theft or substitution and presumably able to realize some sort of profit from disposal of the stolen paintings."

"I suppose we ought to go along, at least until we have more information," Valerie said. "What do you want us to do?"

Desmond took a deep breath. "It's so damned complicated. Valerie, you should get the information about other stolen paintings—start with modern works only, say, post-1850 or thereabouts, because none of the partials we saw were of works any older than that. Contact a reasonable number of insurers, say five or six, and get the information from them. You'll have to find some pretext for the request without telling them why you really want the information, because we can't dismiss the possibility that someone on the insurance end of things is involved, perhaps supplying information about works that will be in transit and vulnerable to theft. I also want to know whether there's any correlation between advance warning and the thefts."

"What do you mean?"

"Well, if you're going to substitute a forged canvas for an original, you need time to prepare the forgery. You don't just fake a picture that takes your fancy and hope that somebody decides to ship it. You find out in advance, and the more warning you have, the better. If there isn't enough time, maybe then you resort to theft, but the less often you do that, the better your chances of getting away with it."

"Jason, if you would make arrangements with the lab and handle the authentication end of things, that would be a big help. If Northamerican won't pick up the tab, I'll see to it that you get paid from my end. I'd also like as much information as you can on private collectors who specialize in modern work, starting with those artists who show up most frequently on the list of stolen works Valerie puts together."

"Surely you don't think serious collectors are involved in this?"

Desmond shrugged. "I'm betting that whoever it is has a passion for art. My guess is that he or she, or they, make legitimate puchases from time to time, or did at one time, until they found a cheaper way. I want to use some papers we got from Jones's loft to see if any of the names on your list show up in those papers. Jones is a pack rat, and there just might be a lead or two from that angle."

Miller sighed. "I guess it's my turn," he said.

Desmond nodded. "Assuming you buy into this, yes."

"Hell, I don't know what to think. But I'll tell you

what . . . if you're right, it'll help clear my caseload. For that reason alone, it's worth a chance. What do you need?"

"Information on thefts other than the twelve we already talked about, to see if there is any correlation. I also want to see if there are any common threads. If we have a larger sample, we might be able to spot a pattern. And, of course, if you get the canvases to the laboratory. I don't know how you go about getting them released from custody."

"You don't. But what I can do is pull a few strings and convince somebody that we need outside specialists. If I can pull that off, I'll move the stuff as soon as I can."

"More than anything else, I think, we have to find Derrick Jones."

"You mean he's disappeared?" Valerie asked.

"No, he's gone to ground. He's scared. Which is another reason I think he's got accomplices, probably heavyweights. Hemenway refused to press charges, so why is he hiding, unless he's made enemies we don't yet know about?"

"That's a tough one. I can't stop every asshole on the street with a few paint streaks on his jeans," Miller argued.

"No, you can't, but Kali might know more than she thinks. You can start with her. And I think she ought to have police protection. Whoever shot at us last night might have been after her, or Jones, or me . . . or all three of us. I am also compiling a list of names and another of phone numbers from the Jones papers. We'll need to find out who the numbers belong to, and cross-check them all with addresses."

Miller nodded. "That it?"

Desmond shook his head. "Not quite. There's one more thing . . . and this can't leave this room."

Miller held his hands out as if to receive something. "So, let me have it. . . ."

"I think we need to know more about Clarence Hemenway."

Handsworth smacked the arm of the chair. "Now hold on, you can't seriously think that he—"

"I can't seriously afford to overlook any possibility. And that means the possibility that Hemenway and Jones are coconspirators. I saw Jones at the opening, and I'd swear that Hemenway knew him, and was nervous about Jones being there."

"Jones is a madman. That would make me nervous, too."

"But Hemenway had no reason to believe that until *after* Jones attacked the paintings."

"If he's involved in any way, I'll be shocked. And if he's not, and he finds out what you've suggested, he'll sue you for every penny you've got. That much I can tell you. Clarence plays hardball in the big leagues."

"So do I, Jason," Desmond said. "So do I."

- TWENTY- - -

DESMOND HANDED A COFFEE TO RAY MILLER. THE
plastic cup nearly collapsing in the lieutenant's big fist
as he took a sip, he gulped down a mouthful of the
scalding black fluid. James Mitchell, looking scholarly
in his white smock, shoved a napkin across his desk.

"Thanks," Miller said, wrapping the cup in the
napkin to sop up the overflow. "Not used to cheap
cups, I guess."

Mitchell adjusted the way his horn-rim glasses sat
on his nose, his blue eyes looking enormous behind
the thick lenses. His white hair spilled over his forehead
in an unruly shock, and he brushed it back before
opening a folder on his desk.

"As I told you on the telephone, we're not quite
finished, but I can tell you a few things that might
interest you."

"Go ahead, Doc," Miller said. "Fire away."

"I'll start with the pigment. We ran spectrographic analysis on several samples from each of the canvases you brought in. We chose pure colors, to try, as best we could, to avoid contamination from blending. The pigments do not match any of the products commercially available. In all likelihood, the artist made his own."

Miller looked at Desmond. "Looks like you might be right, Paul."

Desmond preferred to wait and see. He knew enough about art to know that many painters preferred to make their own pigments. That Derrick Jones had done so meant nothing, in and of itself. He wanted to get a match between the canvases taken from Jones's loft and the two damaged canvases from the Pratt, but getting samples without arousing Clarence Hemenway's suspicion was not going to be easy.

"Anything unusual about the pigments, Dr. Mitchell?" Desmond asked.

Mitchell tilted his head to think. His head nearly rested on his left shoulder, and the odd posture gave him the look of a hunchback. Finally, he said, "It depends on what you mean by unusual."

"I'm not sure I would know what was unusual and what wasn't," Desmond answered.

"Well, one thing might be of interest. I noticed that several of the paintings seemed to be imitations of Claude Monet. That, of course, is not unusual. But I was curious, so I compared the spectrographic results to results we had obtained a few years ago when the Metropolitan Museum was restoring a Monet in its collection. The results were remarkably similar. Not a perfect match, of course, which would be impossible. The purpose of spectrographic analysis, after all, is to discriminate between things superficially similar. But they were very close, close enough that I suspect whoever made the pigments was trying to duplicate Monet's palette."

Miller was skeptical. "How could Jones know what Monet used? He's not a chemist, for Christ's sake."

"Information of this kind is not that hard to come by. Many artists kept detailed notes on their practices, including materials composition. But there are scientific studies done all the time, and the results are published in a variety of journals, some aimed at the art community and others at the scientific."

"But, as you say, Doctor, that doesn't mean much. Not by itself." Desmond wanted more, he wanted a neat fit, one that would convince Miller and Valerie Harrison that he was on the right track. Right now, he felt as if they were simply humoring him.

Mitchell leaned back in his chair. "It's difficult, sometimes even impossible, to make determinations that are anything more than probabilities. Even so sensitive a test as neutron activation is useless here. Using the presence of trace elements, mostly metals, it makes very fine distinctions indeed. It would enable us to determine differences between batches of paint. But that won't help you much because two batches made with Monet's own hand will differ one from another. We could analyze a dozen canvases and tell you which ones were painted with the same batch, but we cannot use that kind of test to say that one painting was painted last month and another last century. This kind of test is better at proving things are the same. That, as I understand it, is the sort of thing you want to know. If I had samples from the paintings damaged at the Pratt Museum, I could tell you whether the pigments used on them match any of those on the samples you've already provided. That would be of some help, I think."

"More than some, Doctor. What about the age? Can you tell the age of a painting?"

"Not precisely. Everyone knows about carbon-fourteen, but that measures the decay rate of a radioactive isotope of carbon. It is useful, but imprecise. And the time period you are concerned with is extremely short for such a test, to the point that it would be meaningless, or very nearly. Again, though, we can measure some other factors, such as the dryness of the pigment, the oils, and so forth. These things might enable us to tell you whether the paintings from the Pratt are old enough to be genuine. They will not prove more than that, however. The fact that a painting is old enough does not prove that it was painted by the purported artist, merely that it could have been. However, we were able to determine that the burned canvas had been painted with the same pigments as the other samples you supplied. I suppose that is useful to know."

Desmond heaved a sigh. It was more than useful information. It confirmed that Jones had not been lying when he claimed the painting was a forgery rather than an original.

"So what you're telling us," Miller said, not working

very hard to conceal his impatience, "is that you can't tell us very much."

Mitchell licked his lips, then tried again to get his hair to obey. "Not exactly. What I'm telling you is that you are asking me to compare apples to oranges, and to tell you the difference, but you have only brought me apples."

"We're working on getting you the other materials, Doctor. We should have them in a day or so."

"Then I suppose we might as well adjourn for now," Mitchell said, getting to his feet. "I wish I could be more of help to you gentlemen, but—"

"Never mind. You've already been helpful," Desmond assured him. "You'll call when the other samples have been tested?"

"Most assuredly."

Mitchell showed them out, and when they were on the pavement, Miller spat disgustedly. "What a crock! All this scientific jive doesn't amount of a hill of beans."

"Not yet," Desmond agreed. "But we're getting there."

"Yeah? I sure as hell don't see it."

"Well, for one thing, we know that Jones has forged at least one of the stolen paintings."

"What's that prove?"

"In itself, nothing. Except it does suggest that Jones tells the truth on occasion. And if that is so, perhaps he tells the truth more often than anyone suspects."

"You won't give up on the idea that he took a butcher knife to his own handiwork in that museum, will you?"

"Not until someone proves I ought to. And we are a long way from that, yet."

"But if those were forgeries, then where the hell are the originals?"

Desmond laughed. "That, if you'll recall, was what I was hired to find out. And unless I misunderstand the role of your Crayon Patrol, it's what you are also supposed to be working on."

Miller grunted. "Yeah. But instead, I keep letting you sidetrack me. Now we're looking at little rainbows from a spectrograph. We ought to be looking in some warehouse somewhere."

"You find the warehouse, and I'll be happy to drive you," Desmond said.

"You know what I mean, damn it."

"Well, I have something that might help," Desmond said as he opened his car door.

Miller climbed into the passenger seat as Desmond reached into the rear seat and grabbed his briefcase. Climbing into the car, Desmond opened the briefcase and reached inside, retrieving a 9X12 manila envelope.

The look on Miller's face as Desmond opened the envelope was more appropriate to the opening of Pandora's box. As Desmond pulled out several sheets of paper Miller said, "Every time somebody opens an envelope like that, it means trouble. Or at least work. And in my line of work, there's no difference between the two."

"Maybe this time is different." Desmond laughed.

"Now, where have I heard that before? Oh yeah, Henry the Eighth said it, right? To Anne Boleyn?"

Desmond laughed again as he put the briefcase on

the backseat of the car, then turned his attention to the papers in his hand.

"I got a list of major collectors from Jason Handsworth. He said it's not comprehensive, because the market keeps changing. People move in and out depending on where they get their money, and how much they have on hand." He handed a sheaf of papers to Miller, who flipped through the three single-spaced pages.

"And we are looking for what, exactly, when we look at this list?"

Desmond shrugged. "Your guess is good as mine. Maybe somebody who dropped out of the market permanently, because he found a cheaper way to build his collection. Maybe somebody with lots of money and no visible means of generating the cash. Maybe somebody with a criminal record. Anything at all that doesn't seem to add up."

Miller bobbed his head. "It'll take some time."

"Whatever. This second list is a more comprehensive list of stolen art that Valerie compiled after talking to colleagues at several insurers. I want to take this to the loft and see if I can find any more that Jones has copied."

"See, I told you it meant work."

Desmond ignored the gibe. Holding up another list, he ticked it with a fingernail. This is the list of phone numbers I found in the loft. I have no idea who they belong to. I don't even know some of the area codes, although I would assume 2-1-2 unless otherwise indicated. Can you find out who they belong to?"

"Sure. Again, it'll take some time. And I think we

might as well get phone records from the loft, too, while we're at it. See which ones he called."

Handing the list to Miller, he picked up a single piece of paper now, a photograph torn from a magazine. He handed it to Miller, who examiend it briefly, then handed it back. "Who is he?" he asked, flicking the man depicted with a fingernail.

"I have no idea. But the picture was in Jones's desk. The caption has been cut off, and I don't even know for sure where the picture came from. It looks like a glossy newsmagazine, maybe *Time* or *Newsweek*."

"I don't see why it's so interesting."

"Look at it closely."

Miller held the photograph in a slant of sunlight through the windshield. As he tilted it back and forth he leaned closer and closer. "What's this circle?" he asked. "It looks like it's drawn around something on the wall in the next room."

"I don't know," Desmond said. "I don't know who put it there, either, but I think I know *why* it's there."

"I'll bite. . . ."

"That looks like it circles a painting. And I think it's a Monet. And unless I miss my guess, it's on that list sitting right there in your lap. But I'll have to do some research to find out for sure."

"Glad to see you don't have to give up all the good stuff. But now it's my turn, Mr. Desmond, and I think this will knock your socks off."

Desmond looked at him expectantly.

"Your little girlfriend is missing."

"Kali."

Miller snapped his finegrs. "Smoke, man. She just flat disappeared. I called her, told her I wanted to talk to her about some things and to arrange police protection. She seemed unsure, but she agreed to see me. When I got there two hours later, she was gone. The girl she's staying with doesn't know where she is. It's only been twenty-four hours, but I thought you might find it interesting."

"You'll let me know as soon as she turns up?"

"*If* she turns up, don't you mean? Because I don't think she will. I think she and Mr. Derrick Jones are in cahoots. This little scam of theirs, whatever the fuck it is, is starting to come unraveled, and they've both headed for cover. That's what I think."

Desmond understood Miller's cynicism, and the reasons for it, but he didn't subscribe to it. He had thought Kali was somehow going to be the key, and now she was gone. He felt a chill creeping down his spine. And he didn't want to think about what it might mean.

— TWENTY-ONE — — —

ON THE BACK OF THE MAGAZINE PHOTO THERE WAS part of an advertisement for a record album and a strip of text from an article. It took Desmond no time at all to determine that the magazine was *Time*. It took him a few hours to identify the album as one by Janet Jackson, *Rhythm Nation: 1910*. A phone call to Tower Records got him the release date of the album and gave him a time frame within which to search the magazine's pages for the photograph.

He wasn't crazy about libraries. The silence was artificial, and it always seemed that some local loon had chosen the time of his appearance to coincide with Desmond's visit. Some of them walked in endless circles, the reek of a month's dirt leaving a noxious vapor trail behind them, others sat and talked to themselves about everything from *Hazel* to Hegel, their voices betraying some implacable anger every bit as noxious.

But like Willie Sutton said about banks and money, Desmond went to the library because that's where they kept the books. The Newburgh library at least had a view. A glass wall overlooked the Hudson and ignored the poverty and ruin surrounding it. Sunscreens kept out the worst of the sunlight, muting the brilliant green on the east bank.

Sitting down at the microfiche reader with several flimsy plastic sheets, each representing a month of *Time,* he steeled himself for a long morning. Since he had no idea of page number, or even the subject of the article, Desmond was resigned to wading page by page through the magazine's notoriously flippant prose. It had been a while since he'd used a fiche reader, and the going was slow for the first half hour or so, until he got the knack of using the pointer. If he had known the name of the man pictured in the photograph, he could have used an index of some kind to further narrow his search, but he wasn't that lucky.

At the back of his mind was the distinct possibility that he was looking for something that, even should he succeed in finding it, would be meaningless to him. It might even be the key to the puzzle, but there was no guarantee he would understand how or why.

Since albums are sometimes advertised in advance, he was starting from the beginning of the calendar year in which *Rhythm Nation* appeared. The first sheet was a dry hole. He'd skimmed an entire month without finding anything remotely like either the photograph or the advertisement.

The second sheet, another month, and still nothing. By now, his eyes were getting tired. The fiche reader was anything but ideal, and the blurred print had him wondering whether he might need reading glasses. He checked his watch, decided to search through March before knocking off for lunch, and a chance to let his eyes focus on something a little farther away than the end of his nose.

By eleven forty-five, he had had enough. Returning the stack of fiche in their envelopes to the desk, he apprised the librarian that he would be back in an hour. The librarian tucked the sheets away for safekeeping, and Desmond walked out into the heat. The area surrounding the library was anything but conducive to a casual stroll, but in his time, Desmond had wandered through some of the worst urban areas on three continents, and Newburgh had nothing to show him that he hadn't seen. Wandering down Liberty Street to Broadway, one of the widest streets he'd seen in a long, long time, he found a sandwich shop, its spic-and-span new front out of place against the bombed-out look of much of the rest of the block.

He indulged his taste for hamburger, ordered it with cheese to appease the cholesterol demon, secure in the knowledge that Audrey would not get wind of his indulgence, and munched his sandwich with a large diet Coke to wash it down.

Sitting there alone, he had time to think, and he realized that he was tiptoeing out on a very slender limb, not at all sure it would support his weight.

Bucking a man with the connections Clarence Hemenway could boast of was playing with a trip wire and not knowing where the mine was buried. And if there was a mine somewhere in the vicinity, there was every possibility that it would cut him off at the knees.

But no matter how he twisted and turned the fragments, holding each up to the light, he kept coming to the same conclusion. Derrick Jones was the key; he had to be. Desmond acknowledged that he had rushed headlong after the tantalizing lead Jones represented, neglecting other possibilities that, while no more or less remote, were no more or less worthy of consideration by any objective standard. But when he pushed hard on the Jones angle, it pushed right back, begging him to push a little harder still.

Much, of course, depended on his intuition that the magazine photograph was significant. Jones was such a squirrel, it could just be that something about the photo appealed to him—perhaps a tint, perhaps an angle, maybe just the composition. But Desmond had to find the original article to be sure.

He left a tip on the counter, paid at the cash register, and wandered back toward the library. The heat was oppressive, and he took his time. As he reached a vacant area on Grand Street, a parking lot on his right and an abandoned red-brick building dead ahead, he stopped for a moment, then decided to walk down Second Street toward the river. He headed down a steep hill, keeping the parking lot on his right. He was across from the library when he heard the sound of screeching tires. He turned, thinking one of the local kids was trying out a new car, or stealing a newer one. But both guesses were wrong.

A black sedan was heading toward him, its right wheels up on the curb. The car's undercarriage was sparking as it scraped the curbstone, and Desmond realized the car was heading right for him. He launched himself up and over a Cyclone fence as the car swept past, knocking a No Parking sign down and dragging it several yards with the shriek of grinding metal, showering sparks like a burning fuse behind it.

As Desmond got to his feet the car skidded to a halt and he saw the backup lights go on. He knew this time they would not settle for trying to run him down. Instinctively, he reached for his hip, but the Browning was in the car, and there was no way he could get to it in time.

He ducked behind a parked car, but the occupants of the black sedan had seen him, and he knew it. Just in case he wasn't certain, a short burst from an automatic weapon hammered the point home. The weapon was silenced, but the slugs chewed at the gray Dodge that provided his only cover, shattering the windshield and punching several holes in the engine compartment.

The police station was just a couple of blocks away, but it might as well have been a million miles. There was nothing about the sound of breaking glass that would even raise a Newburgh eyebrow.

Desmond lay flat on the ground, rolled in close to the Dodge, and trying to cut down his exposure. Another burst of gunfire took out the rear window, and glass rained down on him like hot ice. The black car spun its wheels as the driver reversed direction once more, and as quickly as it had started, it was over. He saw the car disappear down the hill, and scrambled to his feet as it jounced over a bump and skidded another block before veering onto 9W and heading south.

Looking around, he realized that he was alone. If anyone had seen what had happened, he or she was not interested in having it known, at least not to him. It might make for interesting conversation at the bar tonight, but that was different, that would just be back-fence gossip.

Brushing himself off, he walked to a gap in the fence and crossed the street to the library, sprinting up the handicapped ramp instead of taking the stairs. Once inside, out of the hallucinatory heat, he allowed himself to consider what had just happened.

It was the second time that someone had shot at him in the last few days, and he was more than ever convinced that whoever it was believed, as he did, that Derrick Jones had steered him in the right direction. What the gunmen, or whoever had dispatched them, did not know was just how cryptic the artist's counsel had been. Or maybe they did know. Maybe they knew Jones, knew how maddeningly elliptical he could be, but feared that sooner or later Desmond would fill in the blanks.

But as he retrieved the stack of fiche from the checkout desk, he knew that he was not going to be run off—not now, not when he was getting so close.

He went back to the same fiche reader and inserted

the sheet for April. As he worked his way through the pages he felt his heart pounding against his ribs. His ears were ringing, and he found himself thinking about the weapon. He never saw it, but it was definitely an automatic, probably a machine pistol. There were a lot of such weapons, but one thing about them struck him—they were not the weapons of choice for a hired gun. That could only mean two things, either whoever had shot at him was a novice—or he was more than just a hit man. A machine pistol was a weapon that made certain demands on its users. To fire it effectively, you had to fire it often. Drug runners preferred them because they were the ultimate in portable firepower, easier to conceal than an assault rifle, which packed the same wallop. And the typical assault-rifle clip held fewer cartridges. But there was no drug angle to the Derrick Jones story. So who the hell else was interested?

He found the answer in May. Or at least he found the photograph. To his surprise, it was not in the art column. The man in the photograph was identified as Colonel Guillermo Pagan, and the subject of the story was transplanted Latin American politicos, most of them once and future dictators, or adherents thereof. Pagan was not the main subject, which was Somoza of Nicaragua, d'Aubuisson of El Salvador, and Noriega of Panama.

According to the article, Pagan had been influential in El Salvador for a period of three or four years, during the height of that country's civil war, then found a home in the United States along with several other former Salvadoran military men, all of whom were, according to the article, linked to the notorious death squads that had terrorized much of the country for nearly a decade. It was the Salvadoran version of political violence, a local variant of a virulent form of oppression that had also flourished in Argentina, Chile, Nicaragua, Guatemala, and Panama, to name the most significant examples. Pagan was, the article went on to say, nearly an archetype—wealthy family background, quality education on the Continent, military training in the United States, politically somewhere to the right of Attila, well connected in U.S. military and congressional circles and welcome to visit Ron and Nancy or George and Babs whenever he happened to be in the DC area.

Things had changed a little, but Pagan was ensconced securely in Miami now, with a fortune widely believed to be a composite of family money and pirated Salvadoran funds.

It was all very interesting, but Desmond, try as he might, was unable to make a connection between Colonel Guillermo Pagan and Derrick Jones, Clarence Hemenway, or, for that matter, Claude Monet. Maybe he was on the wrong track, after all. But it still didn't explain why the photograph was of such interest to Derrick Jones that he had seen fit to cut it from the magazine and save it. Nor did it explain the faint blue-ink circle around a painting barely discernible in the photograph. There must, Desmond thought, be something about that painting that I have to know. But how in the hell do I find out what that painting is?

He used the printer to make a copy of the entire

article, then returned the fiche to the desk. Outside, he checked carefully before stepping into the street, and when he climbed into his Buick, he set the photograph and the article on the seat beside him. All the way home, he kept looking at them, hoping that inspiration would strike, but as usual, it didn't.

Audrey was out in the garden when he pulled up. She waved, brandished a pair of shears overhead, and hollered, "Come on, buster, the jungle's getting out of control and you haven't been pulling your share of the load."

He didn't laugh, and she realized immediately that he was preoccupied. Standing up, she walked toward the driveway, brushing dirt from her canvas gloves, then pulling them off. "Something wrong?"

He knew better than to tell her about the shooting and the runaway car, so he waved the papers at her. "Can't figure something out."

"Can I help?"

"Don't you always?"

"What's the problem?"

He handed her the photo and the offprint. "I'm trying to figure out what this man has to do with Derrick Jones."

Audrey glanced at the photo. "Who is he?"

Desmond summarized the content of the article, then pointed to the faint blue circle around the visible edge of the painting.

"I have a friend at *Time,* works in the photo research department. Maybe she can check and see if the photo is cropped, or if there are other shots from the same session that show a little more than this one does."

"Do you think she would do that?"

"Sure. It might take her a day or two. I don't know what kind of schedule they're on, but it's worth a try."

- TWENTY-TWO- - -

RAY MILLER OPENED HIS NOTEBOOK. BY HIS LEFT elbow, an ignored cigarette burned, an inch-long ash sagging toward the glass. The breeze from the notebook knocked it loose, and the unbalanced butt fell onto the scarred wood of the desktop. Without looking, Miller groped for the butt, found it, and dropped it into a half-empty Styrofoam cup of coffee.

"I have got to tell you, Paul, you really gave me a shitload of work here."

Desmond started to protest, but Miller wagged a finger at him. "I also have to tell you that it paid off. Maybe . . . just maybe. I know you have something to tell me, but I want to go first. I think I earned it, just because you made me work my little butt off."

"What have you got?"

"For openers, I ran a check on that list of phone numbers you gave me. One of them, the Miami area code, just happens to belong to your Colonel Guillermo Pagan. The funny thing is that there's no indication that he ever called Derrick Jones. We got a look at the records for the last three years, and there is not one instance of a call being placed from Pagan's home to the loft on Greenwich Street. So I wasn't sure what to make of it."

"Maybe Jones called him," Desmond suggested. "After all, it was Jones who had Pagan's number. We don't know that Pagan had Jones's."

"Negative. We checked. No calls to Pagan from Greenwich Street."

"So what are you telling me, Ray? That there's no connection?"

"Hold your horses, Paul. Let me unfold this as it happens. There's a nice element of drama in all this. I think you'll like the ending."

Desmond laughed. "Okay. But don't drag it out, all right, Ray?"

"I got to thinking. You said Jones had another loft somewhere, so I decided to check with the phone company, see what we came up with."

"And?"

"Another dry hole. Nynex did not have another listing for Derrick Jones."

"Maybe it was in another name, maybe Kali's."

"Fine. What's Kali's last name? Or is *that* her last name?"

"I don't know."

"Great, so when we find her, we'll ask her. Unless we happen to stumble on somebody who knows. Of course, the one most likely to know is Derrick Jones, and we don't have a clue where he might be."

"So it's a blind alley?"

"Not so fast. You underestimate my ingenuity. But before I get to the fun part, I want to tell you what else we found in checking the phone numbers." He stopped to light another cigarette, took one drag, and set it in the ashtray where the other had been. A gluey mass of tar held it in place. Through a feathery cloud of smoke, he continued, "It seems that two, not one but two, of those phone numbers you turned up belong to none other than Clarence Arthur Hemenway. So on the surface it looks like you were right. They know each other, at least casually. Naturally, we checked the records on Clarence. And there were a few calls to Hemenway from the loft. Likewise, a few from Hemenway to Jones—unless he's got something going with Kali. It appears he called Derrick Jones quite a few times, at least once a week, sometimes more often. There was a flurry of calls around the time of the hijacking, by the way. I don't know if that's a coincidence or not, but I can't ask Mr. Hemenway just yet."

Desmond had been prepared for Miller to make another attempt to persuade him to change tack. But it was beginning to look as if Miller was slowly coming around to his course. "So are you convinced?"

"Convinced, no. Intrigued, you betcha. The clincher was a nice little wrinkle that I'll bet even you didn't suspect. Pagan and Hemenway each made calls to the other. Once again, there is an increase in frequency around the time of the hijacking. Maybe it was just insider gossip, but I doubt it. I have to think there is some connection, but I'm damned if I know how to prove it."

"Taps?"

"Done. But the boys have clammed up. They are scrupulously avoiding calling each other for some reason. Maybe they're pissed at each other, and maybe they're scared."

"You said there were two numbers for Hemenway. Where is the other phone, at the Pratt?"

"No. We checked that, and there is no call to or from Jones at the Pratt. It was all after-hours stuff."

"Then where is the other phone?"

"Hemenway has a country place, a farm up in Sullivan County, in the Catskills."

"All of this is fascinating, Ray, but it doesn't help us find Derrick Jones."

"No, it doesn't, unless he's decided to woodshed for a tour as a stand-up on the borscht belt."

"Hemenway's place?"

Miller nodded. "It's an outside possibility, but I asked the state police to keep an eye out. I couldn't get a search warrant on what I have, so we'll have to keep digging."

"And the pièce de résistance you referred to?"

Miller smiled broadly, took another drag on his cigarette, and leaned back in his chair, clasping his hands behind his head. "A masterstroke, actually. I'm very proud of it."

"Just cut to the chase."

"Mr. Jones has gone cellular. And guess what, he's placed calls to the good Colonel and to Hemenway over his mobile phone."

"He doesn't own a car. At least according to Kali, he doesn't."

"You don't have to own a car to use a cellular phone. You can put a cellular anywhere you want to. My guess is that Jones has his at the second loft. Unfortunately, the bills are mailed to the Greenwich Street address, so there is no way to be sure. The calls originate from one of the cells in lower Manhattan, but the geography includes Greenwich Street and about six billion other lofts. I'd rather look for a needle in a haystack."

"Any way to monitor the phone?"

"Yeah, but it's hit-or-miss. I've asked the cellular company to notify us of any calls emanating from that unit. But it's not like those old war movies where the trucks ride around the streets trying to triangulate the location of the spy's radio. We'll need a real break to run it down."

"So," Desmond said, "we have a connection among the three men via the telephone. We find a photograph of Pagan in Jones's possession, and Jones attacks two paintings at Hemenway's museum after having an animated conversation with him. And we also find increased contact among the three around the time some paintings are hijacked and a man murdered. It looks pretty certain that we have the hook we need."

"But it's all circumstantial, Paul. Hemenway runs a major museum, Jones is a painter, Pagan is a collector. There is no reason they shouldn't have some sort of relationship. We don't have any *proof,* Paul. Nothing that would stand up in court. It's not like we know what they said on those phone calls. And unless one of them wants to tell us, we probably never will."

"Have you checked the list of collectors? The one that Jason Handsworth compiled?"

Miller nodded. "Yeah, and our boy Pagan is the only one on it who also appears on Jones's phone list. But that doesn't mean anything, either. There is no law against collecting fine art. And Pagan has a reputation. He's plugged in big time, both to the art world and to Florida politics and, not coincidentally, he has friends in DC."

"Are you saying he's off limits?"

Miller shook his head. "No, I'm not saying that. What I'm saying is that with Hemenway and Pagan, we have to take off our shoes and tiptoe. It's worse than walking on eggs. It's more like walking through a mine field. You get their hackles up and they reach for the phone. And, believe me, they know who to call. We have to go slow, Paul, real slow." Miller stubbed out his cigarette without having taken a drag. "Now, you said you had some news for me, too. What is it?"

"I heard from Dr. Mitchell."

"And?"

"He got the samples from the Pratt Monets. There's a match between those pigments and the ones on the samples we got from the loft. Not only that. The canvas fibers match those from a roll of raw canvas from the loft."

Miller whistled. "So, you might be right after all."

Desmond nodded. "Looks like it, but it still doesn't help. I keep coming back to the fact that Jones couldn't pull this off by himself. He had the talent to make the copies, that's pretty clear. But he just didn't have the access he needed. He was not in a position to know when paintings were to be moved. Even if he managed to piece it together from the press, a show being put together—what, where, and when, all that—those were just part of the picture. He had to know precisely when specific artworks were being moved, and *how*. He had to know what airline, what trucker, and he had to get to the paintings in transit, someplace out of the way, where he could make the switch. Unless you want to assume that he managed somehow to buy off dozens of people. And I don't think he had the money for that. Besides, it would take muscle, too, because there is always the chance that things will go wrong, and then you have to be in a position to cover your ass."

"Like the Flannery thing, you mean . . ."

"Yeah."

"So you think Hemenway provided that information, is that it?"

"Yeah, I do."

"But you can't prove it. . . ."

"No," Desmond agreed, "I can't. Not yet, anyway. But I'll have to. If we just get Jones, we have a minnow. And without the big fish, nobody would believe it. You couldn't convict Jones on what we have now. And I don't even care that much about convicting him, as long as I get the paintings back."

"So, once again, we're back to the same place. Unless one of the principals wants to spill the beans, we're out in the cold. And there's another problem with your theory, by the way."

"Which is?"

"Not all the stolen paintings were to be exhibited at the Pratt. If a show is going to Boston or Cleveland, how the hell does Hemenway learn the shipping details? And if he doesn't, how does it get done?"

"I don't know. Maybe he has someone on the inside."

"Inside where? Do you have any idea how many different shippers we're talking about?"

"As a matter of fact, I do. Three."

"That's all?"

Desmond nodded. "That's all. Just three."

"So does Hemenway get on the phone to one of these people and say, 'Listen, I'm thinking about ripping off a Picasso, let me know when you have one in the pipeline'?"

Desmond laughed. "It doesn't have to be like that at all. All it takes is regular contact. And that would be easy enough for Hemenway to establish and maintain. After all, he is the director of a major museum. It wouldn't be that hard for him to get what he needed. Casual conversation with some museum biggie, lunch with a shipper, you name it. The one thing I can't put my finger on is motive. Why would Hemenway do it, assuming he did?"

"I'm not convinced he did. And I agree that motive is important. He doesn't seem to have any unexplained sources of income. And if he has any of the stolen paintings, he's keeping them well hidden."

"Well, do you have a better explanation?"

"Not yet. But I don't think we have all the pieces, either. I think we need to find out a little bit more about the Colonel, because I think somehow he's important. If we can't tie him in, then I think your neat little scheme falls apart."

"I agree, but how do we do it?" Desmond asked.

"I made a couple of phone calls. I have a friend in Miami, a retired cop. Dave Reilly. He used to work for NYPD and then flew south one particularly brutal winter to work for Miami-Dade. The thing is, I can't convince the powers that be to pay for a trip. Can you handle it?"

"I guess I'll have to."

"Lucky bastard!"

"Lucky? It'll be a hundred degrees in Miami."

"Yeah, but while you're down there in the land of silk and money, I'll be looking for a fruitcake of a painter who doesn't want to be found, and a missing woman with enough hair to make a hangman's noose who doesn't want to be found any more than that mad artist. Which would you rather do?"

"Miami, of course."

"I rest my case."

- TWENTY-THREE- - -

BEFORE DESMOND LEFT FOR THE AIRPORT, RAY MILLER had told him to be careful. "Look, Paul, you can't expect to get too close to this guy. Dave Reilly asked around, made a few calls. Everybody tells him the same thing. Pagan is untouchable. And you don't even have proof that he's involved in anything illegal. But if he is, and if he even thinks you're taking a look at him, he'll whack you."

Desmond assured him that he would be careful, but Miller wouldn't let go easily.

"You ever been to Florida?"

"Yeah, and I hated it."

"It's a different world, Paul. Ever since Castro, it's grown more and more like the third world. In some parts of Miami, you'll swear you're in Havana. I might add, the temperature is twenty degrees higher than it is here, and the humidity is so high goldfish can live on the front lawn. You ready for that?"

"I've been worse places," Desmond had told him.

"Look, don't expect too much. Don't think you're going to go down there and find the Dead Sea Scrolls. More than likely, you're wasting your time. I know you think it's all falling together, but I still think you're staring up the asshole of a wild goose. You may be close to the bird, but it don't mean a thing."

Desmond would not surrender. "You tell me why Kali has disappeared. You tell me why people have shot at me twice. You tell me why Derrick Jones has fallen off the face of the earth. If I'm wrong, you explain all that to me."

Miller couldn't, and they both knew it. But he wasn't about to give up easily. "You still don't have a way to tie Hemenway and Pagan into the mix. The phone calls aren't enough to do it. And without them, what have you got?"

"They're in there—you know it and I know it. We just don't know where. Maybe you can dig something up on this end while I'm away."

"You want to go to Florida, take my advice, Paul. Wait till Christmas and take the kids to Disneyworld. You'll have more fun."

"Will you try to find Jones and Kali while I'm away? And peek into a few corners, see what else you can find on Hemenway?"

Miller had shrugged helplessly, then looked at the sky for solace. "Why me, Lord?" he asked. And when the sky ignored the question, he'd nodded. "Sure. If I get a chance, I will. No promises, though. Fascinating as this all is, it's not the only thing on my plate, you know."

"Fair enough."

And now, the plane circling for a landing at Miami, Desmond was beginning to think that Ray Miller had been right after all. It was a wild-goose chase, and he'd lost sight of the goose. The first rush of adrenaline had worn off, and what had seemed like ironclad proof now looked like no more than what Miller had said it was, possibility. But there was still that nagging tug somewhere in the back of his mind. Its grip was tenuous, but persistent. Two days in Miami wouldn't make much of a difference if he was wrong. And if he was right, it might make all the difference in the world.

As the plane touched down, Desmond looked out the window. He hated Florida, hated the very idea of its existence. The mere name conjured images of plaster flamingos on New Jersey lawns, busts of the presidents made from seashells, and inedible candy shaped like firewood. But it wasn't going to go away, and neither was the nagging suspicion. So he stared out the window at the heat shimmering just above the runway, the air currents almost palpable, as if the concrete were covered with a film of clear Jell-O.

Miller had made arrangements for his friend to meet Desmond at the airport. As he stepped out of the jetway into the terminal, he saw a big cardboard sign fluttering in the air at the back of a crowd of waiting families. The bold black letters read DAVE BRUBECK, and Desmond knew he was in for it.

Working his way through the shifting mass of flowered shirts and lime-green triple-knit slacks held up by white belts, he reached the prankster with the sign still in possession of his overnight bag, a fact that struck him as nearly miraculous.

"You Dave Reilly?" he asked.

The man with the sign flashed him a grin. "Figured there could be lots of Paul Desmond's, so this way you'd get the point." He stuck out a tanned fist, the thick wrist bristling with sun-lightened hair like golden wires. "Dave Reilly. How you doin'?"

Desmond took the powerful hand in his own. "Thanks for meeting me."

"No problem. I owe Ray Miller more than a few favors. And since I'm retired, I got nothing but time on my hands. Come on, let's get the hell out of here. I'm parked out front." Reilly led him toward the front of the terminal and Desmond steeled himself for the oven's breath as he pushed through the revolving door and onto the pavement. Mica chips in the cement made it almost impossible to look at directly, and Desmond jammed his sunglasses down tighter on his nose.

"Hope you don't mind a convertible," Reilly called as he skipped through slow-moving traffic to the parking lot across the way. "Always wanted one, and I finally hit pay dirt." He pointed toward a white '61 Impala in the front line.

Desmond tossed his bag into the backseat and climbed in. Reilly cranked up the Chevy and headed for the highway. "Thought we'd take a little ride before we get you settled in," he said.

"Anyplace in particular?"

"You'll see."

The sunlight was blinding, but as long as the car stayed in motion, the heat was bearable. The traffic flowed easily over the network of modern roads, so different from the way Desmond had remembered it. Save for the heat and the palm trees, he could have been on a freeway system in any major American city. The same fast-food joints had put down roots, spreading like triffids. The names of the supermarkets were new to him, but Winn-Dixie was just another Shoprite.

Soon, as they neared the water, the character of the neighborhood began to change. The shops had given way to small homes, and the small homes now were replaced by more impressive residences, complete with broad lawns, sprinklers scattering rainbows in the sun, houses hidden by mounds of rubbery green. No more backboards in the driveway now. Tennis courts had taken their place. The visible cars were in the forty-grand-and-up range. A little farther along, and the houses disappeared behind fences. Some of them were simple grids of wrought iron, backed by impenetrable foliage so perfectly geometrical they must have been cut with a razor. Some of the homes were behind walls—brick, fieldstone, or, less often, mortared block.

Reilly waved a hand like a magician. "You are looking at some of the most exclusive real estate in the world, old son. You need your pedigree to get an appointment with a real-estate agent even to look at a place around here. To buy one, you need more money than God. But nobody cares where the money comes from, as long as you have it. Seems the good neighbors will overlook a few blemishes on your page in the social register, as long as you don't keep a thirty-nine Ford on blocks in the yard." Reilly laughed easily, but it was tinged with bitterness.

"I gather you are showing me all this for a reason," Desmond guessed.

Reilly nodded slowly. They had to raise their voices a bit to make themselves heard over the wind. "You bet I am. Your boy Pagan lives around here. We'll get there in a few minutes. He's right on the water, which is at the end of the road here and about as high on the price scale as you can go."

"What do you know about him?"

Reilly laughed again. "Which one?"

"I don't follow."

"Well, you read his press clippings, you see a pillar of the community, transplanted from more tropical climes, naturally, but flourishing just fine, thank you. He belongs to the right clubs, knows the right people, and says the right things. You got a charity, give him a call and he'll meet you at the door with his wallet already open. You need some political juice to get something done, call the Colonel, he's got more strings in his fist than a puppet master."

"And the other one?"

"Well, it seems that the good Colonel is a bit of a chameleon. I worked narcotics for six years and must have heard his name once a week every week. Nothing you could make stick, but rumors, mutterings, whispers in the night, what have you."

"You look into the rumors?"

"When I could. Never got too far, though. There was always a stone wall at the end of the tunnel, made you wonder how the light got through. Or somebody would call somebody and the mayor would call somebody and . . . you know how it goes. He's on the board of half a dozen corporations, owns a bank, is a trustee for an art museum, for chrissakes. Not bad for a drug czar, wouldn't you say?"

"So maybe it's just unfounded gossip."

Reilly shook his head. "No, it ain't gossip, Paul. That much is sure. I heard too many stories too many times, and they were too consistent. But he's got juice and he's got muscle. Look, you go across the tracks, you hit Little Havana, and you hear a whole other story, not just about Pagan, but about the dozens of men like him. Didn't matter where they were from, it's the same story over and over. They squeezed the orange dry, then flew to Miami and political asylum. We got more once and future dictators and *El Señor Presidente* wannabes in south Florida than a hundred Asturias novels. Pagan is not the worst, either. But I could tell you some stories about him that would make your hair stand on end."

"What kind of stories?"

"You sure you want to hear them?"

"I want to know everything I can."

Reilly nodded. "All right. "You know about the death squads in El Salvador, right?"

"Yeah. I know about them." Desmond had heard more gory tales than he cared to remember. Even old hands at Langley could not believe the depravity.

"Well, word in these parts is that the good Colonel was the genius behind them. We are talking murder by the hundreds, bodies hacked to pieces, severed heads, eyes gouged out with a spoon, corpses stacked like cordwood in a ditch by the side of the road. That is all part of the picture, too familiar to raise an eyebrow anymore. But we are also talking about flat-out torture, especially of women and children, not just by men under the Colonel's command, or his direct supervision, but at his own hands. Chain saws, blowtorches, acid, electricity, razors, anything and everything that can scar, maim, mutilate, or vivisect the human body, and there is a story about Pagan giving it a go. We have, in short, one sick fuck, who, for reasons that escape me, enjoys the glad hand of Uncle Sam."

"And you believe all of it?"

Reilly nodded. "Yeah, I do. I've heard it from too many people I trusted. Look, you work narcotics, you work vice, you come into contact with the scum of the earth, people you wouldn't haul out of a burning building. But after a while you learn who you can believe and who you can't. And believe me, it takes a lot to turn their stomachs, but they were revolted by this man. I'm talking people who used to work with him, some of them. And people who managed to survive his attentions. So when they say he's an animal, I believe them, yes. And when they say he's also, not coincidentally, one of the most influential drug lords in the country, I believe that, too. He's got a small army, mostly Salvadorans, but also Cubans and some former Somozistas from Nicaragua."

"What about—"

"Hang on, we're almost there. You might as well take a look at the place, what you can see of it. I can get you a boat ride for a gander from the water, too, if you want." Reilly cocked a thumb to his right as he hung a left and headed north.

"I ain't gonna slow down, because I don't want to call attention to us. They'll run a check on my license plate if I look like I'm too curious. And I don't want any trouble I can avoid."

Desmond spotted the guard at the security cupola immediately. He craned his neck to look at the house, but there wasn't much to see. Massed flowering shrubs blocked off the ground-floor view, and there wasn't much else but roof tile to look at.

When they passed the main entrance, the road moved a little higher, and they could see over the top of it. A huge lawn, picture perfect and brilliant green, sprinklers splashing rainbows in every direction, ran all the way to the waterline. A pier and boat house sat at one corner of the property, and tennis courts, their clay a perfect orange, their white lines pristine, were surrounded by lawn chairs.

"You see the kind of money we are talking about, here?" Reilly asked.

"I'm impressed, but not intimidated," Desmond said.

Reilly laughed. "You will be, you butt heads with the Colonel."

- T W E N T Y - F O U R - - -

THE EXHIBIT WAS CROWDED BY MIAMI STANDARDS. THAT
meant it was possible to see a painting without
standing on tiptoe or hanging from the rafters. Dave
Reilly was not impressed. Desmond, though, was of
another opinion. As they drifted through the crowd
at the Carson Museum of Modern European Art,
brand new and still smelling of turpentine and
Spackle, Reilly was kept busy pointing out movers
and shakers, the heavies of the Miami-Dade County
social whirl.

Some of the winter residents had flown in despite
the heat, because the Carson was destined to be
something special. And the exhibit of German
Expressionist art was the biggest ever to hit the United
States. That it came first to the Carson still had noses
in New York and Boston out of joint.

"I swear I don't see what the big deal about this stuff is," Reilly kept muttering. "Kids with finger paints can do this shit."

Desmond did his best to keep Reilly amused, and it hadn't been easy. But they weren't there for the art or to hobnob with the rich and powerful. They were there to get a look at Colonel Guillermo Pagan, up close. As one of the prime movers behind the new museum, the estimable Colonel had earned some brownie points with local politicians. Miami was trying to catch up to Atlanta and Dallas as a center of Southern power, but it had a considerable public-relations problem to overcome. The periodic murder of foreign tourists was hurting business and costing the area tens of millions of dollars in lost tourism. Anything they could do to refurbish the local image was welcome, and no one cared to look too closely at the source if it put dollars in their bank accounts.

Pagan's arrival created a stir, and Desmond stood looking on as the mayor and one of the state's two U.S. senators gave him the glad hand.

"Don't look like much, does he?" Reilly whispered as Pagan moved through the crowd, accompanied by a retinue of bodyguards, whose new suits did little to disguise their purpose, or the weapons just out of sight under their tailored jackets.

But Desmond knew that death came in strange packages. During his tenure in the Far East, he had dealt with human cobras, men who would slit a child's throat with one hand and diddle a hooker with the other. They, too, had not looked like much. And he sometimes wondered if it was precisely that ordinariness that enabled them to cut their bloody swaths through the world.

Desmond hadn't expected much from the appearance, and he wasn't surprised when Pagan left quickly, spending just enough time to get his photograph taken and do a cursory tour through the galleries. As he moved toward the door Desmond followed him, Dave Reilly tagging along like a homeless puppy.

Outside in the sweltering heat, Pagan stood on the broad plaza in front of the museum, three bodyguards strategically placed to cover every angle. Desmond moved down the steps, pulling a pack of cigarettes from his pocket. He was angling toward Pagan, patting his pockets, as if looking for a match.

One of the bodyguards moved to cut him off, and Desmond ignored him. "Got a match, buddy?" he asked, looking at Pagan.

Pagan looked at him, his dark eys glittering with reflected floods from the museum's facade. He shook his head. "I don't smoke, amigo."

Desmond moved a little closer. "Thanks anyhow." He reached out a hand while still a few feet away, but the bodyguard grabbed him by the arm and tried to spin him away. Desmond turned the tables, twisting and ducking under, with the bodyguard now in a hammerlock.

Looking Pagan right in the eye, he asked, "You know this guy?"

"He works for me," Pagan said.

"What's he, your chauffeur?"

Pagan shook his head. The other two bodyguards were torn between the desire to teach Desmond a lesson and their obligation to maintain vigilance. They couldn't quite get a fix on what was happening, couldn't decide whether Desmond was a threat or an embarrassment. One of them had his gun out, just in case, and he stared at Desmond, his dark eyes flat and lifeless, but missing nothing.

"My bodyguard, amigo," Pagan said.

Desmond released his hold and patted the body-guard on the shoulder. "No offense, amigo, but all I wanted was a match."

Desmond stuck the cigarette into his mouth and wiggled it.

"Give him a light, Angel," Pagan snapped, turning to go.

Angel scowled, but pulled a lighter from his pocket and clicked it on. Desmond leaned in close, lit the Marlboro, and thanked him. Pagan was already heading for his car, and Angel hurried to catch up, but never took his eyes off Desmond until he climbed into the waiting limousine.

Desmond watched the car pull away, waved merrily, then walked back to the foot of the steps, where Reilly was waiting, his mouth open. "What in the hell was that all about? Are you crazy?"

"Just wanted to get a close-up look," Desmond said. "Push him just a bit, see what happened."

"You want to know what he's like, you pay close attention when I bring you where I'm bringing you."

"And where's that?"

"You said you wanted to get under the public image. Well, I dug up somebody who can tell you all about it. And you're not going to believe it."

They climbed into Reilly's Impala, and as Reilly

backed out of the parking space in the lot, he reached for the radio. When he clicked it on, the sound of salsa blasted out of the speakers. "Might as well get used to the sound," Reilly said. "Where we're going, that's all you'll hear."

He headed down the North-South Expressway, toward Little Havana, the radio blaring. At the interchange for the East-West, he headed west. The closer they came to SW Seventeenth Avenue, the more often overloaded sound systems from passing cars all but drowned out Reilly's own. Most of the time it was instrumental, bright brass sections playing boppish lines over complicated rhythms, and Desmond understood what had drawn Dizzy Gillespie to Cuban music.

They cruised through the heart of Little Havana. Most of the storefronts sported signs in Spanish—cantina and bodega, carnicería and botanica—one after another. As often as not, small knots of young men and women out front stopped what they were doing to watch the Anglo faces drift by.

"This answers the question 'What hath Castro wrought?'" Reilly shouted, trying to make himself heard over Eddie Palmieri.

"I don't see what this has to do with Colonel Pagan," Desmond shouted back.

"You will."

They had circled around and picked up West Flagler, moving toward the ocean now, and the shops gave way to residential blocks, and ahead, the strip of hotels along the beach glowed like a bulwark of light against the advancing waves. Reilly headed south on NE Second Avenue, and they moved into a section of pricey condos and apartment buildings. Some of them belonged to people who used them only three or four weeks a year, whenever the weather at home got too bad, or when the press of making the money that paid for such things relaxed for a week or so.

Reilly pulled into the parking lot of a tall, modern apartment. As Desmond climbed out of the car he could hear the sound of the surf. The thick air smelled of salt, and he walked to a bamboo fence and stood on tiptoe to look out at the beach. Despite the late hour, people still strolled on the sand, and a few moon-bathers lay on blankets, sometimes alone, sometimes wrapped in oiled arms.

Reilly led the way to the lobby, nodded to the doorman on the way in, and headed straight for the elevator.

The place reeked of money spent without concern, and the overwrought decor was typical of nouveau riche tackiness. As the elevator door closed behind them Reilly said, "You wouldn't believe who lives in this place. It's like Appalachin south. You got representatives of the Gambino, Genovese, Bonanno, Lucchese, Maggadino, and Gallo families, and those are just the ones that I know of. That mob guy from Philly, Nicky Scarfo, used to keep a broad here."

"You saying Pagan is connected to the mob?"

Reilly shook his head. "Not exactly. But they do have some things in common, not the least of which is the habit of keeping sweeties in the style they want to get accustomed to. Just stop askin' so many questions and enjoy the ride."

Reilly had punched 22, and both men watched the sequence of round lights move from floor to floor. At 22, Reilly moved to the door and rapped it impatiently with his knuckles. The car stopped smoothly, and Reilly was already stepping out before the doors had fully opened. Desmond followed him into the carpeted hall. A gilt-framed mirror across from the elevator showed him his own baffled expression.

At the end of the hall, Reilly jabbed an impatient finger into the doorbell button, and from the other side of the door, chimes rendered a few bars of "I Feel Pretty."

The door opened a few moments later, and a tall, dark-skinned beauty stepped back to let them inside.

Reilly nodded, then said, "Paul Desmond, this is Maria."

Maria smiled. "Nice to meet you, Mr. Desmond." The voice was a throaty contralto. "I have the quartet's record of tunes from *West Side Story*. I know you're not *that* Paul Desmond, but I'll play the record if you like."

Desmond, who knew the album, said, "Sure, that would be nice."

Maria went into the next room, and a few moments later the familiar opening of "Maria" welled up out of speakers in the walls.

Maria returned, barefoot on the thick carpet. "Care for something to drink?"

Reilly shook his head, and Desmond said no. With a shrug that said, *Have it your way,* Maria sat on the sofa, folding long legs with a slight awkwardness. "Why can I do for you, Lieutenant Reilly?"

"It's just plain old Mr. Reilly now, Maria. I'm retired."

Maria smiled brilliantly. "I'll bet there are a lot of

working girls glad to hear that. I'm surprised I wasn't invited to the party. There must have been a wild one. It probably lasted for days."

"I still have friends on the force, Maria, so don't give me any more guff than usual. Just think of this as being like the old days."

Maria winked. "You don't mean I have to . . ."

Reilly raised a warning finger. "None of that, damn it. None of that, now."

"You used to have a sense of humor, Lieutenant. What happened?"

Reilly sighed. "I got old, Maria, because of people like you. I got old before my time. And a pension doesn't support a sense of humor."

"I'm perfectly law-abiding now, Lieutenant. I don't bother anyone. I even go to Mass on Sunday, just in case."

"I don't think it makes much difference, Maria. Not after the life you've led. You'd need to hire a few dozen people to go to Mass for you, just to come close to getting even."

Maria clucked playfully. "Now, it's not like my line of work doesn't have value, Lieutenant."

"I didn't come here to banter, Maria. Or to discuss theology."

"Then you *are* here on business." The smile was positively radiant.

"Not your kind. Not mine, either." Reilly jerked a thumb at Desmond. "His."

Maria looked interested. "What line of work are you in, Mr. Desmond?"

"I run a security and investigations firm."

"Oh, a *dick.* Private, maybe, but still . . ." The smile

grew even more brilliant.

Desmond laughed in spite of himself. "I guess you could put it that way."

"Honey, when I was younger, I could put it any way you wanted it put. But . . ." The expansive gesture of the hands said it all. "Things ain't what they used to be. So what can I do for you?"

"Tell him about the esteemed Colonel Pagan, Maria."

Maria looked slightly uncomfortable now. "I don't know what I could possibly have to—"

Reilly interrupted. "Come off it, Maria. I know the story almost as well as you do. But I thought he should hear it from the horse's mouth."

"You did say *horse,* didn't you, Lieutenant?" Maria laughed, but some of the bravado was gone.

Looking at Desmond, Maria seemed to be deciding whether or not to speak. Reilly was getting impatient, tapping his thigh with both hands, and Maria finally nodded. "All right. What do you want to know?"

"Anything at all. I'm not sure what might be useful."

"But you want the good stuff, the juicy stuff, right? You want the dirt."

"What I want is enough to understand him."

"No way. I don't understand him. Not at all. But I'll tell you one thing, you don't ever want to cross him. Not if you want to keep on breathing."

"Are you saying he'd have someone killed?"

"That, too. But he'd do it with his own hands, if he really wanted you to suffer. I've heard stories, and I have no reason to doubt any of them. One man, worked for him, I think, but it was drug-related. Willie skinned him alive. I mean literally, from scalp to ankles. Kept him alive for three days, and every day he'd slice a couple of square feet of skin off, pour salt on the raw flesh too. Another time—and I saw this with my own eyes—he crushed a man's testicles in a vise, then tossed him into the Everglades for the alligators. The vise was still clamped on the guy's balls when he hit the water, to hold him under. He had his choice, drown or give up his *cojones*. It was no choice at all."

Maria swallowed hard, eyes darting from Desmond to Reilly and back, as if to gauge whether this was the kind of information Reilly wanted divulged.

"What about drugs?"

"What about them? Does he use them, is that what you want to know?"

Desmond nodded. "And does he sell them?"

Maria exploded in laughter. "Honey, you *must* be from out of town. When it comes to drugs, Willie Pagan is *el número uno* in this town. With that army of thugs, he has a stranglehold on coke and a big piece of grass and heroin, too. But it's mostly coke. It runs through El Salvador from Colombia and Bolivia."

"How do you know all this, Maria?"

The voice dropped a notch or two in pitch. "Willie and I used to be close, if you know what I mean."

"How close?"

"Skin to skin, Mr. Desmond. That's how close. He found me when I was working the street. He set me up in an apartment in Coral Gables, someplace out of the way, you know, where nobody knew him."

Desmond furrowed his brow. "Why?"

Maria laughed again. "He didn't want anyone to know about us. He used to come down on weekends, and I had the whole week to myself. It was a nice arrangement. He played a little rough, and I wasn't crazy about that, but it was better than being on Flagler Street. A much better standard of living, for doing the same thing. Who wouldn't make a deal like that?"

"But I don't understand. Pagan's not married. What difference could it make?"

"It's not macho, Mr. Desmond. You know what I mean?" Maria saw the knit brow and looked at Reilly. "He doesn't know, does he? You didn't tell him."

"Tell me what?" Desmond looked from Maria to Reilly and back to Maria.

Reilly was laughing hysterically now, and Maria scowled at him, then stood up. Grasping the silk blouse in both hands, Maria ripped it open with a dramatic flourish, sending buttons in every direction.

"Now do you get it?" he asked.

"You're a man!"

Maria turned coy. "It all depends on how you look at it, honey." Then, tapping a long scar covering his left ribs, he said, "That, by the way, is a memento of Señor Pagan. He used a razor. Anything else you want to know?"

"I want to know everything, Maria. Everything."

Maria sighed, then stood up.

"Where the hell do you think you're going?" Reilly snapped.

"To put on some coffee. It's going to be a long night."

— TWENTY-NINE — —

DERRICK JONES STOOD AT THE WINDOW. IT WAS
raining, a hot rain the temperature of sweat. The
wind off the Hudson was fetid, smelled vaguely sour,
reeked of swill. The mere scent of it was enough to
conjure images in his mind, the dirty brown foam
coating the water like mucilage, a Coney Island
whitefish drifting like some ghostly latex jellyfish
through the murk, an old man casting, a bucket by
his side, for a fish that no one in his right mind
would want to touch, let alone cook for supper. The
wind carried in its damp embrace everything that
Derrick Jones had come to hate about New York
City.

He could see lights, traffic moving toward the
Battery, off to the south the twin monstrosities of the
World Trade Center, Scylla and Charybdis reduced

to rectangular immobility. He was only sorry the ragheads hadn't done a better job planting their charge. Maybe the city would not seem so ugly with the towers gone.

He'd been trying to paint for three days, but every idea seemed to elude him, like balls of mercury ahead of arthritic fingers, slipping away, hiding in nooks and crannies, dividing to flow around them only to regroup, his scowl of rage rendered a mocking grimace by the tiny convex surface of the quicksilver. He was facing away from the canvas now, not willing to risk confronting the wilderness of empty space that he could not conquer.

Maybe, he thought, maybe I have been kidding myself all these years. Maybe I *can't* paint. Maybe I'm fit only to copy greatness and incapable of creating it on my own. He tried not to think like that, told himself it was a natural reaction when things were not going well, but the fact of the matter was indisputable. Nobody wanted his original work. Nobody. The galleries didn't want it. They were tired, they told him one and all, of wasting wall space for canvases no one bothered to price.

It used to be easy to tell himself that it was just because he wasn't a name. All he needed was a single break, just one, that main chance, to get noticed, to get known, to have his name for just one week on every pair of knowledgeable or monied lips in Gotham. That was all it would take. And when that chance came, he told himself, he would be ready.

But he must have been wrong. Because for a few days his name had been whispered in every ear. People saw his name in gossip columns. Liz Smith reported that he was the illegitimate son of Jackson Pollock. Suzy carried a story that he had taught Keith Haring at the Art Students' League. He expected that before long *The Sun* would reveal that he was from Jupiter. You couldn't get a profile any higher than that. But now he had nothing to paint and, by extension, nothing to sell. If he wasn't there waiting with a stack of canvases, piled like pigmented flapjacks, he would lose his chance.

It was, he told himself, probably already gone. He had made himself a prisoner. His fame was sudden and total, but it was the wrong kind. He had taken a risk, and it was threatening to backfire, may already have done so. Willie Pagan had gotten him out of Bellevue, as Derrick had known he would. Clarence Hemenway had refused to press charges. That, too, had been a factor in his complicated equations. But now he wasn't sure that he had gotten it right.

He hadn't gone to the Pratt intending to destroy anything. All he had wanted was to stand by his two canvases and listen to the oohs and ahs. It would be nice to hear someone praise the brush technique, talk about the masterly eye that had made of light something that no one before or since had managed to do. It wouldn't have mattered that the oglers thought they were talking about Claude Monet when they were really praising the work of Derrick Jones.

But Hemenway had pushed him, asked him to leave, and when he had refused, threatened to have him removed. He had seen the butcher knife at the buffet table beside the roast beef, remembered it, saw its blade flash in his mind's eye like a beacon. It had been a simple thing to retrieve it, simpler still to wield it like some demented Crusader. And why not? The work was his. Who had more right to decide its fate, to let it hang or to slice it to ribbons?

But he had lost control, started raving. Before he knew what he was doing, he had claimed pride of authorship, and it all came tumbling out in a single unstemmable flood. The years of neglect had filled him with a corrosive acid that had eaten away the valves without his even realizing it, and once he started, he couldn't stop.

Once he realized what he had done, the risk he had taken, he had no choice but to shape it, make of it a performance, turn his rage into a piece of theater. It was his only chance. He knew what Pagan was, what he would do. To save himself he had feigned madness. Or so he had told himself. Now he found himself wondering whether he had merely succeeded at long last in revealing his true self, after years of feigning sanity.

Leaning out into the night, he let the rain saturate his hair, felt its weight, felt the warm trickle down his neck. He had wanted it to feel cleansing, a kind of sacrament, a baptism that would wash away everything that had gone before so that he could start over again. Instead, he felt only the tepid wash of reality. He could wash nothing away. Not now, and maybe not ever.

He was being hounded by Furies now. Pagan would kill him, he was certain of that, and not quickly. Unless he could think of some reason to convince the Salvadoran bastard that he was more valuable alive than dead. He had not, after all, said anything about Pagan, not to anyone, not even to Desmond. That ought to be good for something, buy him some small mercy. And if only he could think, he might be able to buy the rest. But he needed time. Time to think. Time to frame his defense.

And time was the one thing he didn't have.

It might be better to throw himself on the mercy of the wind, drift down through the sticky rain like a piece of paper, sail with the wind until gravity and cement conspired to put an end to his misery. It sounded logical, even attractive. It would free him from the inexorable squeeze, the pressure that threatened to crush his skull as if it were frail as an egg.

Fuck Pagan, he thought. He can't hurt me if I'm dead. And for a moment he realized that that was all he really wanted out of the rest of his life, however short it might be—not to hurt. The pain was indescribable, incessant. He tortured himself with wanting, with desire for things he knew he couldn't have, and knew, too, that he didn't really want or need. Having them was the thing, knowing that you could if you wanted. He remembered a story about Grace Slick, when the Jefferson Airplane first made it big, going into a Mercedes showroom, barefoot, wearing a long, flowing caftan, the quintessential flower child, and telling the car dealer which one she wanted. And when the car dealer went to throw her out, pulling out a wad of bills and paying cash.

It must be nice to have that ability, even once. To do it, to be able to do it, was more important than the Mercedes. It was the gesture, the act, that provided the joy, not the car. Charles Foster Kane never quite learned that. Able to buy the world piecemeal, he had spent and spent and spent, and nothing mattered. No matter how much he owned, there was still more to be owned. And in the end, it was not the castle, not the opera house, not the treasures of a continent that mattered, but a simple wooden sled.

But who am I kidding? Derrick thought. I am not Charles Foster Kane or Grace Slick. I don't have their money. And even if I did, it wouldn't do for me what I need done. To have his work hang in the great museums, not pseudonymously, not pretending to be the work of another, more famous hand, but under his own name, that was what he wanted. And as the blank canvas behind him brought so forcefully home, he was not deserving, not equal to the simple task of making something real from cerulean blue and cadmium yellow. He had been defeated, perhaps even crushed, by a simple expanse of empty linen.

He wondered if he had spent so much time pretending to the work of others that the fakery had crowded out his own imagination, the way crabgrass insinuates itself into a lawn until finally the grass is all gone and nothing but weeds remains.

Turning back to the canvas, he hauled himself up on the window ledge. He felt the warm rain soak through his jeans and dampen his underwear. For a fleeting instant the sensation brought him back all the way to childhood, and he was overwhelmed by an unspeakable fear that someone would punish him.

He shook it off, resting his weight on his hands on the sill. The slate slab was slippery and warm, barely felt like stone. He glanced over his shoulder at the traffic again, watched the twin blades of head lamps carve a tunnel out of the night. He tried to hear the hiss of tires on the wet pavement, but he was too high, too far away. He heard only the wind and, far off, a foghorn out in the harbor.

Taking a deep breath, he dropped to the floor, landing with a jolt that seemed to compress his skeleton from ankle to skull, every joint rattling and scraping together. He walked closer to the canvas, staring at its off-white infinity. He could cram a whole world into thirty-two square feet, if only he could unlock himself again.

He picked up the palette, took a brush from a labelless can on the floor beside the easel, and stared at the blobs of color. It was all there, an entire universe, just waiting for him, the way *Guernica* had waited in the paint for Picasso. But where? How did he get to it?

Unlike some painters he knew, he couldn't just start, get in touch with something from a simple line or smear. He had to have a shape, a plan, an *idea*. That was why the forgery had been so easy for him. He could see through the finished work to the skeleton underneath, find the inner structure, the master plan. One quick look, and he could see it all clearly, the perfect audience for the canvas, apprehending in a split second everything the canvas had to offer, as if his eye were insatiable, a voracious beast, swallowing whole like Jonah's whale what others could see only through repeated viewings, painstaking examinations of square inch by square inch.

He held the brush as if it were a sword, dipped it in a color without looking, and made a blind swipe. But when he looked at what he had done, he saw nothing but a smear of paint, a random blur of color without meaning. It came from nowhere and went nowhere. It simply was, amorphous and empty.

He turned away, scaled the palette like a Frisbee, and watched its lopsided flutter toward the window. It struck the frame and wobbled, then bounced off the sill and teetered for a moment. He ran toward it, not knowing whether he wanted to pull it back from the brink or push it out into the night. But gravity had its say before he reached the open window and the palette tipped over and slid off the sill. He leaned out to watch it fall but saw nothing at first. Then, as it passed a lighted window two stories below, it took shape for a moment, the blobs of color winking like jewels for a split second until it fell back into shadow.

Once more, he saw the palette, moving faster now, slipping sidewise, held up by the wind, and it flipped over, showing him its back, snubbing him like a woman walking out of his life, then it disappeared into the darkness. He listened for the slap of wood on pavement, but heard nothing but the hiss of rain and the far-off foghorn.

Again he wanted to jump, to follow the palette ten flights, down one hundred and twenty feet, into oblivion and darkness. But the urge passed as quickly as it came. That was not the way. He didn't think it cowardly, just ineffective. It would prove nothing, not to the world that survived him, and certainly not to himself. It was better to stay and fight, if only he knew how.

When the phone rang, he was grateful for the distraction. He backed toward it, still staring at the open window and the darkness beyond it. He could see a few winking lights out on the river, marking the stately drift of a garbage scow on its way out to sea. The phone rang again, and he reached for it without looking.

He held it to his ear for a long moment, uncertain what to say, as if words had deserted him as surely as paint and palette. Finally, he managed to croak, "Hello?"

"I have Kali, Derrick. Do you understand? I have Kali."

"Who is this?"

"Think about it, Derrick, I think you know."

"Willie?"

"I have her, Derrick, and you know what I will do to her if you don't come to me."

"Let her go, Willie."

"Oh, I will, Derrick, I have nothing against her. It is you that I am angry with, Derrick. It is you that I want."

"Then let her go."

"She is my leverage, Derrick. The cheese in my trap, the worm on my hook."

"What do you want?"

"You know the answer to that, Derrick. Think about it. I will call you again in one hour. You have until then to make up your mind."

"How do I know you have her?"

"I can make her scream for you, Derrick, if you like. But I don't know if you would recognize her voice."

"No, no, I believe you."

"One hour, Derrick."

And there was nothing but dead air.

- TWENTY-SIX- - -

GUILLERMO PAGAN PACED NERVOUSLY IN THE unfamiliar surroundings. Angel and Raul sat on the front porch, smoking and talking quietly. He could see them through the large mullioned window, silhouettes against the gray sky. The sun was almost down, and Pagan knew he would feel more comfortable once the dark had settled in.

The woman was a nuisance, but she was his trump card, and he had no choice but to play the hand the way it had been dealt. He sat down, got up again, then sat down once more, crossing his legs at the knee. He could feel his pulse beating behind the top knee, see the slight tremor of his foot with every beat of his heart. He was not in control, and he did not like the way it made him feel.

The woman watched him. She was tied to a chair,

- 2 3 6

an expensive one from the look of it, Pagan thought, one of those delicate constructions of wood so brittle no one was ever allowed to sit on it. But Pagan didn't care about antiques, and there was a kind of perverse pleasure in listening to the occasional creak of the ancient joints of the chair every time the woman shifted her weight.

"You know, chica, none of this had to happen. You know that, don't you?"

Kali looked at him with wide eyes. She seemed uncertain whether to respond and finally moved her head in a compromise between yes and no.

Pagan laughed. "Cat got your tongue?" he asked.

Kali shifted her weight again, and again the chair creaked, making a brittle sound like the joints of an old man. She stared at Pagan so intently that she wondered whether her eyes were blinking normally and tried to remember the last time there had been a momentary interruption of her vision.

Pagan got up and walked to the chair. Kali's braid hung over the back of the chair, and he picked it up, hefted its heavy weight in both hands, then looped it around her neck. "Like a rope, chica, like a rope. Fit for a hangman, no?" He pulled the braid snugly up under her chin, tightened it until she started to squirm, then let go. The braid lay on her chest now, its weight in the hollow between her breasts.

Moving in front of her, Pagan reached down and stroked the bronze rope as if it were a living thing, a serpent perhaps. The backs of his fingers brushed against her breast, but he seemed not to notice. Kali shifted again, trying for the impossible, to get comfortable.

"You know, chica, this is all Derrick's fault. I am not a bad man. I tried to help him. He has talent, I won't deny that. He is a very talented man. So I tried to help him. I paid him well to work for me. You know that. You spent the money, too. But he betrayed me. He made a fool of me. And that is the one thing I cannot forgive."

He looked at her again as if he expected her to respond. When she did not, he grabbed the tape covering her mouth by its curled edge and peeled it back in a single rip. The pain made her eyes tear, but she wouldn't give him the satisfaction of uttering a sound.

Rolling the tape into a ball between his slender fingers, he tucked it into the pocket of her denim shirt. She expected him to hurt her then, to squeeze her breast until she cried out, but he pulled his hand away and turned his back.

"I will have to kill him, chica. You know that. You think he cares for you, and that he will come for you, to trade himself, his life for yours. I am not so sure. But it is the only thing I can do."

"You'll kill me, too," she whispered. "You think I don't know that?"

Pagan turned, a smile on his face. "You are not so dumb, chica. What about your friend Derrick? Is he as clever as you are? Do you think it will occur to him that I cannot allow either one of you to live?"

"It doesn't matter."

"Of course it matters. Because if he doesn't come, I will still have to kill you. How would it feel to go to your death knowing that this man does not care enough about you to trade his life for yours? Wouldn't it be so much better to have company as you cross that one great threshold?"

"It doesn't matter."

"You say that now, of course, because you still think there is time. But there is not much time, chica. Twenty-four hours is not much time, and it is already slipping away. If I had a glass full of sand and set it in front of you, you would see that almost half has already gone."

Pagan walked back to the sofa and sat down. Once more he crossed his legs. "It was such a simple thing. He had all the time he could want to make me masterpieces. But he wasn't satisfied. He was greedy, he wanted more, more even than I could pay. Not money, but recognition. And that was the one thing, of course, that he must not have. I couldn't permit that. And he knew it when he accepted my offer. But he changed his mind, chica, and now he will have to pay the price."

Pagan got up again and walked to the front door. Pushing aside the screen door, he stepped onto the porch. He stood beside Angel's chair, letting his hand rest on the cold metal. The line of trees across the yard was already turning black as the last few blades of sunlight cut through the distant clouds. It grew suddenly dark, so abruptly that he expected to hear a thud, as if the sun had fallen to earth and sputtered out in the sea.

But it was perfectly quiet. After a few moments the crickets started to chirp. He saw the drunken flutter of a bat against the sky, saw it dart and dive then disappear against the trees. A lightning bug flashed, another answered, then a third and a fourth.

He was waiting, and he did not like to wait. A man of his money and influence should not have to wait, he thought. It was demeaning. But he was not in total control, he remembered. That was why he was so angry. That would change soon, if everything went as he planned it. All he had to do was be patient just a little longer.

"Angel," he said, "go around back and make sure the other men are not sleeping. I don't trust them."

Angel got up and walked off the porch, flicking his cigarette in a high arc. The ember glowed brightly for a moment, and when the butt hit the ground, it exploded in a burst of sparks and winked out on the damp grass.

Stepping off the porch, Pagan walked toward the trees. He wanted to be alone, but knew that it would have to wait. There were times when he wished he had never come back from Europe. El Salvador was such a backward place, a cesspool, really. It had been so much better in Madrid. Staying up all night, drinking coffee with the other students at the university, reading Góngora and Lorca, Cervantes and Unamuno.

He remembered seeing Dali once, riding in a Cadillac convertible. The top was down, the backseat full of peeled cauliflower. The vegetables looked like preternaturally white human brains. He had waved to the great painter, and Dali had given him a brilliant smile, then twisted his mustache and honked the horn. As if in response to Pagan's greeting, Dali had then clapped a pith helmet on his head and driven off. The encounter had been pivotal, made him search for everything he could learn about Spain's most outrageous artist. The search had taken him to others, to Gris and Miró and to the greatest of them all, Picasso. He discovered early on that he had no interest in the old masters, Velasquez, El Greco, Goya. They did nothing for him. It was the moderns who struck a responsive chord in him. They did not quite fit into the world in which they found themselves, and neither did he. He felt a kinship with them, one that had grown more intense when he had returned to the rancho in El Salvador.

He had almost refused to come home, wished still that he had somehow found the courage to say no to his father, to tell him that he was not interested in the family business, in the army, in politics. It was art that mattered to him, and poetry. But he had not had the courage, and now it was too late.

Looking back at the house, at the tiny glow of Raul's cigarette, he wondered where it would all end for him. He knew that he was walking on a tightrope now, and that one false step would send him tumbling into an abyss so dark and so deep no light could find the bottom. He fancied that he might fall forever, drifting through the darkness and the cold like some dark star in the vastness of infinite space.

But there was still a chance that he might avert disaster, if only that stupid painter would have the *cojones* to come here, to save his woman. Jones was a fool, but he was a romantic fool, had to be to paint as he did. And there was that one slim chance that he would find a way to find the courage for that one grand gesture, that he might come to the rescue of his fair maiden with the hair like Rapunzel. And if he did,

Pagan told himself, he might yet walk away unscathed.

He saw headlights on the road coming over the mountain behind the house, a single pair of head-lights. It was too soon for it to be Derrick Jones, but he knew the car was coming to the house. There was nothing but forest for miles in any direction, and it was not the time of night for a casual ride in the country. Anyone on that road at this time was there for a purpose.

Pagan watched the lights for a moment longer, then walked back to the house. Angel was already on the front porch again, a glass of water in his hand. Pagan could hear the ice tinkling against the side of the tumbler. "He is coming," he said. "Angel, you and Raul go inside. I will tell the men out back and be right in. Tape the woman's mouth again, to keep her quiet."

Angel got to his feet and carried his glass inside. Raul followed him, a glass in his own hand, and when the screen door banged, Pagan walked around the back of the house. "Listen," he said, "Felipe, he is com-ing. We are going to wait inside. Be ready for trouble, but don't make a sound unless you know for sure that we need your help."

"*Sí*, Colonel," Felipe said. "Not a sound. Like the mice, we will be. Quiet as the mice."

Pagan walked back to the front and climbed onto the porch. He could barely make out the headlights now as the car had crested the mountain. The road dropped down the mountainside in a serpentine wiggle, and soon the car would reach the long, wind-ing lane that led to the house, and he would know if he was right.

He curled one arm around a porch pillar and watched the steady approach of the headlights. He knew who it was, he was sure of that. One more piece falling into place, just as it was supposed to. And it was best this way. Sooner or later he would have had to address this separate piece, so why not do it all at once? It was cleaner and neater that way. And why not? Why not get it over with all with one blow from the sword?

He saw the car slow now, then turn into the lane. The headlights swept past him, but he was too far away for the driver to notice him. The entrance to the lane was uphill from the house, and the trees were few on the road, and very tall. It was almost a mile to the road, and the woods were too thick for anything but the slenderest of rays to pierce through the foliage once the car entered the lane and began to wind downhill. Pagan heard the car shift gears, then went inside, letting the screen door bang closed. He closed the front door, locked it, and walked to the small lamp in the living room and reached for the switch.

For a moment he let his gaze linger on a Mark Rothko canvas, its soft blues somehow comforting, like a precursor of the darkness that would envelope him as soon as he flicked his wrist.

The light clicked off and Pagan felt his way to the sofa and sat down. Reaching into his pocket, he removed a 9mm Walther automatic, slid the safety off, and whispered, "Angel, you and Raul wait in the kitchen. I want to receive our company alone."

He saw their bulky shadows moving toward the kitchen door, heard their feet clomp on the wide wooden planks of the floor as they stepped off the Chinese carpet.

"So, Kali, we are alone again, eh? Things are beginning to happen now. Pretty soon we will see what your Derrick is made of. But first we have to receive another guest. I hope you don't mind." He laughed, feeling as if he were on the edge of hysteria. His voice sounded high-pitched, quavering, barely controlled. He chose to say nothing more rather than listen to the fear beginning to creep into his voice, and expose his weakness to the woman.

He could hear the sound of an engine as the car approached, sometimes coasting, downhill, sometimes laboring a bit to climb a small rise in the undulating lane. After two minutes light bathed the front of the house. He heard the car stop, then it went dark again. A car door banged, the heavy thud of a well-made machine, probably German. A moment later he heard keys rattle as the driver approached the house. Pagan listened for voices, but heard nothing. The driver was alone. As he was supposed to be.

Steps creaked and a heavy tread climbed to the porch. The hinges of the screen door squeaked, the thick spring whining as the door was pulled wide. A key scraped in the lock, the latch clicked, and the door bumped open.

Pagan closed his eyes to protect them from the sudden onslaught of illumination he knew was seconds away. There was a thump, something being set on the floor just inside the door, then his lids turned red, and he opened his eyes. He held the automatic almost casually.

"Clarence," he said. "How nice to see you."

Hemenway looked stunned, then noticed Kali, took in the ropes, the silver tape, and buried his face in his hands. "Oh my God," he moaned.

Pagan chuckled, then said, "He can't hear you, amigo. Believe me, He isn't even listening."

- TWENTY-SEVEN - - -

THEY WERE IN RAY MILLER'S OFFICE. MILLER WAS munching on a hamburger, talking through the glutinous mush of meat and roll. "You mean to tell me that our swashbuckling Colonel Guillermo Pagan is actually our *swish*buckling Colonel Pagan?"

"That's what I said." Desmond was still confused by the revelation twenty-four hours later. At first, he had found it difficult to accept, but by the time Maria got finished laying out the details, there was no way not to believe it.

"You're sure?"

"I'm sure," Desmond said.

"So what's the angle, do you think? You think maybe Pagan and Jones had a thing? Is that it?"

"No. According to Maria, Pagan was—"

"Wait a minute, let me get this straight, so to speak. Maria is a man, right?"

"Right. And according to him, Clarence Hemenway and the good Colonel moved in the same circles."

"You think that's the angle, then? Blackmail, maybe? Pagan decides to use what he knows to force Hemenway to cooperate, or else he blows the whistle?"

"I don't know. All I know is I'm still trying to find a reason for Hemenway to cooperate with Pagan. So far, we don't have one. Hemenway's sexual preference probably isn't enough. The art scene is full of gender benders, and that probably wouldn't be enough to persuade him to cooperate."

"But his finances are aboveboard, as far as we can tell. I don't see what—"

The phone rang, and Miller swallowed another mouthful of burger and picked up the receiver. "Yeah, Miller . . . Yes he is, he's right here. Hold on a minute."

Miller covered the phone. "It's your wife. She says it's urgent." He handed the receiver to Desmond, who immediately assumed the worst—an accident, one of the kids in the hospital, something terrible.

"Hello, Audie, it's Paul. What's wrong. Are you and the kids all right?"

Miller watched Desmond sigh with relief, then reach for a pencil from his jacket pocket. Miller turned a pad around and shoved it across the desk. Desmond nodded, scribbling an address as he listened. "And you're sure it was Jones?"

He tapped the pencil on the pad and said, "All right. Thanks for calling. Yes, you were right to do it. I'll call you as soon as I know anything."

He handed the phone back to Miller, who hung it up without taking his eyes off Desmond. "What is it?"

"It's our mystery man. Jones wants to see me. As soon as possible. Want to come along?"

"You bet your sweet ass I do. Where is he?"

Desmond looked at the pad. "Twenty-three Barclay Street, down in TriBeCa."

"Maybe it's the other loft. What'd he say to your wife?"

"Just that he had to speak to me. That it was a matter of life and death and that there was no time to waste. She's sure it wasn't a crank, because he told her some of the things that he told me when I visited him in Bellevue."

Miller stood up. "Then let's get our asses in gear, Paulie. We'll take your car, if you don't mind, since the company car is a little under the weather."

Miller opened his desk drawer and took out his service revolver and a couple of speed loaders. He clipped the holster to his belt and pocketed the loaders, then snatched the last of the hamburger from its cardboard plate and picked up his Coke. "Growing boy," he said, with a sheepish grin.

Desmond was parked in a lot across the street from the precinct house. He paid the attendant on the way in, to save time, and took the keys. He was in the front row, and they were out on Eighth Avenue thirty seconds later. He headed crosstown, picked up Eleventh Avenue, and turned south.

"What the hell do you think this is all about?" Miller asked.

"Damned if I know. Audrey said he sounded terrified, but he refused to give her any details. I guess we'll have to wait until we get there."

Miller looked at the address. "I know the building, I think. An old dressmaking firm. Big ugly gray thing."

"Ideal for an artist's studio, right?"

"Right. It almost has to be the second loft that Kali told you about."

Desmond drove without regard to traffic laws, dodging in and out among the streams of sluggish cars and taxicabs. Twice he ran a light, and grinned at Miller. "Always wanted to be able to do that," he said. "If I get a ticket, can you fix it?"

Miller punched him on the arm. "You civilians are all alike. All you think about is me, me, me. No social responsibility."

At Canal, Desmond left Eleventh and picked up West Street. The streets were clogged now, and he drummed on the wheel in his impatience to get through. It took another ten minutes before they turned into Barclay, and Miller pointed to the building. "There it is. That's the place I was thinking of."

Desmond left the Buick in front of a hydrant and Miller was already in the vestibule by the time he reached the sidewalk. "What floor?" Miller hollered. "There's no names on the bells."

"Top floor," Desmond said, stepping into the vestibule.

Miller jabbed the button and a familiar voice crackled over the intercom. "Desmond, is that you?"

"It's me, Derrick."

The door lock buzzed, and Desmond pushed inside. The elevator was right there, and the car was open and waiting. The two men stepped inside. As the door closed, Miller drew his pistol. Desmond looked at him with a quizzical expression.

"It could be a setup, you know," Miller explained.

He was right, it very well could. Someone could have been using Jones as bait to make sure Desmond didn't dodge another bullet. But he didn't think it likely.

The elevator was old and cranky. The gears groaned and the cable sang as the car rocked and bumped toward the top floor. The last few feet seemed to be almost more than the old elevator could stand, but finally it reached the top and moaned to a halt. When the door opened, the two men had to step up a foot to reach the floor.

A heavy steel door directly opposite was the only one on the floor, and Desmond rapped sharply on it with his knuckles. To be on the safe side, Miller stood on the opposite side, his pistol ready.

The scrape of the fisheye was followed by a quavery voice. "Who is it?"

"It's me—Desmond."

"Are you alone?"

"No, I have someone with me, a police officer, Lieutenant Miller."

"I told you to come alone."

"You're not in a position to make demands, Mr. Jones. Now, are you going to let us in or are we going to go home?"

The fisheye scraped again, and a symphony of

rattling chains and sliding bolts was followed by the click of a latch, and the door swung open slowly.

Desmond stepped inside cautiously, Miller right behind him. Derrick Jones looked terrible, as if he hadn't slept in days. His eyes were puffy and red-rimmed, his hair even more unruly than usual. He licked his lips as he pushed the door closed, almost knocking Miller over in his haste to get it secured again.

Desmond watched as bolts and chains were reattached, then the heavy bar of a police lock was slipped into the floor bracket. Only then did Jones turn around.

"They have Kali," he said. And before Desmond could ask who, Jones broke down. Tears welled up in his eyes, and he rubbed at a runny nose with the cuff of his wrinkled shirt.

"Who?" Desmond demanded. "Who has Kali?"

"Willie. The Colonel. Colonel Guillermo Pagan."

"Who is he?" Desmond asked, not sure why Jones expected the name to mean something to him.

"I thought you would have stumbled on him by now."

Desmond nodded his head. "Yes. Are you sure he has Kali?"

Jones bobbed his head. "Yes, I'm sure."

"How do you know?"

Jones exploded then. "Because I saw it on *Oprah*, you flaming asshole. I heard it through the grapevine. My mama told me. How the fuck do you think I know? He called me. He told me. He said—"

Miller stopped him. "Hold on. Mr. Jones. Why don't you start from the beginning?"

"There's no time. He said he would kill her. He said I had twenty-four hours. And he means it. He *will* kill her."

"What does he want, Derrick?" Desmond asked, trying to be less stern than the lieutenant, working on Lincoln's theory about the difference between vinegar and molasses.

"Me," Derrick said. It was abject, almost a moan, barely intelligible. "He wants *me*. He wants to kill me."

"Why?"

Jones looked up sharply. "You know why. I told you why. I told everybody why. And that's why he wants to kill me."

"Because you told the truth about forging the paintings? Is that it?"

Jones nodded, the movement all but imperceptible. "Yes."

"Tell us about it, Derrick. How did you work it?"

"There's no time."

"Tell us, or you can handle this yourself," Miller snapped.

Jones gave him a look of contempt, then sneered. "Did you work this out beforehand—good cop, bad cop? Or are you winging it?"

"You want our help, you start talking, and I mean now. Hemenway is in this, isn't he?"

"Yes."

"Why? What's in it for him?"

Jones started to laugh, a hyena shriek that told Desmond just how close to the edge the little artist was. "You want to know, all right, I'll tell you. His career. That's what's in it for him. Money, too, I guess, but not much. Pagan didn't need to pay him, because he had something better. He had a hook, and it was buried about as deep in Hemenway's gut as it could get. You want to know, I'll do better than tell you. I'll show you. Come on."

He backed away from them, still watching their faces, his head swiveling from one to the other and back again. Desmond looked past him, into the dimly lit interior. This loft was smaller, and far less elaborate than the one on Greenwich. Rather than a fashionable living space, there was just a small cubbyhole set off from the rest of the loft by metal partitions, the kind used in offices to demarcate work spaces. The rest of the place was clearly devoted to its main purpose: art. Canvases were everywhere. Industrial racks held dozens of jars of paint, and as many containers of solvents, pigments, oils, and assorted other materials. Desmond read the labels of some of the jars—Picasso (pink), Picasso (gray), Monet (light blue), Monet (thalo green), Beckmann (cerulean)—and he didn't have to ask whether this is where the forgeries had been painted.

"Come on, come on," Jones urged. "You want to know, I want you to know. Maybe then you'll see what he's like. Maybe you'll understand." He walked to the far end of the loft and turned on a lamp. Desmond noticed a rack of electronic components and looked at Miller, mouthing the words, "What's he up to?" Miller shrugged his own incomprehension.

Jones stood in front of the rack, pressed a button, and a large-screen television came on, filling the room with a buzz. The picture was a salt-and-pepper haze. Jones pushed another button, and the screen flickered. An instant later a face filled the screen. It was a face of indeterminate gender, either that of a tomboyish girl or a slightly effeminate young man. In either case, it was elaborately made up, the soft mouth a garish red gash, the eyes darkened with mascara and outlined with eyeliner of a dark bluegreen. The cheeks were heavily rouged, like the cheeks of a clown, but the rest of the skin was ghostly white. The camera zeroed in on one wide eye, the pupil dilated almost to its outer limit.

"Whoever she is, she's zonked," Miller whispered.

Desmond nodded in agreement. He glanced at Jones, who was watching the screen almost rapt and, sensing Desmond's eyes on him, turned with a sick smile. "Zonked, yes," Jones agreed.

The camera pulled back, then panned down a naked chest, and there was no doubt now that it was a man, not a woman. The camera lingered over the navel, almost tantalizingly dropped an inch or so, then rose again. A cheap trick, but well done. Whoever handled the camera knew what he was doing.

In a reverse zoom, the view was broadened just enough to take in the biceps, leather straps binding them so tightly that flesh bulged above and below, and a white line marked the edge of the strap separating it from the engorged flesh on either side.

Again the camera pulled back a bit, taking in the restrained man all the way to the knees. There was sound for the first time now as a whip cracked, once, then again, off camera. The man looked away from the camera, probably toward the whip, Desmond guessed, then in the other direction. The face was gelid now, beginning to quiver as if the man realized for the first time just how much trouble he was in. The whip cracked again, this time its lash snaking across the screen and landing with a sickening splat, then dropping off camera, leaving an ugly white welt behind. The welt began to redden, and the camera moved in. Only then did the whip strike again, and this time they could hear the man moan.

Miller was uncomfortable, and he muttered, "Come on, get to the point, Jones. What's this all about?"

Jones cackled, stabbed the remote at the VCR, and pushed the tape into fast search. The image was too jumbled to be seen clearly, and Jones held the button down for nearly a minute. "It's slow, but steady," he said.

When he let go of the button, the picture stabilized and revealed two figures now. The wielder of the whip was standing with his back to the camera, raising the ugly black leather over his head. He was naked, except for a wide, studded leather belt around his waist. Again and again he lashed at the restrained man, whose head now lolled to one side, as if he were unconscious. His entire front was visible to the camera, and the whip had made a bloody moonscape of the pristine flesh, an ugly tracery of interconnected welts, many of them oozing blood.

"Turn around, damn it," Miller whispered. And it was almost as if the man onscreen had heard him. Because he flicked the whip one more time, playfully, almost tenderly, grazing the battered genitals of the whipping boy, dropped the whip to the floor, and turned to face the camera with a broad smile.

"Well, hello, Clarence," Miller whispered. "You naughty boy, you."

Another naked figure, this one masked in black leather, stepped past Hemenway and approached the unconscious victim. An instant later the newcomer turned around, his red lips leering through the mouth hole of the mask, and the camera pulled back. In his hands, crosswise over both palms, he held a silver dagger. Astride the blade lay a hunk of bloody flesh, almost unrecognizable for what it was—the severed organ of the victim. The camera pulled back farther, and the tableau was complete—Clarence Hemenway, his face contorted with disbelief on the left side, the neutered victim, blood soaking both thighs, in the middle, and the masked figure on the right. Then, with a sudden jerk, the masked man ripped off the leather concealing his face, and Guillermo Pagan leered into the camera once more, licking his lips in a kind of mock lasciviousness worthy of a superannuated rock star.

"You wanted to know," Jones whispered. "And now you do."

"Where in hell did you get that tape?" Miller asked.

"Does it matter?"

"No, I suppose not." Miller looked at Desmond. "You wanted a motive, Paul. Now I guess you've got it. Hemenway was hooked for life."

"Where's Pagan now, Derrick?" Desmond asked.

"I don't know."

"If you're supposed to meet him, where did he tell you to go?"

"That animal you saw on that tape has my Kali. Will you help me?"

"Do you have to ask, Derrick?" Desmond whispered.

— TWENTY-EIGHT— —

IT WAS LATE ON A FRIDAY NIGHT, AND THE WORST OF the northbound traffic was far ahead of them as they took the thruway through Westchester and headed for the Tappan Zee Bridge. On the way, Desmond and Miller debated the pros and cons of involving the state and local police.

Miller, aware that he had no jurisdiction outside of the five boroughs, was concerned, and argued for at least limited participation by the state police. Desmond wanted to keep it small, knowing that Pagan would be more manageable if he were not backed into a corner. Derrick Jones ignored the controversy and slumped in the backseat of Desmond's Buick like a condemned man on the way to the gallows. He had nothing to say and stared out the rear window, oblivious of the discussion in the front seat.

In the end, they agreed to stop by Troop D and pick up a couple of troopers. Miller knew Captain Stan McCarthy, the commander of the troop, and it was McCarthy who had been monitoring Hemenway's country house, so at least he was already plugged in.

Miller used the car phone to contact McCarthy and made arrangements to meet him in Ferndale, with two men. McCarthy's first instinct had been to go federal, since Kali had been kidnapped, but Miller talked him out of it. "We are talking about a guy with real juice, Stan. He's really wired, and if thinks he's been painted into a corner, he could go ballistic."

McCarthy had been skeptical, but finally acquiesced. "All right, Ray, but if this goes sour, it's your ass as well as mine."

"If it goes sour, I have a feeling we'll have more than our asses to worry about." When Miller had hung up the phone, he looked at Desmond. "I hope you're satisfied, Paul."

Desmond looked at him without responding. The look on his face said it all. Once they crossed the Tappan Zee, they had a wide-open run. Desmond nudged the speedometer toward eighty and let it sit there, since McCarthy had agreed to alert the cruisers on the thruway to leave them alone.

"I hope we have enough firepower," Desmond muttered. "We don't have any idea what we're up against. You know Pagan will not be alone. And I saw the kind of goons he keeps around him when I was in Miami."

"Dave Reilly told me about that. He thought you were a crazy man. And I'm beginning to agree with him."

Desmond tapped the wheel, but didn't answer. He was already questioning his own sanity. He didn't need outside commentary on so debatable a point.

By the time they crossed the Rockland County line, it was already after midnight, and they still had a long run through Orange and up into Sullivan. Another hour, at least. Jones had been given eight A.M. as a deadline for giving himself up, and Pagan was sure to be up early, and expecting trouble, so the sooner they got to the house, the better.

"I wish I knew where Hemenway was," Miller mumbled as they left the thruway at the Harriman interchange and picked up 17 West for the Catskills. "I called his office this afternoon, and they claimed not to know where he was. I left a call on his answering machine, but he never called back."

"He could be there with Pagan. It's his house, after all."

"Think about it. Would you be there if you were Clarence?" Miller argued.

"Clarence may not have had a choice, Ray. From what I've seen of Pagan, anything is possible."

"Anything?"

Desmond nodded. "He's desperate, and that's not a condition he's used to. I just hope we can talk some sense into him."

"How do you talk sense to a man capable of doing what we saw him do on that videotape?"

Desmond shrugged. "Maybe we offer him immunity, work out some sort of deportation arrangement."

"We don't have that authority."

"We'll lie, if we have to. The main thing is to get

Kali out of there, and avoid bloodshed."

"I think it'll depend on the firepower. If he thinks he can blast his way out, he'll try it. That's why I think we should have pulled out all stops. Bring in a SWAT team. Show him we mean business."

"I think that's an invitation to a shoot-out that would make Butch and Sundance in Bolivia look like a turkey shoot."

"That's all right by me. It wasn't the *federales* who got wiped out, if you remember the film."

"They didn't have a hostage," Desmond reminded him.

"Hey, you want my opinion, you got to use the Israeli approach. Outgun the bastards and let the chips fall where they may."

"Why don't we wait and see what we're dealing with before we get ourselves all worked up. I don't want to go in there looking for an excuse to shoot somebody."

"Even Pagan?"

"Even Pagan. You want to get rid of animals like him, you can't use his methods."

"That sounds like bleeding-heart liberalism at its most pussyfooted."

"What are you, a Rush Limbaugh type? Destroy the village in order to save it?"

"No, but I've lost a few friends over the years, some in 'Nam and some in Nueva York. I don't like the way it feels, and I don't like waking up in the middle of the night thinking it could have been different, if only this or that. You give scum an inch, and it covers the whole planet before you know what happened."

The sides of the highway were dotted with billboards for the Catskill resorts now—Kutsher's and the Concord Hotel, Grossinger's and Davidman's Homowack. They were getting close, and Desmond felt a tautness in his stomach, as if it contained a giant spring that was being wound tighter and tighter.

At Ferndale, they left 17, and McCarthy was waiting for them at the end of the exit ramp. He had three cruisers with him, and Desmond was concerned. "I thought we were going to try to keep this small, Captain," he said.

McCarthy nodded. "We are. But the farm is in an isolated area. There's no way we can get in in the dark without calling attention to ourselves. I figured I'd bring extra men as drivers. They'll get us as close as they can, and we'll hop out. The cars'll move on. If they're watching from the farmhouse, they'll see the lights move on. Maybe it'll buy us a little time."

Desmond got out of the car and locked it. All he had was the Browning automatic. Miller had his service revolver. But McCarthy had thought of just about everything. In the trunk of one of the cruisers, he had Kevlar vests for everyone, including Derrick Jones. And he had two M-16s, one of them equipped with a Star-Tron nightscope. He handed the rifles to Miller and Desmond. "Either one of you ever use a nightscope?"

Desmond nodded. "Yeah. I have."

Miller looked at him with a puzzled expression. Desmond, sensing it, said, "It's a long story, Ray. Maybe I'll tell you about it when this is all over."

"No maybes, Paul. You *will* tell me. And lunch is on you, too."

The men laughed, relieved at a chance to let off a little of the tension. Once they had put on their vests, Jones wearing his under his loose-fitting shirt, they piled into the three cruisers for the last ten miles.

McCarthy, Desmond, and Miller rode in one car with a driver, Jones was in another. To be on the safe side, the painter was locked in. "In case he changes his mind," McCarthy said, winking.

"Swan Lake is just up the road, but the house is back in the woods, and there's nothing but trees and mountains for miles in every direction. Beautiful place, the kind of place I hoped to retire to when I was young and didn't know any better," McCarthy told them.

The drive took fifteen minutes. McCarthy's car was in the lead, and he pulled over to the side of the road at the beginning of a long, winding trip up the side of a mountain. The drivers of the other two cars pulled up behind and got out of their cruisers and walked to McCarthy's window for last-minute instructions.

"I want to be in the middle," he said. "We'll run without lights, and we'll fall out just below the top of the mountain. I want to have a communications post." To his driver, he said, "Billy, we'll stay in touch with you. I've already told you what to do if we run into more trouble than we can handle." The driver nodded.

McCarthy continued his briefing, addressing himself to the remaining two drivers. "If there was a moon, we could do this without lights, but there isn't and we'll just have to make do. I don't want you men to stop, not under any circumstances. Slow down, but don't stop. Make sure your men get off clean. Have them sit on the trunk with the rear windows open so they can have handholds. I want this smooth, and I want you to keep rolling. Anybody in that farmhouse sees you, what they'll see is two cars taking it easy, and that's all. Understood? We could try it without lights, but if they hear the engines, that'll tip them off, so this is the way it has to be."

The two drivers nodded.

McCarthy turned to Desmond. "One of you two will have to go in another car, because I don't want Jones trying to jump from a moving vehicle, no matter how slow. He turns an ankle, we'll have to carry him a mile through the woods."

"I'll switch," Miller said.

"Tell the men to put all their weapons in the trunk of this car. I don't want them losing anything, and I don't want them falling off trying to hang on to a rifle."

When the weapons were transferred and the men were ready, one of the three cruisers pulled in front of McCarthy's. To avoid the risk of being picked up on police band, they were using handsets to communicate. McCarthy gave the order, and the odd caravan lurched into motion. As they wound their way up the mountainside Desmond reached up and unscrewed the lens over the domelight, pulled the bulb, and set in the lens before replacing it.

"Never thought of that," McCarthy said.

"You can't be too careful," Desmond answered.

The road cut back and forth across the side of the mountain in a series of sidewinder loops. The forest on either side was thick, and impenetrably black, except for the small swath of brilliant green picked out by the two pairs of headlights. Heavy undergrowth made a solid wall nearly six feet high, and Desmond was thankful he didn't have to deal with hiking through it.

The two men on the trunk deck of the lead car looked almost like circus monkeys, clinging to the slowly moving cruiser by the light rack. Ray Miller, his jeans and ponytail even more incongruous than usual beside the fatigued trooper to his left, was grinning back at Desmond, and once waved a hand. "Looks like he's having a grand old time," McCarthy grunted.

"You know him long?" Desmond asked.

"Yeah. And I knew his father before him. Dick Miller was NYPD, too, back when I was a rookie, before I switched to the state. Ray's an oddball, not exactly what you'd call a model policeman, but he's just possibly the best cop I ever saw, except for his dad. He does things his own way, gets his ass in a sling when he does, but he gets the job done. And that's the bottom line."

"It seems like a waste to have him chasing stolen paintings if he's that good," Desmond said.

McCarthy snorted. "He's on that damn Crayon Patrol as punishment, you know. The brass hats don't like a man who thinks for himself, so they stuck him with it. They thought it would make him quit, but Ray's a tough nut. He'll wait them all out, unless I miss my guess."

They were getting close to the top of the mountain now, and McCarthy turned his attention to the handset. "All right, the next turn is where we drop, fellows. Make it clean, and be careful."

The car negotiated a hairpin, slid between two walls of broken orange shale that reached almost to the shoulder of the road, then back into the trees. McCarthy's driver pulled off to the side into a small clearing, and in the headlights of the second car, Desmond saw Miller and the state cop let go of the rack and slide off the deck. They landed awkwardly, but kept to their feet.

The second car rolled past, two more troopers repeating the maneuver.

McCarthy opened the trunk of the parked car and handed out the weapons. Desmond took the M-16 with the Star-Tron, then walked over to Derrick Jones. "This is it, Derrick. This is the one chance Kali has. Don't screw it up."

"Let's go," McCarthy hissed.

Jones looked at the captain then at Desmond. His eyes were wide, but he swallowed hard and whispered, "I won't."

— TWENTY-NINE ——

THE HOUSE LAY BELOW THEM. IT WAS DARK, ALL BUT black against the thick forest behind it. A late-model Mercedes sedan sat in the semicircular driveway, but there were no other vehicles in evidence.

"If Pagan's here, he must have walked in," Miller whispered.

"Not necessarily. There could be a car behind the house," Desmond answered.

"Maybe so, but we can't make a move until we know what we're up against."

"Even that won't be enough. We have to know exactly where Kali is. She's got to be our first priority. As soon as they realize we're here, they'll make sure we can't get at her. She's the only leverage they've got. It's ironic, in a way. She was supposed to be the bait that got Jones here. But now she may be their only way out."

"How do you know Pagan won't just kill her? He's not your ordinary kidnapper, to say the least. It won't take much to push that son of a bitch right over the deep end. If that happens, who the hell knows what he'll do?"

"I don't think he'll panic easily," Desmond said. "He's used to political wheeling and dealing. Tit for tat. If he thinks he can use her to buy his way out, then he'll keep her alive. And no matter what we do, we have to let him keep on thinking that way."

McCarthy was scrutinizing the house with a pair of French-made infrared binoculars. Lowering them, he shook his head. "Don't see a damn thing. Most of the windows have curtains on them, and I don't see anybody out front."

"They must have posted guards," Desmond said. "We're just not looking in the right place."

"How many men do you think are in there?"

"We don't know. Pagan said he had Kali, and if we accept that at face value, then there are at least two people. But Pagan wouldn't go anywhere without muscle. How many men, I don't have a clue."

"Can you make a guess?"

"Yeah, I can guess, but I don't want to try to pull this off by the seat of my pants. In Miami, he had three bodyguards and a chauffeur when I saw him. I would assume that the chauffeur is also a bodyguard and therefore armed. I would guess at least five armed men, at a minimum. And there is a strong possibility that Clarence Hemenway is in there as well."

"A minimum of seven people, then," McCarthy muttered. "At least five of whom pose a threat. What about Hemenway? Will he fight?"

"I don't know," Desmond answered. "Given a choice, no, I don't think so. But he may not have a choice, or may not think he has one. In that case, it's anybody's guess."

"I'm going to position my men at the corners. Then we'll make a circuit. If there are sentries, we have to find them before we do anything else."

Desmond nodded. "How long will it take?"

"Twenty minutes, tops. And if we find sentries, we're going to take them out, if we can do it quietly. We'll take them alive, if we can."

As McCarthy was about to move, the sound of a door opening echoed across the clearing. "Hold on, Captain," Desmond hissed. "Let's see what happens. Maybe we just caught a break."

"You don't catch breaks in this kind of situation, Mr. Desmond. You make them." But he stayed put.

Desmond took the night glasses and trained them on the front porch. He could see the figure of a man in the shadows on the porch. Something very bright glowed in front of him, and Desmond resolved the focus; he realized by the floating blobs of light that the man was holding something hot, probably cups of coffee. The man stepped off the porch and down onto the front lawn, then moved toward the corner of the house and disappeared behind it. Desmond cursed under his breath. He was a good five hundred yards away, and he didn't have an angle to see where the man had gone.

"I think he was bringing coffee to the troops," Desmond whispered. "You better go ahead and get your men in position."

"You want to wait until daylight, when we'll have more control?" McCarthy asked.

Desmond shook his head. "I don't think so. I think the sooner we move, the better. Maybe we can catch them while some of them are asleep."

"That only gives us an edge if we get inside. If we hit any resistance before we get in, the others'll be up anyway."

"We'll get in. Or at least I will."

"I don't come out in the middle of the night to ride shotgun on a black-bag job, Mr. Desmond. If we're going to make this work, we have to pull together."

Desmond nodded. "I know. But we have to locate the woman. That's paramount. And to do that, somebody has to get inside. We don't know the layout of the house."

"If you go, you take a man with you."

"I'll take Ray."

McCarthy whispered his commands over the handset. Desmond watched the troopers through the night glasses, dim shadows all but invisible as they worked their way through the groves of pines surrounding the house on all sides. There was a broad lawn on flat ground out front, and open fields sweeping up and away in every direction. Behind the house, the trees came to within fifty yards, not as close as Desmond would have liked, but if he was going to go in, that would get him the closest without having to cross open space.

The mysterious figure reappeared at the corner of the house, its hands now empty. It moved up the steps. Ill defined in the infrared, it looked less like a man than some large unicellular beast oozing uphill and into the house. The door closed again, and the figure was gone.

"Time for us to get a little closer," McCarthy suggested.

They moved downhill, losing sight of the house temporarily once they entered the trees. Even though the handsets were silent, employing earplugs rather than speakers that might alert those inside, the three men who were approaching the house had been told not to break radio silence unless absolutely necessary. Until Desmond reached the bottom of the mountain and the edge of the meadow overlooking the house, he would have no idea what was happening ahead of him.

Derrick Jones was still silent, even withdrawn. He had been cooperative, but his presence clearly made McCarthy uneasy. He kept looking at the painter as if trying to measure him in some way, wondering just how long he would remain a neutral presence rather than a liability.

Desmond, too, was worried. The painter was unstable, even if one interpreted everything he'd done in the best light, and that was giving him too much credit by far.

When the house reappeared, it was as dark and silent as before. But it had gained in size. From the high vantage point, it had seemed small, a cozy cabin in the woods. Now it was more imposing, and the larger it seemed, the more daunting became the prospect of getting inside and finding Kali without alerting her captors.

But it was the best way. Even Stan McCarthy knew that. He didn't like it, and there was no reason he should. But he was willing to let Desmond make the calls until Desmond screwed up. At that point, whatever Desmond wanted to achieve would happen by chance, rather than design, and everybody on the side of the mountain knew it. Except possibly Derrick Jones.

McCarthy slipped in beside him and whispered, "There's two guards out back. No sign of anyone out front. I don't figure it."

"There's got to be somebody watching the front from inside. They must have wanted the guards on the outside in back because the trees are so much closer."

"Makes sense, I guess," McCarthy agreed.

"Can your men get the guards without alerting the house?"

"They think so."

"Do you believe them?"

"I didn't get where I am by doubting them."

Desmond gave the assent with a bob of his head. "Alive, if possible," he whispered.

"We'll have to see about that."

McCarthy gave the order for his men to move in. Once they started, communication would be temporarily suspended, and he reminded them to be aware of that fact. The men were trained in a variety of penetration techniques, and they would have no trouble taking out both guards without a sound if their only intention was to kill them.

It struck Desmond once more how much harder it was *not* to take a human life. Doing it the quick and easy way was something he had hated about his years in intelligence work. Time had done nothing to quell his antipathy. Ends and means were too readily balanced on the point of a knife. It was not that he couldn't find a way to justify death, make it efficient, even expedient. He could do that with the best of the Company cowboys. But it was precisely because he could do it so easily that he had begun to doubt his intentions as well as his methods. It had come to seem as if human life were just one more bargaining chip, as if human beings were no more than pawns, simple obstacles to be disposed of simply. It reduced cold-blooded murder to a negligible factor in a deadly calculus whose equations seemed to have imperatives of their own.

That Guillermo Pagan was the end product of such a mathematics did not make death more palatable, but, on the contrary, made it all the more to be scrupulously avoided lest in looking Pagan in the face, he see nothing more than a self-portrait.

It seemed an eternity until McCarthy clapped him on the shoulder, then whispered, "It's done. One dead, one captive. We'll see how much juice we can squeeze out of the orange before we decide what next."

"Where?"

"Behind the house. We'll move in as close as we can. They'll question the captive while we circle around. With any luck, we'll have a pretty good idea of the layout by the time we're ready to go."

McCarthy got to his feet and started on the circuitous route that would bring him into the stand of pines behind the house. Ray Miller hung back a moment. "Are you all right, Paul?"

Desmond didn't know how to answer, so he said nothing, giving the lieutenant a noncommittal wave of his hand. Miller took it as an okay and started through the trees in McCarthy's wake, one hand firmly grasping Derrick Jones by the elbow.

Desmond started after the odd couple, aware of nothing so much as the tang of pine, the whisper of his shoes on a carpet of stiff needles, and, overhead, through the crowns of the trees fifty feet above him, the silent twinkle of a million stars. For a moment all he could think about was how lucky Clarence Hemenway was to have a place like this. He knew the thought was incongruous, perhaps even grotesque, but he couldn't push it aside.

Then, as he recalled the image of Hemenway on the videotape, sweating and naked, the bloody whip in his hand, the envy turned to disgust, then to blind hatred, and for a moment he wanted to tell McCarthy that he had changed his mind, that a frontal assault was the best thing, maybe even send Jones on ahead to take his chances, use him as he had used so many others. They were, after all, every one of them—Jones, Hemenway, Pagan—users. And he was sick to death of the lot of them. Death, no matter how violent, was no more than they deserved.

Then he thought of Kali, how terrified she must be, and he realized once again that wisdom sometimes demands compassion for the few at the expense of justice for the many. It was the only way the equations would balance. It made for lousy math, but it was how it had to be.

— THIRTY— —

"YOU SURE YOU WANT TO DO THIS, DESMOND?" McCarthy asked.

"I don't know of any other way to avoid unnecessary bloodshed."

"From what I hear of Pagan, shedding his blood would not be unnecessary. It would probably be a profoundly moral act."

"I don't want to expose the woman to any more danger than we have to."

"Suppose we set up an exchange and pop Pagan when he comes out?"

"He won't come out. And once we let him know we're here, the ball is in his court. That's what I want to avoid, if at all possible."

McCarthy looked at Derrick Jones. "We got a perfect minnow here to hide the hook. Hell, what'd we even bring him along for, we're not gonna use him?"

"He's our fallback position, Captain," Miller said. "If all else fails, then we can dangle him, see what happens. But he's too unpredictable. We can't afford to let him screw things up, which he almost certainly will do, whether he means to or not."

McCarthy looked at Jones again. "Hell, why not just shoot him? Put him out of his misery. Make our job a whole lot easier, I think."

"Too late for that, Captain," Desmond said. "I think we better get going."

"Well, if our prisoner told the truth, and if he knows his ass from his elbow, you know where the woman is. If you can get into the basement, she'll be in the room right at the top of the stairs. Pagan's with her, according to Pancho or whatever the fuck his name is. The owner of the place, Hemenway, is upstairs. He's not tied up like the woman, but he's locked in, so you can probably forget about him until it's all over. My advice to you, since you insist on trying this, is go right for the woman. Get her the fuck out of there, and let us call for plenty of backup."

"I'd like to get Hemenway out, too, if I can."

"It's up to you, but I think you're biting off a little more than you can chew. Once you go to the second floor, you'll have a bitch of a time getting out. Pagan's got four men in there, and they're all armed to the teeth. The two watching the front will be awake, so you'll either have to neutralize them, or bear-trap 'em. Whatever the hell you do, be damn careful."

Desmond nodded. "We will."

"The first gunshot I hear, I'm calling for help, and

I'm coming in. I got people on standby, and I won't wait. Understand?"

"We understand, Stan," Miller said. "Come on, let's get moving. I can't stand the suspense."

Desmond took the point. The fifty yards of open space between the trees and the house were the easy part. Getting inside would take a little luck. Getting out again would take a whole lot more.

At the back of the house, two low windows, set in concrete wells, provided some sun and ventilation for the basement. The windows were not very large, and the wells made for an awkward entry, but it was the best way in, since the back of the house had a heavy wooden door that was bolted and chained. It would not be possible to get through without alerting everyone inside.

Desmond headed for the window on the left, which was partially screened from the rear windows by some dense shrubbery at the corner of the house. His legs felt like lead as he neared the house, and by the time he reached it, he was already beginning to second-guess himself.

Ray Miller skidded to his knees beside him. He hefted a heavy-bladed knife and leaned close to the window to slice through the wire screen protecting the glass. He cut an X in the center and reached inside to unhook the screen frame, then pulled the frame away and leaned it against the side of the house. "Now comes the hard part," he whispered.

He had a large suction cup with a handle attached to its rear, but on his first attempt to stick it to the glass, it wouldn't take. "Too much dirt for a good vacuum," he muttered, wiped the glass with his palm, then spitting on his fingers and moistening the edge of the suction cup. Once more, he pressed it against the glass, and this time it took.

Quickly, he cut a circle in the glass and pulled it free with the handle. The disk was still clinging to the suction cup when he set it down. Reaching through the hole in the windowpane, he found the slide bolt, right where Pagan's man said it would be.

They could push the window open now, but Desmond held up a hand to wait. He listened at the opening for nearly a minute, and only when he heard nothing did he push the window in. It ground on sandy dirt as it opened, but that was the only sound. They couldn't risk a light yet, not until one of them was inside. Desmond went first while Miller held the window open. The top of the masonry well scraped against his Kevlar vest as he slid backward into the basement, holding on to the cement until his toes found the floor.

"All right," he whispered, "come on."

He stood to one side and held the window open while Miller handed the two M-16s through, then waited for Miller himself to come sliding in backward like some befuddled snake. Not until Miller's feet were on the ground and he could lower the window again did Desmond use the tiny light. He cupped it in his hands for a moment before letting its tiny beam probe the recesses of the basement. They were in a halfhearted rec room. The walls were paneled, and there was some shabby lounge furniture. The place smelled of mildew, a thick, musty scent that reminded Desmond of old damp laundry.

The stairs were to the right, and Desmond moved

toward them, holding the torch in his teeth and slipping the safety off on the M-16. The Star-Tron was bulky, but it still might come in handy, so he was willing to work around it.

The stairs were wooden, and likely to be noisy. Desmond moved cautiously, placing one foot at a time, then shifting his weight slowly, ready to stop at the first creak. The third step was loose, and he had to step up to the fourth, and pointed to make sure Miller realized it. It took nearly ten minutes to get to the wooden door at the top of the stairway. Desmond placed an ear against the lower door panel and listened for a couple of minutes. He heard nothing and reached for the doorknob, squeezing it and pressing down to guard against a rattle. When he had it firmly in his grasp, he put out the light and waited to let his eyes adjust to the gloom. Once he was confident that he would be able to negotiate the darkness, he turned the knob.

It turned easily, and he could feel the resistance of the latch spring until the latch finally recessed and he was able to ease the door open an inch or two. There was no sign of light from the first floor, but he waited, just to make sure. The next part was tricky, because he had no idea whether the hinges were going to squeal as he pushed the door open far enough to slip through into the small hallway beyond it.

He could hear the slight hiss of air with every breath Ray Miller took. He slid one hand around to the outside and pressed the other against it. The rifle was slung over his shoulder, and he would have to open the door wide enough to get through without bumping the weapon into it.

Gently, and so slowly he wasn't sure he was doing it at all, he eased the door outward until it was halfway open. He slipped the rifle from his shoulder and stepped out into the tiny hall. Ray Miller was right behind him and closed the door as quietly as he could. When he felt the latch against the jamb, he let go. The door started to swing open again, and he reached into his pocket for a matchbook, folded it once and shimmed the door snug against the jamb.

It was not possible to talk now, and they were going to have to have something akin to ESP to find Kali. According to the description given by the captured bodyguard, there was a large room full of bookshelves just beyond the short hall. Facing the front of the house was a sofa fronted by a coffee table. When Pagan was in the room, he was on the sofa. It was possible he was there and asleep. But if not, he would be on the second floor, in the master bedroom. Clarence Hemenway was in a smaller bedroom adjacent to it. Two guards would be sleeping in the third bedroom. The two on duty were supposed to be in the library next to the main room where Kali was being held.

The two rooms were connected by a hallway, with a third room at the far end of the house. The kitchen, and the rear door, were behind them, and the only way to reach them was through the main room. Going out the front was not an option, because the guards would see them, even if they didn't hear them.

Desmond reached the end of the tiny hall and lifted the rifle to his shoulder. He used the nightscope to scan the room. He saw Kali, tied to a rickety chair in the center of the room. He could just make out the tape over her mouth. The sofa was empty, and Desmond assumed that Pagan must have gone up stairs.

Getting Kali out would not be easy. But they had to try. Desmond moved into the room and put a hand on Kali's shoulder, then bent to whisper in her ear, "Kali, it's Desmond. Don't make a sound. We're going to get you out of here. If you understand, nod your head."

He felt her head move, the scent of her hair filling the air around him. He was going to leave the tape on her mouth, just in case. Miller knelt beside her and pulled the knife while Desmond watched the door to the hallway. Behind them, against the west end of the room, was the stairway leading to the second floor. Another stairway was at the east end of the house, from the hallway just off the kitchen. If Pagan was upstairs—and Desmond had no choice but to assume he was—he would not know which stairs the Colonel would use should he decide to come back down. Desmond could only hope it would be those at the east end.

He heard the rasp of a knife blade slicing through the ropes binding Kali to the chair. Miller was trying to avoid even the slightest sound, but Kali was restless, and as she squirmed on the chair it creaked. In the quiet, it sounded like a rusty gate swinging open, and Desmond sucked in his breath and held it, canting his head toward the second floor and listening intently.

For a moment he thought he heard a voice, but the sound was not repeated, and he couldn't be sure. Miller, too, had frozen, clamping the knife between his teeth and pulling his service revolver. His rifle was on the floor beside Kali's chair.

Again, Desmond thought he heard a voice, then he heard a thump, something bumping the floor above. It was repeated, and he realized that someone was beginning to move around. He wanted to whisper to Miller to hurry, but was afraid to risk it. If the guards heard the noise, they might come poking around to see what had caused it.

Miller sliced away the ropes, and Kali was free of the chair, but her ankles were still bound together and she could stand, but not walk. Her wrists, too, were still tied behind her. Miller turned his attention to the ropes holding her feet. He had to be careful not to cut her accidentally, and the going was excruciatingly slow.

Another bump on the floor above set Desmond's pulse racing. Miller finally got through the foot rope, and helped Kali to her feet. She teetered unsteadily in the dark as he bent to grab his rifle, but that couldn't be helped. He was pulling her toward the short hall when something clicked, and the room was suddenly flooded with light.

Steps sounded on the stairs, and Desmond waved to Miller to get Kali into the hall, but he was too late. Someone, maybe Pagan, saw Desmond, and shouted as he ducked back up the stairs and out of sight. Footsteps pounded in the long hall and Desmond swung the M-16 toward the entrance to the room. Upstairs, someone ran, then knocked on a door. The hollow sound of the rapping seemed to cascade down the stairs like a flood, filling the room with thunder.

Two men burst into the room, machine pistols in their hands. Desmond saw them at the same instant they saw him. He fired his M-16, sending them skidding into a stop, then fired again, hitting one man in the shoulder and knocking him backward into his companion, whose machine pistol exploded in a wild burst as the two guards fell to the floor.

That tears it, Desmond thought. McCarthy will be calling for his backup now, and Kali was still in the house. Another burst from a machine pistol swept through the room, blowing several panes of glass from the front windows. The crash of breaking glass was drowned out by the echo of the weapon's hammering.

Desmond switched the M-16 fire-control lever to full auto and ducked behind a leather easy chair. It wouldn't offer much cover, but they had to see him before they could shoot at him, and he held his breath as Miller shoved Kali into the hallway. Desmond heard the door open, then footsteps, as someone, presumably Kali, went down to the basement.

Outside, someone was calling his name, but the voice was too far away to hear it clearly, and his ears still rang with gunfire. Miller started to come back, but Desmond waved him away. "Get Kali out of here," he said. "I'll go out the front way."

Miller nodded, then ducked out of sight. One of the two gunmen reappeared in the doorway, and this time Desmond was ready for him. He fired a short burst, saw three scarlet boutonnieres suddenly bloom on the man's shirtfront, and he knew the opposition was down by one.

He backed toward the front door, reaching for it with one hand, but as his hand brushed against the knob the second gunman darted into the room, and Desmond had to use both hands to bring the M-16 to bear.

Once more, he scored, and once more he reached for the knob. It rattled in his hand, and he felt the thumb key of the latch, pressed it, and started to pull the door open when a gunshot from his right brought him up short. The bullet narrowly missed him, but he jerked the door open as he dove for the chair and cover again.

"Mr. Desmond," a voice said. "Mr. Desmond, I am coming down. I have Clarence with me, and I want you to pay close attention to what I have to say."

Desmond saw feet on the stairs, first one pair, then another, the first were bare, and above the ankles were stripes from what could only be pajamas. The second pair were shod in expensive Italian loafers.

A moment later the tangle of legs jitterbugged down the steps until two faces came into view. Guillermo Pagan had one arm around Clarence Hemenway's neck. His other was cocked at the elbow, its hand holding a pistol against Hemenway's temple.

"Have I got your attention, Mr. Desmond?"

"Yeah, Pagan, you have my attention."

"I was trying to set my affairs in order, to tidy up an unexpected little mess, but you have seen fit to prevent me from doing so. I see now that I will have to revise my short-term goals, as it were, settling for something a bit more modest."

"What do you want?"

"I want what everyone wants—to live his life in quiet."

"How about the boy in your little home movie, is that what he wanted, too? Or didn't it matter what he wanted?"

Pagan's face was frozen in shock for a moment, but

it was nothing compared with the look on Clarence Hemenway's face. The Pratt's director seemed to sag toward the floor, his whole body collapsing, and Pagan had to struggle to maintain his grip on his hostage.

But Pagan recovered quickly. "I see Mr. Jones was capable of copying more than Monet," he said.

"You are one sick bastard, Pagan," Desmond snapped. He heard his voice, heard its brittle, almost metallic tone, and realized that he hadn't sounded like that in years, not since decompressing in Langley after his last tour abroad. Something was happening to him, he was reverting, as if Pagan carried some kind of viral plague and Desmond had lost his immunity. He was changing, and it terrified him.

For a moment he thought about emptying the rest of the clip into both men and putting a neat, not-so-clean end to the matter. His finger tightened on the trigger, and Pagan saw the movement, started to back away; with the movement, Clarence Hemenway threw himself forward, slipping from Pagan's grasp.

The automatic in Pagan's hand tried to home in on Desmond, but he had lost his balance, and as he fell he lost the pistol. At the same instant his chest seemed to explode, and his body was thrown back against the steps. He bounced down two, then a third, and slid the rest of the way to the floor.

The screen door swung open and Desmond looked up in time to see Ray Miller stepping through it. Just past Miller's shoulder, Desmond saw a hole in the screen where Miller's shot had passed through.

Stan McCarthy and his men followed Miller inside, and Desmond shouted, "There are two more upstairs." McCarthy nodded, started up the stairs, and sent two of his men to the other end of the house.

Clarence Hemenway lay on the floor, moaning. Desmond thought for a moment that he had broken a bone in his fall down the stairs. He knelt beside the moaning man, who looked frail and ludicrous in his striped pajamas. Desmond put a hand on his shoulder and said, "Let me help you up, Mr. Hemenway."

Hemenway turned to look up at him, his face contorted by something that could have been sorrow or hatred, or an amalgam of the two. He started to shake his head. "I . . . I . . .—" he stammered, trying to find the words, but they eluded him.

He buried his face in his arms again. Once more Desmond tried to coax him to his feet. He leaned forward, but the sound of a muffled gunshot sent him sprawling for his rifle. It took him a moment to realize what had happened. Only the blood seeping out from under Hemenway's folded arms explained it. He turned Hemenway over and saw the man's hand still holding Pagan's pistol.

Desmond got to his feet. It's over, he thought, then walked out into the darkness.

— THIRTY-ONE ———

DESMOND STOOD THERE IN THE COLD, DIM LIGHT OF
the warehouse, the stink of decay seeping in off the
river. Derrick Jones paced nervously, and he seemed
small, almost an absence, the empty eye of a hurricane.

Valerie Harrison kept rubbing her hands, staring
alternately at them and at the ceiling, a novice over-
playing Lady Macbeth, the friction of skin on skin
surrounding her like strange music.

They were waiting for Ray Miller, and when the
sound of a car engine drifted in through an open
window, Desmond was only too willing to walk to the
door to see if he had finally arrived. He saw the car, a
nondescript gray with cheap hubcaps that could only
be an unmarked police car, and felt as if some great
burden were being lifted from his shoulders.

Miller climbed out of the car and waved. "Sorry I'm

late," he shouted. "I'm tempted to say better late than never, but I hate when people say that to me."

Desmond stood aside for him to enter the warehouse. Just inside the door, Miller stopped, looked around, his nose twitching at the ripeness of the air. "So, this is where it all ends, is it? This is where we learn the secrets of the universe . . . not much to look at."

He walked past Desmond, scowled at Derrick Jones, and shook hands with Valerie Harrison. "This better be good, little man," Miller warned. "You have about run out the string, as far as I'm concerned."

Jones nodded apologetically. His lips twitched, as if he wanted to say something, but all he could manage was another shake of his head.

"All right, Derrick, let's have it," Desmond said. "You promised some answers, and I think they're long overdue."

Once more Jones nodded, swallowed hard, and began. "It was complicated," he said. "But it worked. I mean, it did, didn't it? It worked." He looked at each of them in turn, as if he expected some hint of approbation, perhaps even admiration. What he got was three cold, blank faces.

He shifted his feet. They scraped on the cement, and the echo bounced back at them from every corner of the warehouse, like the ghosts of sounds long dead— the slap of a moth against a screen, a rat's claws tearing at old wood, the slither of a snake on wet rock—noises fit only for cold, dark places.

"The way it worked, Clarence found out what paintings were going to be brought to this country for shows. He could find out way in advance, because the museums always work together on organizing big exhibits. The Colonel would decide which ones he wanted, and then I would start making the copy. Sometimes there wasn't enough time, or Clarence couldn't find out how the canvases would be shipped. It all hinged on that. We had to have advance knowledge of the shipping. Then we would arrange for the substitution, if we could get to somebody on the inside. We could do it pretty easily, usually through the trucking. We'd bring the originals here and substitute the copy. It was so simple. You're expecting a Monet; you open a package, and there it is. You don't think it might be a fake. You don't test it. It's a Monet. Period. You hang it, and you send it back after the exhibition. It's the kingdom of the blind, after all. And you know what they say about that. It doesn't take much to be king."

"What happened to the originals?" Miller asked.

Jones gave him a queer smile. "They went to the Colonel, of course. He was financing the whole thing. He had the money, and he had the lust for the paintings. He was a greedy son of a bitch."

"I assume you were well paid?"

"Yeah, I was. I should have been. I'm a good painter, even a great one." He moved his shoulders as if the mantle of greatness were somewhat uncomfortable, but one he would learn to wear.

"That picture, the one from the magazine . . . why did you have it? What was the circle around the Monet for?"

"That wasn't a Monet. It was one of mine, an impression of Impressionism. I kept the picture to show Kali that somebody paid good money for my own stuff."

"So," Desmond asked, "why did you decide to blow the whistle?"

"I got scared. Pagan was getting greedier by the minute. He wanted everything. I couldn't paint fast enough. He wanted so much, and he didn't understand that my work had to be the equal of the original. I mean, you were expecting Monet, you saw it, but that didn't mean I could just slap things together. I worked on a Picasso—it took me six months to get it right. First, I couldn't get the colors right, and when I finally did, they changed in the aging, got darker, so I had to start all over again, brighten every tone a bit so when I aged it, it looked right. It was a bitch."

"I don't understand what that has to do with—"

Jones waved an impatient hand. "Look. He didn't understand. He thought it was like making sandwiches or something, like anybody could do it. When I tried to tell him he had to be more selective, he went around the bend. Then, when I saw that tape, I knew what I was dealing with. I should have known earlier, I guess, but I didn't want to see it. The money was too good."

"How'd you copy the tape?"

"I didn't copy it. I substituted a blank for it and smuggled it out of his place in Miami. He has a hundred of them, more even."

"All like that?"

"What tape?" Valerie asked.

"Never mind. You don't need to know that," Miller said. "It doesn't have anything to do with the paintings."

She looked at Desmond, as if to enlist his support, but he shook his head no, and she surrendered.

"Anyway," Jones continued, "I figured the tape was my insurance policy. I figured there would come a time, and it wasn't far off, when he would start to lean on me. I figured that the tape would buy me some time to disappear."

"What changed your mind?"

"When they killed that truck driver. I mean, I didn't know they were going to lift those German things, but as soon as I read about it in the papers, I knew what had happened. Pagan had a guy worked for him who used to work for that shipping outfit. I figured he was out of control."

"And that you were likely to get whacked yourself?"

Jones nodded. "Look. I am very good at what I do. But I don't think Pagan understood just how good, or how difficult it would be to replace me. I started to figure he'd just cash me in and get somebody else. I didn't really plan on going public, not the way it happened. But Clarence was getting antsy, too. At the museum that night, he was really losing it, and we had an argument. I didn't realize how close to the edge I was myself. It just sort of happened."

"You understand, don't you, Mr. Jones," Valerie Harrison said, "that you are admitting to being an accessory in the theft of millions of dollars' worth of valuable art?"

Jones gave her the same queer smile he had given Miller a few minutes before. "Remember," he said, "what I told you about the kingdom of the blind. It's all expectation. What you see is what you think you're going to see. That's why the switch worked so easily."

"I don't understand."

Jones smiled. "I know you don't. But you will. Come with me." He walked toward the rear of the warehouse, where a small room, its walls half glass, had served as some sort of office.

He opened the door and clicked on a light. Against one wall, a large canvas was draped over what appeared to be a shapeless mound. Jones grabbed one edge of the canvas and looked at Miller. "Grab the other end, Lieutenant," he said. When Miller complied, together they tugged the canvas free of the mound.

"What is this?" Miller demanded.

"What do you think it is? Maybe that will determine what it actually is."

The mound was composed of several rectangular packages wrapped in waterproof paper. Jones reached into his packet for a small knife and slit the paper on the end of the frontmost package, leaning against the front of several larger packages.

Beneath the waterproof paper was a cardboard box, sealed with tape. Jones slit the tape and opened the flap. "Somebody hold the box, please," he said.

Miller grabbed the end of the box and Jones reached in to remove the contents.

Valerie Harrison gasped. "My God, it's the portrait of Madame Monet!"

Jones laughed. "Sure. They're all here. There's forty-one. Everything I copied for the Colonel. All of them except the German ones. They're probably at Pagan's place in Miami."

She was still stunned. She looked at him in disbelief. "I don't understand. How did . . . ?"

"Any more questions, you can talk to my attorney, Walton Henry."

Desmond started to laugh. "I think I get it." He

looked at Jones with something like sneaking admiration now. "You did two copies, didn't you? You gave Pagan the other forgery. He was expecting the original, so he didn't look too closely either."

Jones smiled. "That's right. I figured he was as blind as anyone else in the kingdom, why not take advantage of it? I figured that someday I might need an ace in the whole. This was sort of my nest egg."

"You didn't keep them here all this time?" Valérie asked.

"No, of course not."

Miller stood there shaking his head in disbelief. Valerie knelt in front of the canvas almost as if it were some sort of altar. Desmond watched the two of them, wondering whether one nagging little question ought to be given voice. Finally, he decided that it deserved an airing.

"How do we know *these* are the originals, Derrick?"

Jones gave him that same queer smile. "You don't." Then he started to laugh. "But you can trust me. Can't you?"

■ HarperPaperbacks *By Mail*

Seven epic stories of POWER AND JEALOUSY,
AMBITION AND REVENGE, LOVE AND WAR
from the critically acclaimed bestselling author
JEFFREY ARCHER

KANE & ABEL

William Lowell Kane and Abel Rosnovski are two men from widely
different backgrounds whose driving passions are overshadowed only
by their obsession to destroy each other. Across three generations and
a rapidly changing world, their battle rages unchecked for the love of
a dream, the loss of an empire, and the lure of a fortune. "With *Kane
& Abel* Jeffrey Archer ranks in the top ten storytellers in the world."
—*The Los Angeles Times*

THE PRODIGAL DAUGHTER

The #1 bestseller and stunning sequel to *Kane & Abel*. Florentyna
Rosnovksi, daughter of a powerful Chicago baron, and Richard Kane,
son of a blue-blooded millionaire, are the children of bitter enemies.
Through a chance encounter, they fall passionately in love and strive
to win it all—against insurmountable odds. "Archer is an expert
storyteller....Sure to be a smash." —*Washington Times*

FIRST AMONG EQUALS

A spellbinding tale of four extraordinary men, sharply
divided by their backgrounds, who battle for a prize
that only one can win. Through three tumultuous
decades of fierce personal and political rivalry, they
vie for Britain's most powerful office—a rivalry that
sets love against hate, honor against deceit, and faith
against betrayal. "Fascinating."—*Boston Herald*

In its complete
& original form
—first U.S.
publication

A QUIVER FULL OF ARROWS

In this dazzling collection of stories, Jeffrey Archer creates an enticing
world of glamor, wit, and stunning surprise from London to China,
New York to Nigeria. Embracing the passions that drive men and
women to love and to hate, this magnificent showcase resonates with
the timeless rhythms of life and the powerful twists of fate.
"Exciting....Everything a reader could want." —*Baltimore Sun*

A MATTER OF HONOR

When Adam Scott opens the yellowed envelope bequeathed to him in his father's will, he triggers an incredible drama that sends him on a tailspin flight across Europe. For the terrible secret that shadowed his father's military career is now a ticking time bomb of intrigue, passions, and greed—one that could forever change the balance of global power. "Sizzles along at a pace that would peel the paint off a spaceship." —*The New York Times Book Review*

A TWIST IN THE TALE

A philandering husband and a very dead mistress…A game of strip chess with a sexy stranger…A wine expert put to the acid test. Jeffrey Archer now unveils a richly woven tapestry of fateful encounters. With deft, urbane style and witty sophistication, this dazzling collection suitably crowns his brilliant reputation as a master storyteller. "Cunning plots….Silken style." —*The New York Times Book Review*

AS THE CROW FLIES

When Charlie Trumper inherits his grandfather's vegetable cart, he also inherits his enterprising spirit. But before Charlie can realize his greatest success, he must embark on an epic journey that carries him across three continents and through the triumphs and disasters of the twentieth century. "Archer is a master entertainer." —*Time* magazine

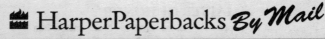

CAMPBELL ARMSTRONG

Agents of Darkness

Suspended from the LAPD, Charlie Galloway decides his life has no meaning. But when his Filipino housekeeper is murdered, Charlie finds a new purpose in tracking the killer. He never expects, though, to be drawn into a conspiracy that reaches from the Filipino jungles to the White House.

Mazurka

For Frank Pagan of Scotland Yard, it begins with the murder of a Russian at crowded Waverly Station, Edinburgh. From that moment on, Pagan's life becomes an ever-darkening nightmare as he finds himself trapped in a complex web of intrigue, treachery, and murder.

Mambo

Super-terrorist Gunther Ruhr has been captured. Scotland Yard's Frank Pagan must escort him to a maximum security prison, but with blinding swiftness and brutality, Ruhr escapes. Once again, Pagan must stalk Ruhr, this time into an earth-shattering secret conspiracy.

Brainfire

American John Rayner is a man on fire with grief and anger over the death of his powerful brother. Some say it was suicide, but Rayner suspects something more sinister. His suspicions prove correct as he becomes trapped in a Soviet-made maze of betrayal and terror.

Asterisk Destiny

Asterisk is America's most fragile and chilling secret. It waits somewhere in the Arizona desert to pave the way to world domination...or damnation. Two men, White House aide John Thorne and CIA agent Ted Hollander, race to crack the wall of silence surrounding Asterisk and tell the world of their terrifying discovery.